ev
N

700020519323

Murder is a Pretty Business

Also by Anthony Masters

FICTION
A Pocketful of Rye
The Sea Horse
A Literary Lion
Conquering Heroes
The Syndicate
Red Ice (with Nicholas Barker)
Rig (with Nicholas Barker)
Murder is a Long Time Coming
Confessional
Death's Door
The Men
The Good and Faithful Servant
    (Insider One)

NON FICTION
The Summer that Bled
Bakunin
Bedlam
Inside Marbled Halls
Nancy Astor
The Man Who Was M
Literary Agents
The Newall Murders

CHILDREN'S FICTION
Badger
Streetwise
Dream Palace
Frog
Mel's Run
Nobody's Child
Shell Shock
Travellers' Tales
The Transformation of
    Jennifer Howard
Dead Man at the Door
Raven
Bullies Don't Hurt
Bypass
Wicked
Day of the Dead

INSIDER TWO

MURDER IS A
PRETTY BUSINESS

Anthony Masters

Constable · London

First published in Great Britain 2000
by Constable, an imprint of Constable & Robinson Limited
3 The Lanchesters, 162 Fulham Palace Road
London W6 9ER

Copyright © 2000 Anthony Masters

The right of Anthony Masters to be identified as the
author of this work has been asserted by him in
accordance with the Copyright, Designs and Patents Act
1988

ISBN 0 094 80250 5

A CIP catalogue record for this book is available from the
British Library

For Robina with love.

PROLOGUE

As Rowland Griff bled to death, he gazed up, seeking comfort from an old friend.

'Who's a pretty boy then?' croaked Hamlet.

Dr Griff didn't think he had ever been a pretty boy. Jumbled images of childhood filled his mind, overlapping, making little sense. He felt no physical pain, and as he lay on his back he saw the estuary he had sailed as a child.

Rowland was at the helm of the *Walrus*, his brother Jed on the jib. Mother sitting amidships. The water sparkled, and the sky was turning meridian blue as the cloud lifted. Eleven a.m. A spanking breeze, the fluttering of the tell-tale, the rattling of the pennant.

The dinghy bounced over the waves. Rowland hadn't remembered any of this in years, but now the intensely familiar setting made his spirit soar. Was this the after-life? Could there be such a possibility after all? Rowland had always rejected the idea; how could he accept it now? Surely it was only a mocking illusion? Mother and Jed had died of cancer within weeks of each other. Had they really come to collect him now, pale ghosts in the morning sun, heading away from the shore towards an eternity that might or might not exist? Extinction had come so unexpectedly. Rowland had never thought his assailant would go that far.

'Who's a pretty boy then?' croaked Hamlet yet again.

What a way to go, Rowland thought, with only a parrot for company. Then he decided that Hamlet wasn't such bad company after all. At least he had never let him down.

Rowland smiled up at Hamlet.

The parrot peered down. He looked confused.

The image of the *Walrus* returned, the sunlight sharp, beams like splinters over the sea.

The blood from Rowland's neck ran in a steady stream. How could he have so much in him? he wondered. He was like a stuck pig. But it was rather academic now.

'Brace up, Rowley,' Mother said. 'Brace up.'

Her face grew huge, blotting out the sun.

PART ONE

1

Sunlight lit the early-morning garden. It was early June with the heat increasing, and St Clouds was ready for another baking day.

Kate Weinstock strolled along the path from her own modest apartment in the school grounds to Rowland Griff's. She was feeling frayed round the edges, which was unusual, for Kate took a pride in her reputation for moodless stability. But this morning she knew she couldn't push the situation to one side any longer, and Rowley had to stop avoiding the subject too. It was unpleasant – more than unpleasant – one deeply repugnant to her. But the rumours – and she was sure that was all they were – couldn't be allowed to continue.

They always met together at 8 a.m. to talk about the day-to-day running of the school – just she and Rowley – much to the annoyance of Noel Bundy and probably most of the other senior staff.

Soon Rowley was to retire, but Kate knew the board of governors had already agreed to her succession. She felt confident of that at least, but not much else, as she briskly made her way along the cliff-top path she always took for her morning walk to the meeting.

Overweight but handsome and statuesque, Kate Weinstock was a magisterial figure as she stood watching the waves break on the chalk cliffs, gulls screaming behind a fishing boat, a cormorant wheeling over salt-encrusted, spray-lashed rock.

Kate had always been self-possessed, the daughter of a Headmistress, with a single focus of ambition that no potential husband or child could be allowed to sabotage. A Latin scholar, a formidable and much feared teacher, a figure of considerable authority, Kate had no friends amongst the staff of St Clouds – except for Rowley. But she also kept him at a safe distance – an arrangement she enjoyed and found comforting. The thought of a marriage of convenience had never been allowed to enter her head, although she was sure it had entered Rowley's. Kate Weinstock placed a premium on private space. She needed a lot of that.

Sometimes she wondered if she'd been conditioned to be an isolated person by her parents. They were both academics and only connected when there was mutual need. She, their only child, had been born into an arid world, but found aridity had its own advantages. Human beings had to be kept in their place. There was no need to make unnecessary contact. It was good to sit on the edge of the universe.

Colleagues – the formal word suited Kate – colleagues would certainly lunch and dine and attend the same conferences together, even stay in the same hotel, but there could be no more to it than that.

In the holidays, Rowley and she took the occasional Swan Hellenic cruise together and would listen to the visiting lecturers with questioning discernment, just as they would to the hot-house gossip in the staff room. But they would be apart. They wouldn't connect, and to ensure they remained self-contained islands, she and Rowley would take cabins at opposite ends of the ship. They never sat at a table for two. Nothing intimate would ever be allowed to ruffle the even tenor of their lives.

Glancing at her watch, Kate was startled to see she was a little early, so she remained gazing down at the tide-washed rocks, contemplating Rowley's retirement and her own elevation. She had looked forward to this for a long time, but now she felt uneasy. Sole responsibility was what she had wanted, but there were difficulties. Rowley and she had had a good partnership and Kate would have preferred the alliance to continue, partic-ularly at this difficult time. Heading up the school alone at a time like this was not going to be easy.

But Rowley's angina was worsening and his younger sister, Angela, who had just spent a week looking after him, was not a favourite with Kate. Despite the fact that all three of them were single, she regarded Angela as a 'typical spinster', with her yapping pekes, her fussiness about detail and her blatantly insensitive intrusion into the cloistered atmosphere of Rowley's bachelor apartments. Now, even in Angela's absence, his rooms stank of henna rinse, dog and Dettol, when once there had been only the heady perfume of lavender furniture polish.

Kate strode the steep little path that led past St Clouds to the lawn at the rear of the Headmaster's house and the french windows of Rowley's sitting-room.

The crenellated Gothic pile had huddled on the Swanage cliffs, overlooking the Old Harry Rocks, for more than two centuries. Previously an educational establishment for the sons of the clergy, St Clouds was now a school for the damaged sons of dysfunctional families – or so she classified them. At school, the pupils were in her charge, under a different set of controls, and with some of them she could be surprisingly successful.

Kate Weinstock placed little reliance on psychiatry or psychology. Instead, she believed in her pupils conforming to her own regime. Her rules were simple – hard work, hard play and positive thought. Her enemies were self-indulgence, self-abuse and self-centredness, and she was confident that if the boys in her care followed her dictates, conformist behaviour would become a habit. Over the years, staff had compared Kate Weinstock to a cross between Baden-Powell and the Queen Mother, with a generous helping of *Tom Brown's Schooldays*.

Built into the side of the cliff, St Clouds had originally been the over-ornate seat of an eighteenth-century shipping magnate, enabling him to contemplate the shipping lanes in retired vigilance. After his death, the building had become a boys' boarding school – spartan, uncomfortable and windswept.

Although conditions had since improved, the three Gothic wings, the stunted towers, the rambling thirties additions, the seventies science block, the brutal shape of the gym all made St Clouds resemble a turn-of-the-century asylum, high above the rolling breakers of the English Channel.

This morning, the waves sighed lazily in the hazy sunlight as Kate tried to work out what she was going to say to Rowley. The serpents' heads were growing and Kate felt increasingly powerless. Surely Rowley couldn't be allowed to remain aloof? Conscious of his imminent retirement, he had been trying to put matters on hold, to let her shoulder the burden alone.

13

As she turned and approached the house, Kate grew increasingly despondent for she knew how deliberately blinkered Rowley was being. Despite his reserve and deliberate distancing, he had far more perception about the boys than she had, and in this present crisis she needed him. Otherwise, his retirement would leave her rudderless.

Rowley's lawn was forbidden territory to the boys so Kate was surprised to notice two of the flowerpots had been knocked off the terrace and were lying on the grass.

The french windows were open and she could hear Hamlet squawking. Kate hated the parrot, with its moth-eaten feathers and rheumy eyes and festering repetitive question. She could hear it clearly even now.

'Who's a pretty boy then?'

This was the only phrase Hamlet had ever been able to memorise, a croaking cliché repeated dozens of times a day, never getting on Rowley's nerves but always on hers. Kate had hated Hamlet from the moment she had arrived at St Clouds, and the thought of the school without the mangy-looking bird was elevating. Rowley had inherited Hamlet from his mother so how old did that make the wretched creature? And would all Rowley's retirement days be rent by Hamlet's squawking?

Kate hurried over the velvet, close-cut lawn, wanting to shake Rowley out of his complacency, even call an emergency staff meeting – an unheard-of event – to examine the serious nature of the crisis. The situation could close the school and Kate felt a ripple of fear for if St Clouds was no more, then her own life would be over too.

'Who's a pretty boy then?'

Kate smiled grimly. How she would love to wring the bird's scaly neck.

'Rowley? Where are you?'

The sitting-room was empty. When Angela had been in attendance she had served coffee and then ostentatiously withdrawn. Thank goodness she had now returned home to Wareham and they were spared her unctuous discretion.

14

Kate cleared her throat as she always did when she was about to make a difficult decision, all too well aware that both staff and boys referred to the guttural sound as 'the Kraken wakes'. Yet these little epithets pleased her, reinforcing a craving for affection that she could never give nor show.

Why hadn't Rowley made the coffee himself? He was usually punctilious and painstaking and it wasn't like him to be so remiss.

Kate walked across the Axminster, viewing the familiar and pristinely tidy sitting-room, with its faded chintz and cricketing memorabilia, including a signed bat, a ball on a plinth and serried ranks of team photographs. Rowley had always had a passion for the sport and, in his heyday, had been a first-class batsman for the county. Wisdens lined the bookcase and on the wall, like an intrusion from Angela, there were a few gloomy Victorian portraits that had belonged to Rowley's mother. Suddenly the room, as tidy, orderly and arid as their friendship, seemed inexplicably alien.

'Who's a pretty boy then?' Hamlet croaked from the study. Rowley usually shut the parrot in there while they had their meetings in the sitting-room, but she always heard him just the same.

'Rowley? Where are you?'

The house was unnaturally quiet and her voice seemed exceptionally loud and coarse.

'Rowley?' Kate hurried up the passage with the Samuel Palmer prints on the walls that led past the study to the kitchen.

She paused at the study door, breathing heavily, startled, with unfamiliar butterflies in her stomach that she hadn't remembered having in years. Had Rowley slipped out for a moment? If so, why? Day-to-day crises were dealt with by the Second Master, Noel Bundy, or Bundy as she always thought of him. Could Rowley be ill?

His study door was almost closed but not quite, just left a little ajar. Kate paused, her heart beating faster, anxiety almost overcoming her.

'Rowley?'

The bedrooms were upstairs. Should she check them first? But

15

why didn't she just push open the study door? It was all so simple yet suddenly impossible. Kate was frozen, mentally and physically, unable to make up her mind to move, to do anything at all.

The silence was a suffocating blanket. For once even Hamlet wasn't making a sound.

With a huge effort of will, Kate pushed open the door, immediately noticing the dark red patch on the carpet, and her sense of alienation was replaced by one of numbed unreality. What had Rowley done? Upset a glass of wine? Or a bottle? Then she saw waxen ankles and the familiar tartan carpet slippers. One of the slippers was half-way off. Could he have had a heart attack?

A loud buzzing sound began in Kate's head and her body was suddenly clammy, sweating under her summer print dress. Beads of perspiration stood out on her forehead and the buzzing was making her feel sick and dizzy.

Clearing her throat again and again, Kate stumbled into the room, smelling faeces, awkwardly aware that something dreadful had happened to Rowley. The stench was overpowering and deeply, deeply embarrassing. She shook her head, incredulous, and then moved further on into the room, the nausea increasing and a void of disbelief opening up inside her.

Rowley was lying flat on the carpet, but because the curtains were still drawn his head was in shadow. Stumbling away from the stain, Kate pulled them aside, allowing the bright light to flood the room.

In the revealing sunlight she saw Rowley's wide open mouth, displaying a clean white plate, discoloured lower molars – and a jagged cut at his throat that had ripped away shards of darkly bloodied flesh. Blood was encrusted over his chest and had flowed in a long trail down to the saturated carpet. Now it was like a dry river bed that had run rust.

Kate gazed down at him.

'Who's a pretty boy then?' demanded Hamlet, perking up again.

She turned to the parrot, the fury welling up inside her, breaking into the numbness and causing Kate to emit little squeals of shock that sounded absurd – even to her. The unfamiliar panic was almost worse than the carnage.

'Rowley? Please, Rowley – don't – don't –'

Suddenly, in a terrible flash of realisation, she knew she'd loved him. And then lost him. She also finally understood that she had only lived half a life – and would now never have the opportunity to live a full one. What a fool and coward she had been.

Kate went down on her knees on the carpet, oblivious of the crusted layer of blood, cradling Rowley's head which seemed oddly loose, as if he was a rag doll.

'Don't go. Don't leave me now,' she begged him, pawing at his cold, hard cheek and then kissing him over and over again.

2

'What have you been up to?' asked Creighton.

'Nothing much,' replied Boyd.

'Any easier?'

He shrugged.

'Do you want to work?'

'I'll go out of my mind if I don't. Every time the phone rings I've been praying I'd hear your voice.'

'You make me feel like God.'

'As far as I'm concerned you *are* God. You can change me – with your mighty word. Maybe you're a magician after all – a magician on the darker side, of course.' Boyd realised he was babbling on, but often he didn't speak to anyone for days at a time.

They were sitting in Creighton's New Scotland Yard office on a battered black plastic sofa. In front of them was an equally battered black coffee table on which rested two mugs of mauvish-grey liquid. Neither had been touched.

Creighton noticed that Boyd had put on weight and had a slight paunch, while his shock of blond hair was thinning on top. He looked beaten.

Boyd was sure that Creighton had lost weight. He was still slightly stooped, with half-moon glasses, but his arms and legs looked painfully thin and his shirt collar was too large for his bony neck with its pronounced Adam's apple.

Boyd wondered if Creighton was well.

Creighton wondered if Boyd was drinking.

There was a doubtful silence which Boyd eventually filled. 'I've been decorating the house. There are so many layers of paint on the walls the rooms have got smaller.'

They laughed uneasily.

'Socialised with anyone?' asked Creighton. 'Friends and neighbours?'

'Not if I see them first. So when are you going to say it?'

'Say what?'

'Start moving on. Put it all behind you.'

'Your family was killed, Daniel.' Creighton sounded hurt and misunderstood. 'I don't expect you to snap out of that.'

'Not ever?' Boyd was genuinely surprised.

'You'll always carry them with you.'

'I'm not going anywhere.'

'How about Dorset?'

'Why Dorset?'

'There's work for you.'

'For how long?'

'As long as it takes.'

Boyd felt a rush of gratitude.

There was a long silence.

'What kind of shape are you in?' asked Creighton.

'I can start to work out again.'

'There's no time. So answer the question. What about the booze?'

'It's under control.'

'That's what they all say.'

'I'll get a grip.'

'You'll have to.' Creighton hesitated. 'Is there anything else?'

'No women. No song. What kind of work are you offering me?'

'Ever thought of becoming a pederast?'

18

'Now that would be a challenge,' said Boyd. 'Although I'm not sure if I'd be very convincing.'

Creighton continued as if the question had been answered acceptably. 'An army base in Swanage may be involved and there's also a school and this youth club.'

'Bees round a honeypot,' said Boyd.

'The Royal Rangers at Bantry Bay, St Clouds School for Boys, Ballard Youth Club. We need to clobber these nonces, and now there's been a development that might help us.' Creighton sat back and closed his eyes, looking excruciatingly weary, as if the subject was as distasteful to him as it was to Boyd. 'Headmaster's had his throat cut. Have you seen the papers?'

'I don't read them.'

'The speculation is that he surprised an intruder.'

'But he wasn't surprised?'

'He might have been, but quite likely by someone he knew. There's this teacher at St Clouds. Head of English – Gaby Darrington. She approached Swanage CID alleging one of her students had been sexually assaulted by an army officer.'

'One of our chaps, shagging for his country? Haven't you got anything else on offer? All this sounds nauseating.'

'It is. That's why I thought of you.'

'You're as flattering as ever.'

'You can merge. You're the invisible man.'

'I've always had a strong personality. Why didn't this Darrington woman go to the Head?'

'Because she thought the Head wouldn't be able to cope. Mrs Darrington decided to make a direct approach to Swanage CID. But now her allegations can't be substantiated.'

'Why not?'

'Because the student's withdrawn the allegations.'

'Under threat?'

'She thinks so.'

'How long have these nonces been around?' asked Boyd.

'We don't know. We've been talking to the military police, but they've been fairly dismissive. Until now.'

'You want me to go undercover on an allegation that's been withdrawn?'

'These rings – these nonces – they're getting stronger all the

19

time, popping up everywhere, shitting in other people's nests. We've wanted to get at a ring for a long time. Ted Mason at Swanage CID reckons there's one operating locally.'

'Based on?'

'Rumours.'

'Who from?'

'Locals.'

'Nothing much to go on, is there?'

'There wasn't until Griff was murdered.'

Boyd had been seriously contemplating suicide over the last few weeks, often toying with the idea too long. The theoretical concept had been curiously pleasurable, although he knew that he didn't really have the nerve for it. But it was what he wanted. His nearest relative was a brother he had no time for, and their parents were dead.

Boyd's wife, Abbie, had been an only child too, but although her mother was still alive Boyd had never got on with her, particularly after the accident. Anyway, she now had Alzheimer's. Family life was a little thin on the ground. He wouldn't be missed. The self-pity made him wince.

'Griff's body was found by his deputy, Kate Weinstock,' Creighton continued.

'Signs of a struggle?'

'Two flowerpots knocked off the terrace. Nothing else.'

'What was the name again?'

'Rowland Griff.'

'Long-serving?'

'Just under twenty years.'

'And you believe the murder is connected with a ring of pederasts?' Boyd sounded incredulous.

'That's what we want you to find out.' Creighton was testy, beginning to be aware how much Boyd had deteriorated. Was he really going to be up to this?

'Any more pupils come forward?'

'No.'

'What about this Darrington woman?'

'She's married to the Commanding Officer of the Royal Rangers at the base in Bantry Bay.'

'Now that's awkward.'

'The Rangers are a new peace-keeping force and they're meant to be red hot. Commando training – special services and all that.'

'When was the murder?'

'Yesterday. But I've been considering this placement for some time. Maybe too long. Swanage CID are out of their depth and the military police are shit scared now.' Creighton paused. 'You were a teacher before you joined the force?'

Boyd nodded uneasily.

'Were you any good?'

'No.'

'*Could* you be any good?'

'If I set my mind to it. I just didn't like the feeling of being institutionalised.'

'Isn't the force the one great institution?'

'So I discovered. Maybe I've always wanted a safe job.'

'How long were you a teacher?'

'A couple of years. I read English at Leicester. But you've got that on file.'

'We may have got the stuff, but have *you* got the stamina?'

'You know what I feel about Boyd.'

Creighton nodded, not meeting his eyes, and Boyd wondered what he might have guessed. 'One of the English teachers at St Clouds is sick and there's a short-term contract in Gaby Darrington's English Department. She's shown a great deal of initiative.'

'I wonder why. What about the marriage?' asked Boyd.

'They're separated. No children.'

'Any ulterior motives?'

'I expect so.'

'When do I go?'

'Tomorrow? I don't think we've got time to hang around, but there's the problem of your new identity. Last time you had a long briefing.'

'Are you saying I'm going to add noncing to my life skills?'

21

'Only in an emergency. Teaching might do just as well for a while.'

'Suppose I don't get the job?'

'I'm told it's a dead cert. St Clouds is a draughty Gothic pile in the middle of nowhere which doesn't attract staff. Neither do the management. Kate Weinstock is *in loco parentis*. Shall we say her educational policy is out of the ark, if Mrs Darrington's an objective witness.'

'Will I get complete co-operation from Mason?'

'You bet you will. He's not getting much co-operation from the military police. They're looking to self-protection and closing ranks.'

'And my identity?'

'Alan Soames. Nice and bland, but not too bland.'

'I have to learn a life in a night?'

'We know how retentive you are.'

'You mean anally so?' enquired Boyd.

Creighton got up, pulled an envelope out of his desk drawer and gave it to Boyd. 'Alan's not a complicated sort of chap. Divorced with no kids and been time-serving at a prep school in Surbiton that got closed down.'

'Nonces?'

'Incompetence.'

'Substantiated?'

'You won't be blown. If you see what I mean.' Creighton had the grace to blush slightly. 'But you need to give yourself some time out of teaching since Surbiton. Why don't you say you've been trying to write a novel?'

'I didn't realise Soames was that immature. Do I have nonce on my CV?'

'Take heart,' said Creighton. 'You'll be fighting the killer bees. Just don't get stung, that's all, but you may be lucky enough to score without playing and you've got the old bill on your side. Ted's a good man. Dogged endurance – that kind of stuff.'

'Mr Plod?'

'We need Mr Plods.'

'When do I get to meet him?'

'When you've settled in.'

'What about Mrs Darrington?'

'She knows you're on the way.'
'Isn't that knowledge a risk?'
'It's one we've got to take. She's *your* insider.'

When Boyd left Creighton he bought a paper and went into a greasy spoon café to order a massive fry-up. Strangely, for the first time in months he had an appetite, which even the grisly details of Dr Griff's murder couldn't spoil.

HEAD SLAIN ran the tabloid headline. Boyd read on, pouring tomato ketchup liberally over his fried bread, two eggs, three sausages, slightly burnt bacon and mushrooms.

> Dr Rowland Griff, Head of St Clouds Boys' School in Swanage, Dorset, was found in his study, with his throat savagely cut, by Deputy Head Kate Weinstock. 'He had no enemies,' she stated. 'He was loved by both staff and boys and was just approaching retirement. This is a terrible loss.'
>
> DI Ted Mason of Swanage CID gave us this statement: 'We are treating Rowland Griff's death as murder, possibly as the result of a confrontation with an intruder.'
>
> St Clouds has just over a hundred and twenty pupils, most of whom board at the school. The St Clouds Foundation awards scholarships to boys with special educational needs.

Boyd put down the paper and buttered some toast, gazing blankly at the steamed-up windows. Creighton hadn't told him about the 'special needs' aspect of St Clouds, but no doubt the information would be included in his briefing.

Boyd felt a wave of irritation, remembering how he had hated teaching. Maybe Creighton was right and he *had* simply gone from one institution to another, ending up in the CID with its male freemasonry of shared danger and shared prejudice. Did he really lack individuality?

Kate Weinstock, at last freed from police interrogation and all too conscious of the forensic team in Rowley's study, sat in her office, quite unable to accept his death. All she could keep thinking about was a school drama production a few years ago where Rowley had played a murdered theatre critic. She could see his body lying on the stage now, but she couldn't accept his real corpse lying on the study floor. In the back of her mind was the continuous sound of Hamlet's squawking tirade mingling with the sigh of the summer waves drawing at the shingle on the beach below.

Rowley had been the centre of her life, that quiet, reserved, reclusive man who had only demanded the quiet, detached companionship she had thought she had needed.

But now Rowley was dead, Kate realised that she had wanted so much more. She felt cheated, as if waking from a long dream that had had no end. They had hardly reached each other, like two strangers in the fog of mutual sterility, shyness and the fear of being touched in every possible sense of the word. It was all such a waste.

Kate Weinstock's shoulders bowed but she still couldn't cry.

Instead, she got up and went to the window to view the police incident caravan drawn up in the school drive, together with the statutory requirement of Land-Rovers, squad cars and other unmarked vehicles.

The phone rang and when she picked up the receiver there was yet another parent on the line.

Wearily, Kate Weinstock switched on her muddling-through voice, sensible and comforting and courageously matter-of-fact.

'Hello, Mrs Beale.'

'I've just heard about the tragedy.' Mrs Beale was flurried and nervous.

'It's been devastating – for us all.'

'I gather there was an intruder.'

'So I understand.'

'It must have been dreadful for you.'

'It is.' Kate Weinstock's nerves began to scream as she waited for the next predictable question.

'Should you be working?'

'I'd rather work. I'm sure you'll understand.' Kate Weinstock waited for Mrs Beale to come to the real point of her call – her son. As if given permission, she began to express the kind of disquiet that so many other parents had confided.

24

'Leonard's seemed very jumpy for the last few weeks.'

'Really?'

'He's said nothing of course. Never does. But what with – with – we've decided he'd be better off at home for a week or so. I'm sorry.'

'I quite understand.'

After a while Kate Weinstock managed to ease the guilty, embarrassed and platitudinous Mrs Beale off the line. She had been the fourth parent of the morning to withdraw her son.

Kate buzzed her secretary and told her she would take no more calls that morning. Then she went back to the window and gazed down at the police presence again. An officer was standing on the steps of the incident caravan talking to someone inside. Another was walking towards the cloisters. Everything has come to a head, she thought. The orderly life had vanished, perhaps for ever. Then she tried to pull herself together. It was order that would rescue the situation and it was up to her to reimpose it. She had to reimpose it now. Rowley was gone and the school was her legacy.

Then she began to wonder how big the problem was. Who *had* killed Rowley? And was a sense of order going to dismiss the enemy who had penetrated this far? She shuddered at the extent of it all and then decided with reassuring simplicity that the threat was the police's job now and not hers. Definitely not hers. All she had to do was to hold fast.

There was a knock and she started.

'Yes?'

'Detective Inspector Mason wants a word.' Mrs Cubitt was barely able to carry out her tasks this morning. She had been Rowley's secretary as well as her own. 'Shall I show him in?'

'Of course.'

'Are you all right, Miss Weinstock? I can always –'

'Show him in,' she snapped, seeking the control that had been so badly undermined – but must be regained whatever the personal cost.

'Just thought I'd give you a progress report, Miss Weinstock.' Mason was reassuringly deferential and wore the kind of suit she thought he should wear – grey with a slight check. He sat down heavily, making her feel better, safer. 'The pathologist puts Dr Griff's death at somewhere just after midnight. We can't find any fingerprints – except Dr Griff's of course – but someone left in a hurry, leaving the doors open, knocking over the flower-pots.' He paused. 'I'd also like to talk to you about Lofts.' Mason made eye contact with her for the first time. 'Could there be a connection?'

At once the safety zone sharply contracted.

'Why should there be?' She was immediately on the defensive.

'So you think Mrs Darrington was over-reacting?'

'I wish she'd spoken to me personally.'

'Would you have believed her?' persisted Mason.

'Lofts withdrew his allegations.'

'That doesn't necessarily mean they were untrue.'

'Are you suggesting he was lying?'

'I'm not suggesting anything at the moment.' Mason paused. 'We have some reason to believe there could be a paedophile ring operating in Swanage.'

'How very unpleasant,' she said dismissively. 'But I'm sure it has no connection with any of our pupils.' Again, Kate Weinstock took evasive action. This was the police's job, not hers, she reminded herself.

'You haven't heard of any complaints?'

'Of course not. I would have known if there had been.'

'So it was just Lofts.'

'He's a very disturbed boy.'

'I was wondering about that.'

'Far less so than when he came to us,' she added hurriedly.

'It's all a bit worrying, isn't it? Rumours of a ring – and Lofts's accusations.'

'He needs to claim attention. He's made accusations against members of staff over the years. All sexual. All disproved.'

'You haven't mentioned that to me before.'

'You didn't ask.'

'I am now.' Mason was impatient.

'Bernie Lofts has had a lot of problems in the past, when he was much younger.' Kate Weinstock decided not to expand on the problems. 'But we've had very little trouble recently. I see

26

this as a lapse. A one-off lapse. He merely seized an opportunity for attention-seeking. The psychiatrist has a word for his mode of behaviour, but I just prefer to try to reassure him that we're all in support – and that he has to control himself. We're a very close community here, Mr Mason. Close and loving. We all share responsibility for each other. We have to realise –'

'Suppose Dr Griff had identified a member of the ring?' Mason cut into the propaganda.

'That's most unlikely,' she replied. 'This dreadful ring has no connection with St Clouds.'

'Did Dr Griff ever talk to you about local pederasts?'

Kate Weinstock hesitated. 'Only in the context of rumour.'

'Was any action recommended?'

'That we should all be vigilant.'

Mason got up. 'This is a very serious business, Miss Weinstock, and it's not going to go away.'

'Is Dr Griff still in his study?' she asked.

'He's been taken away.' He tried to be gentle with her, despite her obtuse attitude.

'Where?'

'The mortuary in Swanage.'

'Can I see him?'

Mason didn't reply immediately. 'I think you'll have to wait until they're ready.'

'He's not in a drawer?'

'He won't be there for long.'

She moved towards the door. 'When will he be in a chapel of rest?'

'After the autopsy. I'll let you know.'

'Thank you.' Kate Weinstock paused. 'You don't think you're leaping to conclusions about this – this ring?'

'Anything's possible at this stage, Miss Weinstock,' said Mason, anxious to get away.

3

As Boyd drove towards St Clouds he felt increasingly uneasy. He had sat up late last night, trying to absorb Alan Soames's identity, realising that he would have to work much harder on the detail tonight. As a result he felt apprehensive and full of self-doubt. Going back to school was an unpleasant thought and to actively teach seemed much worse than anything he had encountered in his last investigation.

Facing children, with Rik and Mary dead, was a deeply distressing idea, and mixing with them worse. Why in God's name had he accepted the job? Or was this Creighton's way of trying to help him face up to his loss? Boyd was suddenly sure that Creighton had seized an opportunity.

Other cars hooted behind him and Boyd realised he'd been driving so slowly that he'd practically ground to a halt. He speeded up, sweating despite the open window.

'Alan Soames? Welcome to St Clouds. I'm so sorry you've arrived at such a dreadful time.'

Kate Weinstock stood in the black-beamed, mock Gothic hallway. She kept clearing her throat.

The ceiling had been painted with white clouds in a dark blue sky. Strangely, they didn't clash with the heavy dark oak of the sweeping staircase that led to the first floor, or with the beaded wooden panelling around the walls. Glass cases filled with trophies and a Headmaster's Notice Board took up the remainder of the space. A wooden hatch on the right-hand side served as Reception while the panelling on the left bore a number of green felt boards announcing sporting fixtures.

Kate Weinstock stood rigidly, staring ahead.

'Would you like to see me another time?' asked Soames.

'The school has to continue with its routine. You'd better come up to my office and tell me something about yourself.'

He prayed that he would sound consistent in his new role.

Somehow he had to ditch Boyd and rapidly give birth to Soames.

Kate Weinstock's office was large and sunshine was streaming in at the window which faced out on to the drive. A side window overlooked the cloisters and students could be seen hurrying along with books under their arms, looking dutiful as they passed the Headmistress's vantage point.

The boys' hair was strictly regulation length and they wore blazers, white shirts and blue ties, dark, narrow trousers and polished shoes.

Soames recalled Boyd's school-days at a rough secondary in Edmonton. Then he remembered Soames shouldn't be thinking this way. Boyd no longer existed. So what *was* Soames's educational background? For a terrible moment his mind went blank until he remembered that he had supposedly attended St Augustine's Prep School in Eastbourne, once again conveniently closed, and Crayford in Bristol, a minor public school where there had been quite a few boys by the name of Soames.

'Do sit down.' Kate Weinstock was already at her desk, shuffling papers which no doubt included his references. Her hands were trembling slightly. 'I gather you can join us at short notice?'

'I took a year out. It didn't work.'

'What were you doing?' She looked up at him, her face blank. How perceptive is she? he wondered. Her pale china-blue eyes rested on Soames as if he was a faintly interesting exhibit, and he sensed her detachment. He wondered if it was caused by the shock, or if she was always at this kind of distance. There was a capability to her that was formidable.

'Writing a novel. Lifetime's ambition.' Soames made himself grin self-consciously and, at the same time, seem shame-faced. He was rather pleased with the effect.

'And now you want to stop writing your novel?' For a moment he was sure she was ever so slightly amused, but in a second the impression had vanished.

'I was going stir crazy.'

'I'm sorry.' She shuffled the papers again and Soames noticed her hands were more under control.

He decided to emphasise his sensitivity. 'This is a very painful time for an interview. Would you like me to come back later in the week?'

'We have to fill the position,' she said. 'We can't delay. Dr Griff wouldn't have wanted that. We ran the school together. Would you like coffee?'

'Thank you.'

She got up and went to a cafetière on a table behind her.

Soames began to examine the room, which was dominated by dozens of shelves stacked with books with Latin names. There were some good prints on the opposite wall and a couple of original landscapes, but there was an anonymity to the place, an overall blandness that was off-putting. It was as if Kate Weinstock was sitting in front of a backdrop.

He watched her as she placed his coffee cup on a small table beside him and then moved slowly back behind her desk. For a big woman, he thought, she has poise. Soames began to wonder how popular she was with the staff. There was something very rigid about her self-control.

'Of course, we've had other applicants, but no one is as free as you are. Mr Blenheim's gone into hospital for a heart bypass.'

'I'm sorry.'

'He was a good teacher and used to our boys. As you've probably guessed, they can be difficult.'

Soames was silent. He didn't want to sound too glib. Then he asked cautiously, 'Difficult?'

Kate Weinstock sat back, hands folded on her ample bosom, while sunlight streamed on to the scarred polished oak of her desk. She suddenly seemed more approachable.

'St Clouds was founded by a priest for the sons of priests. Perhaps he felt that they might have a calling too, but that was all a very long time ago. Nowadays our pupils are largely children from broken homes.'

'Is this a policy?'

'You've read our brochure?'

Had he missed something? 'Of course,' Soames replied firmly.

30

'You'll see there's no mention of that. The brochure simply underlines our policy of hard work and hard play. We have simple rules. There must be no bullying and we must show each other mutual respect.' Kate Weinstock paused. 'Naturally, we have trained counsellors who are as important as the teaching staff. Some of the children who come to us are badly damaged. It's our job not only to heal, but to motivate them as well, and we do get some excellent A-level results.' She stood up. 'End of pi-jaw.' She used the old-fashioned phrase with relish, glancing down at her watch. 'Would you like a brief tour of the school?'

'Have I got the job?'

She gazed at him rather absently, as if he was only of passing importance – as of course to her he was. 'When can you start? Would Thursday be convenient? I've found your references perfectly adequate.'

That gives me two days more mugging up, thought Soames as he smiled at her gratefully. 'I'd be delighted.'

'Will you?' she asked absently.

The tour was short and bland, with visits to classrooms where Kate Weinstock politely knocked on doors which were opened to reveal polite classes with their eyes down, ostensibly learning from polite teachers.

The clearly cosmetic impression didn't change when they visited the gym to see politely restrained acrobatics, to the pitch to view a polite game of cricket and finally the library where students were politely engrossed in their reading. Soames was amazed at the restraint. Did Weinstock's cold eye really strike such terror?

The tour concluded in the cloisters with impeccable timing, and as she glanced at her watch again Soames knew he was being dismissed.

'I'll have the bursar send you an employment contract and some more details about our little community. You can find your own way out, can't you?'

They shook hands and he noticed that her palm was hard and dry while eye contact was brief.

'Thank you.'

'We're so grateful you can join us at such short notice.' Then she paused, looking apologetic, as if his presence had suddenly recurred to her and she had had a twinge of conscience. 'You haven't asked me about accommodation. I'm so sorry . . .'

'I live in London. At the moment.'

'I'm afraid what's happened . . .'

They both seemed at a flurried disadvantage.

'Of course. I quite understand,' said Soames. 'Is there staff accommodation available?'

'You can have Mr Blenheim's flat on a temporary basis. I know he'll be only too happy for you to rent it from us as he did.'

'Are all his things still there?'

'Most of them.' She was becoming brisk now, with just an edge of impatience. 'Would you like to see the flat?'

'I'm sure it'll be fine.'

'Good.' Kate Weinstock nodded and turned away. 'We'll all look forward to seeing you on Thursday. And thank you again.'

'Thank *you*.'

She was off, striding through the cloisters, giving a brisk wave without looking back. Soames didn't know what to make of her. Kate Weinstock was so focused, so locked in, that she didn't betray anything – and he was certain there was a lot to betray.

'I'm deeply sorry,' he called out instinctively, and she half turned. 'About Dr Griff.'

'I can't . . .' She looked suddenly vulnerable and he was shocked that he had caught her out actively betraying emotion.

He stared at her in silence. His action had been deliberate, but Soames felt oddly ashamed without quite knowing why.

Kate Weinstock gave a helpless gesture and hurried through the door.

You're a control freak, aren't you, he thought as he stood in the cloisters, staring up at Weinstock's shadowy figure in her latticed office window. Then Soames realised that she was watching him.

32

He walked away too casually through the corridors of the main building, into the hall and out on to the drive.

That afternoon, Boyd went for a walk in the park near his house in Croydon. The day was sunny and warm, with a strong breeze picking up the scent of stocks and geraniums as they grew in regimented lines in the council flowerbeds, not a leaf out of place or a weed in sight. The sense of order always gave Boyd a feeling of despair. It had been a year now, but his isolation was far worse, far more painful than before.

The sound of the bursting tyre had been like a gunshot and the truck had loomed up out of nowhere on the sunlit motorway. Boyd had twisted the wheel but there had been no response and the Rover had felt as if it was floating. Then they had hit the truck. Abbie and Rik and Mary had been killed on impact.

Boyd had gratefully accepted Creighton's offer to leave his job as a DI in the CID and work as an undercover officer on a case that had been highly volatile. Once it was over, however, there had been too long a period deskbound.

'You're on call for the creative jobs,' Creighton had told him after Boyd had complained. 'You're too old to hang around the drugs scene and you're too familiar to the villains – at least for a while.'

'So I'm a little limited in scope,' Boyd had commented sourly.

Creighton had not denied it.

Boyd yearned so deeply for Abbie and the children that he would spend painful hours standing by their graves in the cemetery in Purley. But he couldn't cry.

Boyd knew he had become an empty husk, sitting, drinking, watching daytime TV, occasionally visiting Abbie's mother in her rest home. She barely recognised him now, but she had developed a vigorous fantasy life, a role play that had a farcical link with his own, except he had never imagined himself playing Marilyn Monroe and Abbie's mother did that all the time.

She spoke unceasingly about filming, the perks of stardom, the exigencies of show business, gossip and of romances with men in high places. The flow of false memory rarely withdrew and

33

was as frightening as it was absorbing. Abbie's mother was hiding behind a seamless false identity from which she rarely strayed. She had the ultimate alias in which she totally believed and his own efforts to create identity seemed puny beside hers. He had to work at it. She didn't.

Boyd sat on his usual park seat, overlooking a gazebo and the snooker-smooth lawns of a bowling club. Men and women, on the whole elderly, were inspecting the woods intently as they were rolled over the cropped grass. Boyd had watched them for a long time but had never been able to grasp exactly how the game was played.

He knew he had become a fixture in the park and suspected that boys kicking balls, joggers and cyclists, vagrants and park attendants, lovers and silent thinkers alike, all regarded him as someone to set their watches by. Maybe he should have bought a dog.

Boyd got up and stretched, realising how unfit he had become, knowing how much Creighton disapproved. He should have 'put it all behind him'. He should have 'moved on'. His grief should have 'flattened out' by now. But it hadn't and probably wouldn't and his only escape was to go undercover, to survive by role play. But why bother to survive at all? Why not join his beloved dead? After all, he had thought about suicide long enough.

Boyd set out for yet another round of the well-worn, well-known walk through the park, from sandpit to gazebo to bowling green to disused band-stand, via the long, broad, black tarmac path that wound past the serried ranks of corporation flowerbeds to the empty fountain where cheeky corporation cherubs had once spouted water from every orifice.

Good old shadow man. Good old familiar figure. Good old fat white man that no one loves, always wearing those white gloves. Boyd had smiled at the absurdity of the loneliness, the time-filling that he indulged in until he could safely, at least by his own rules, go home and open a bottle. The alcohol would soothe the hollow man, giving temporary oblivion from the emptiness of a house that seemed to have been frozen in time, ever since the burst tyre had taken away the meaning of life. He didn't even bother to wind up the clocks any more.

Despite the booze, Boyd was aware that once its effects had worn off he would wake to a grey morning, and in the bathroom, as he shaved and showered, the hangover heavy as lead, his mouth dry as grave dust, he would hear mocking voices telling him to 'look on the sunny side', 'muddle through', remember 'every cloud has a silver lining', 'stand up straight', recall 'so many are worse off than you', 'grin and bear it' and so on and so on. The clichés rattled in his head, and when they temporarily withdrew Boyd heard the sound of an old and familiar hymn he had sung as a child. 'Ten thousand thousand are their tongues and all their joys are one.' When the hymn ended, the voices returned, ringing out with a final cliché: 'after all, life's a great game'.

Well, it was, wasn't it? Creighton had offered him the greatest game he could ever play, and the harder he played the faster those dear, dead faces would temporarily become a blur.

'Good afternoon,' said the little old lady with impeccable timing, as she always did when they met by the dried-up ornamental fountain with the fresh vomit at the bottom, spread amongst the litter.

'And good afternoon to you,' said Boyd as he thankfully left the park for what he hoped might be a very long time.

4

'Who spoke?'

Soames stood by the board, the squeaking chalk setting his teeth on edge, determined to catch and outsmart the culprit. Outside the sky was grey and sullen and the waves seemed to sigh with the sheer boredom of so relentlessly coming in and going out again.

There was silence and then a smothered laugh.

Soames had only been at St Clouds for a morning, but it was long enough for him to realise that he was being tested.

He gazed down at the serried ranks of clean-cut fourteen-year-olds and was forcibly reminded of the corporation flowerbeds in the park. Only a few had the blight of acne. But all were practised at recognising weakness, and all unerringly went straight for the jugular. A far cry from – but Soames was determined not to think about the other world. Boyd's world.

Of course it only needed one pupil to be the catalyst, and this one had just made animal noises behind Soames's back when he was writing on the board.

'Who spoke?'

The silence became a murmur.

'Be quiet.'

He scanned their faces. If he was to survive he had to single the culprit out and make an example immediately.

'I would have expected you to behave better in the light of Dr Griff's death.' Well before he had brought out the last word, Soames knew he had made a fatal move.

'Sir?'

'Yes?' He had no idea who any of them were yet, despite the fact that he had called a register, desperately trying to match names to faces.

'Who murdered him?'

'How should I know?'

'You might be Sherlock Holmes, sir.'

Soames froze although he knew he was only being wound up. The boy smiled up at him innocently, his heavy jowls making him look older than he was.

'Why are you joking in such bad taste?'

'I only wondered, sir.'

'Don't bother.'

The same animal noise, extended to become a flat fart, blurted out from the other side of the room. Less restrained laughter rose and took a long time dying away.

'OK,' said Soames. 'Let me tell you something. My last job was in London. It's tough there.' He was sure he sounded weak, especially when a camp scream rang out. 'The next interruption I get, that boy is for the high jump.'

There was a short expectant silence until his original questioner asked, 'What did you do in London, sir?'

'What do you think? Run a fish shop?' Too late, he realised he was falling into their hands by feeding them jokes.

'I just thought you might have been Hercule Poirot, sir.'

'What makes you think that?' Soames wiped away beads of sweat from his brow and hoped they hadn't noticed. He was torn between an urge to lash out, to pulverise the little bastard, or to run screaming from the room. He had never felt like this before and suddenly Soames began to wonder if he was going to break before he had begun. Broken by a fourteen-year-old? What would Creighton think? Yet the boy was the same age as Rik would have been now. Soames felt himself going hot and cold and his eyes filling with tears.

'What's your name?' he asked quietly, deliberately pacing himself.

'Altrin, sir.'

'And your first name?'

'Edward Altrin.'

The animal noise came again, but this time Soames saw the boy's contorted lips and felt a rush of triumph.

He strode over to the boy and leant against the wall, looking down at him with angry contempt.

'And *your* name?'

'I didn't do anything, sir.' Surprised, the boy was beginning to panic, and Soames felt his adrenalin soar. The moment when he could have been broken had passed. Hadn't it?

'And your name?'

'Martin, sir. Tom Martin.'

'So you make animal noises. *Are* you an animal?'

'I didn't do anything, sir.'

There was silence now. Could it be the silence of the defeated? Soames knew he shouldn't risk any hint of faltering now, but could there be an element of doubt about Martin? Could he have got the wrong boy? Soames knew he shouldn't let it matter. Doubt had to be thrown aside in his baptism of fire.

'Martin and Altrin. Get out.'

They both stared at him blankly.

'Did you hear me? I want you to get out and stand in the corridor until we're finished. Then I'll take you to the Head.'

'You can't, sir,' piped up a voice.

'Why not?' Too late, Soames realised the trap had been sprung again.

37

'He's dead, sir. He was murdered, sir.'

There was laughter but it was uneasy. Soames guessed they were waiting to see whether he was bluffing or not.

'Your name?'

'Bob Grant. And by the way, sir . . .'

'Yes?'

'It was me who made the noises. Not Tom.'

Soames felt a sudden vulnerability as he realised he *had* made a mistake. How was he going to handle this admission? Was it all part of the wind-up? What in God's name was he going to do?

'That's honest of you,' he managed to get out.

'Thank you, sir.'

Knowing he was being cheeked again, Soames glanced across at Tom Martin. 'Is he right?'

'It wasn't me, sir. I told you, sir.' Martin took refuge in moral outrage.

'So the culprits are Altrin and Grant.' Soames swung round.

'We should take our punishment,' said Grant.

'We did wrong,' added Altrin.

The expressions on the faces of the others were of controlled glee. Soames knew the game was still on.

'Get out. When the bell goes, I'll take you to the *Acting* Head – Miss Weinstock. I'm sure she'll be able to sort you out.'

With immense satisfaction and a certain amount of curiosity, Soames watched the two boys' expressions change.

'Don't do that, sir,' stammered Altrin.

'Why not?'

'She's strict, sir.'

'You should have thought of that before you started playing me up, shouldn't you?'

'She's more than strict, sir,' said Grant. 'She's out of order.'

'How?' Despite the danger of being outflanked, Soames was curious.

'She canes us, sir.'

'When caning isn't allowed,' put in Altrin.

Soames was surprised. Was Altrin telling the truth? He had no idea whether caning was still allowed in private schools.

'I'm still taking you to Miss Weinstock.' Soames knew he was winning now, and maybe the news of his victory would get round St Clouds sufficiently quickly to make his life much easier. 'As I said, you should have thought of the consequences before you started winding me up.'

'You don't have to take us, sir,' said Grant. 'Standing in the corridor's enough. She'll come prowling and find us. She always does that.'

Soames gazed at Altrin and Grant, wondering what part of the game they had reached. Were they still ahead of him?

'We'll see about that,' he snapped. 'Get out of my class and wait for me in the corridor.'

They got up and began to walk slowly to the door while the others watched them with gloomy relish. Soames knew the feeling – self-indulgent peeking through the lace blinds, drinking good wine while the TV screen blazed the horrors of Kosovo or East Timor.

'Please, sir,' said Grant. 'We're sorry. Can we stay?'

But Soames knew they had to be sacrificial lambs and if the lioness was on the prowl, so be it. In another part of his mind he was wondering when Ted Mason would contact him. He needed to know how the investigation was proceeding as soon as possible. And why did the St Clouds pupils seem to regard Griff's death as some kind of gruesome joke?

'I told you to get out,' insisted Soames.

Grant opened the door and he and Altrin shuffled out into the corridor as if to immediate execution.

The door closed quietly and Soames turned to the rest of the class. 'Let's get this straight. I don't want to have to do this again, but I will if I have to. Do you understand?'

There was a murmur of assent and Soames knew he had finally won.

When the bell rang for mid-morning break, Soames checked the corridor and found Altrin and Grant with their backs against the wall. They looked defeated.

'Did Miss Weinstock find you?'

'Yes,' said Grant.

'What's going to happen?'

'She told us to come to her office at eleven.'

'Will she really cane you?'

'It's fifty-fifty, sir.'

Soames glanced at Altrin to see that he was almost in tears.

'Whatever happens, you did the right thing by owning up, Grant.'

'Yes, sir.'

'Your testing went too far.'

'Yes, sir.'

'It mustn't happen again.'

'No, sir.'

Soames paused. 'Does Miss Weinstock always inspect the corridors?'

'All the time, sir.'

'I see. Now do you know where the staff room is?'

Grant began to give him a series of rather complicated directions and Soames felt so insecure that he wondered if he was being wound up all over again.

5

The staff room was crowded with ancient armchairs, each one, no doubt, belonging to an individual teacher and therefore 'out of bounds'. In another area, members of staff were hunched around a large square table, marking books and planning lessons, and in a few cases desultorily reading copies of the *Telegraph*. There didn't seem to be any other newspapers available.

A large urn in one corner gave the room a suitably institutional feel. There were ragged notice boards on the walls, stacks of box-files on the floor and a large overflowing bookcase.

Predictably, most of the tattered chairs were taken and the smell of stale coffee impregnated the whole space.

Soames suddenly felt a sense of total isolation, and wondered when Gaby Darrington was going to make herself known to him. Surely she should have met him when he first arrived? He had been told where his classroom was by a teacher who was so casual and laid-back that Soames had been surprised the comparatively young man had been able to stand up at all. For reasons that were now clear to him, he had smelt of stale coffee. He hadn't even bothered to introduce himself, thought Soames, and his indignation rose. Here were the staff of St Clouds, presumably trying to educate emotionally damaged boys, and they didn't have any manners or sensitivity at all. Now he was expected to wander into the cliquey atmosphere of the staff room and fend for himself.

Soames entered self-consciously, heading awkwardly for the urn, wondering what he was meant to do. Should he offer to pay for his no doubt abysmal coffee and what about the plate of digestives on the table? Once again he felt the irony of it all. His previous assignment had been life-threatening, yet he was just as traumatised by this secret micro world full of rituals he didn't understand, littered with booby traps he had to avoid by instinct.

'Mr Soames?'

An overweight, balding man in a scuffed dark suit and white shirt with a floral tie was moving towards him, a hand outstretched, a look of determined welcome on his broad, fleshy features.

'Do call me Alan.'

They gripped hands too hard and held on for too long.

'I'm sorry there was no one to meet you this morning. We're all at sixes and sevens at the moment, and now I hear you had trouble with the Lower Fourth.'

So the news was already out, but why shouldn't it be? This was a small community and Soames knew he had to learn to swim in its unpredictable currents.

'They were a baptism of fire and I had to send a couple of them out. They were much easier after that.'

Soames tried to sound jovial but authoritative, at the same time wondering whether this man who still hadn't introduced himself considered his action a demonstration of strength or weakness.

'The name's Noel Bundy. I'm the Second Master. Welcome to St Clouds.'

There was something both challenging and cynical in his over-stretched smile.

'I'm sorry you've come at such a dreadful time. The police have been very discreet, but I still can't take it all in.'

Soames thought of the incident caravan outside and the rows of parked vehicles. Did he really consider that discreet?

'Any conclusions been drawn?'

'We haven't been told anything, but then we never are. Would you like some excruciatingly filthy coffee?'

'Thanks.' Soames's spirits lifted. The disgruntled Bundy seemed friendly if nothing else. He followed him to the urn where his new acquaintance slopped hot water into the already prepared scum in the bottom of a plastic cup. Why weren't the staff allowed to dole out their own coffee? Suppose he had wanted it black? Soames felt annoyed again, as if he was a deprived child himself.

'Do I pay?'

'There's a coffee kitty. We pay into it once a month and that covers biscuits too.'

Soames wondered if, once the preliminaries were over, Bundy would bustle off for he seemed the bustling type. But, instead, he still hung around.

'Don't worry too much about the Lower Fourth. They're a noxious bunch at the best of times. There are better classes at St Clouds. Not that much better, though.' Bundy laughed uproariously, as if he had just put on a lavish display of wit.

'They didn't seem to care too much about Dr Griff.'

'They wouldn't. He was very remote and didn't teach.'

'What was he like?'

'Withered academic. Coasting towards retirement. Did everything Weinstock told him.' Bundy spoke in staccato phrases, as if they were so familiar to him he repeated them automatically, without thinking or ever revising his opinion. Weinstock and Griff had obviously become stereotypes to him. Soames had seen Bundy's type before in the force. They were prejudiced, bitter, and made up for their own inadequacies by criticising management.

'But who on earth would have killed him?' asked Soames in deliberate bewilderment.

'I've no idea.'

'Was he single? I assume Miss Weinstock is . . .'

Bundy gleefully responded. 'The old dears were probably knocking it off in their own desiccated way, like a couple of neutered water buffaloes mating in a sandstorm.'

Soames laughed dutifully, delighted that Bundy indulged in internecine warfare, wondering to what extent he had hated them both. Suddenly the difficult morning seemed a little brighter.

'I didn't mean –' Soames began, simulating embarrassment, but Bundy swept on.

'Look, if you're going to teach here, even temporarily, you need to understand that Weinstock rules. She rules the boys. She rules the staff. She ruled Griff. She rules – but she doesn't understand a sodding thing.'

'Bit of an autocrat?'

'Bit of an arsehole.' Bundy laughed but without humour. 'Please don't think I'm usually so unprofessional or so vindictive. But we're all of a common mind about Weinstock. She's a control freak.' Bundy grinned again, this time more self-consciously. 'Bet you didn't expect to hear all that.'

Bet you've got another agenda, thought Soames. What sort of promotion has Weinstock blocked for you? Why this bitter loathing?

'Anything else I should know?' he asked mildly, watching Bundy's expression become less easy to read. 'I've heard all this stuff about a ring of pederasts moving in on Swanage.'

'There've been some nasty rumours, but you'll pick those up on the grapevine.'

'Can't you give me a short cut?'

Bundy was silent. Then he said hesitantly. 'I just don't know. If the rumours are true, then it's a very serious matter. Naturally I've been keeping my ear to the ground.'

Soames backed off. 'What's it like here?'

'A safe billet if Weinstock takes a shine to you.'

'And she doesn't take much of a shine to you?' Soames risked, laughing to keep the sting out of the question.

'Does she hell! But I'm a good poker player.' Bundy paused. 'I knew I was never in line for the Head's job, but it doesn't stop me feeling bitter. I've been here too long, and I don't want to shift. My wife's Head of Art and I'm in charge of pastoral care.' He paused reflectively, then spoke, for once, with genuine warmth. 'The kids are worth looking out for despite the fact they can be bloody difficult.' They made eye contact and Soames felt more open-minded about him. He might be a cynic, he might hate the management, but maybe he really did have the students' welfare at heart.

Soames changed tack. 'Do the St Clouds kids go to the youth club in the town?'

'Miss Weinstock's been on about that, has she?'

Soames didn't say she hadn't.

'It's the only organisation the boys are allowed to attend in Swanage – so it's an escape, however cruddy the facilities are. I know what you're going to say – why are the lads still going there if even a whisper of doubt exists? I would have put the club off limits – but Weinstock feels differently.'

'Why?'

'She's always reckoned the leader – a Jesus freak called Hinton – is spot on. Nice and compassionate. Listens to all the kids' problems. She's even thinking of asking him to join the staff, to run a youth wing here. Once Weinstock's convinced about something, there would have to be a world catastrophe to change her mind. Local priest speaks highly of Hinton, but personally I find him a creep.'

'You don't think this ring might have spread its tentacles to the school itself?'

Bundy paused for a moment, but the pause seemed false, as if he wanted Soames to notice he was thinking hard.

'I know they say pederasts are cunning, but they'd have to be *very* cunning to get past me.'

'I've been told there was an incident.' Soames tried another cautious risk, taking a sip of his filthy coffee.

Bundy paused again, and for a moment it seemed as if he didn't want to continue. 'Gaby Darrington will fill you in, but there's this kid called Bernie Lofts. Bit of a head case. He's made accusations before when he was younger and then withdrawn them, but this time they weren't about a member of staff.'

'Does Miss Weinstock know?'

'So Gaby says. Weinstock would never confide in me or anyone else, but I expect she told Dr Griff. This CID bloke, Mason, has interviewed me, but I couldn't tell him much – just what I've told you. The trouble is, this horrible business could close the school. The parents have already started taking their kids away.' There was a slight edge of panic in his voice and Soames began to realise he was, in his own way, as buttoned-up as Weinstock.

'Do you think Dr Griff confronted an intruder?'

'It's impossible to say.' Bundy looked uneasy. 'He and Weinstock check on the boys all the time. They're like a surveillance team. There's no privacy for anyone and they're not above going through the boys' lockers.' Bundy gave Soames a wry smile and seemed to reflect for a moment. 'Have you heard about Griff's parrot?'

Soames shook his head.

'Name of Hamlet. Can only say one phrase and repeats it monotonously. Fortunately, Dr Griff kept Hamlet to himself.'

'What was the phrase?'

' "Who's a pretty boy then?" ' There was an awkward silence and Bundy looked embarrassed, obviously thinking he'd gone too far. 'You must think I'm a callous bastard.' He didn't wait for a reply. 'I've just had one hell of a shock, that's all. Griff and Weinstock acted as one – like a closed cell – which has always made them difficult to work with. But it feels weird now one of them's gone – and with the school being hit so badly . . .' His voice trailed away and then returned with brash jocularity. 'You think your job's temporary – well, it could be a lot more temporary than you think. Like everyone else's round here.'

'What's Miss Weinstock's attitude?'

'She's just devastated by Griff's death. As I said, she can blind herself to anything – except what happened to Griff.'

'Have you talked to her about the ring?'

'Of course, but she just closes her mind to it all and goes on about the evils of the modern world. What about the Romans, I said. I mean – she's an expert on that lot and they fancied boys, didn't they? But I couldn't get through to her at all.' Bundy looked at Soames unhappily, rather more flustered than he had been before, no doubt thinking he'd been talking wildly. 'Sorry to bend your ear like this, Alan. Sometimes it seems – if you talk to a stranger across a crowded room – do you know what I mean? It's liberating – contact with someone on the outside – and that's where these perverts are if you want my opinion. Well on the outside.' He shrugged and glanced down at his watch. 'The bell will be going in a sec. Never send to know for whom the bell tolls, eh? Nice to have you aboard.' Bundy paused. 'Ah – here comes Gaby – Gaby Darrington. Your Head of Department. I expect she'll want a quick word.'

He moved away, heading for a group of teachers round the table who were all staring at him expectantly. Were the staff put out that Bundy had spent so much time talking to a new teacher? wondered Soames. Was he going to have to account for his actions, to hurriedly reassure them that all would be well with their right, tight little world?

Gaby Darrington was somewhere in her late thirties, slim with auburn hair. She was attractive and gave the impression of being confident.

'Please call me Gaby. I'm so sorry not to have been here to greet you on your first morning. I've been with the police for hours. But I don't think they're getting anywhere. Who would want to kill an old man? He was such a sweetie. It *must* have been an intruder.' Gaby Darrington paused, conscious that she might sound gushing. 'Look – will you come and have lunch with me at my house? It's almost next door to your flat. We could have a talk.'

'What time?'

'Say twelve thirty? That will give us an hour. I gather you had a problem with the Lower Fourth, but you took the right course of action. They can be very difficult.'

'I was impressed with Grant. He owned up and took the blame.'

'Yes – he's a decent boy,' she replied a little vaguely.

The other members of staff were slowly beginning to leave now and they were surrounded by a gently milling throng.

'I met Miss Weinstock in the corridor,' Gaby Darrington continued.

46

'*Did* she cane them?'

'I don't think so.'

'But she does dish out corporal punishment?'

'Occasionally.' Gaby Darrington looked uneasy.

'I thought it was illegal.'

'Only in state schools,' she said even more vaguely. 'Anyway, St Clouds is a world of its own. You'll soon see what I mean. I've got to dash.'

As Soames walked back to the classroom with a feeling of trepidation, he saw a group of boys whispering together in the locker-room. They were not members of the Lower Fourth, but there was something so anxious about the group that he almost stopped to ask them what was wrong. Then he realised how stupid that would be and, anyway, he could well be over-reacting to the clandestine world of childhood.

Soames hurried on, uncomfortably aware that they had all stopped talking and were gazing at him. Somehow they reminded him of Kate Weinstock watching him from her office on the day of his interview.

'Do come in.'

Gaby Darrington looked much more apprehensive than she had in the staff room and Soames had the feeling that she was wondering if she had taken on too much, that the reality of his appearance had made her anxious.

Soames was feeling anxious himself. Both his classes after break had been well behaved and attentive, but unfortunately he was rusty, not sharp enough with the syllabus, and he had made a couple of obvious mistakes.

Still feeling shaken, he followed Gaby into a tasteful, well lived-in room, with good prints on the walls and a clutch of military photographs and portraits. A glass case displayed medals and trophies while the sofa and chairs were blue hessian which was picked up again in the lampshades and in the pattern on the carpet. A collection of gentle Dresden shepherds and shepherdesses were contrasted by a military sword slung along the wall.

'Will you have a drink?' she asked.

'What are you having?'

'A dry sherry.'

'That'll be fine.'

'Make yourself comfortable. Lunch should be ready in about ten minutes.'

As Gaby poured the sherry, Soames said, 'I think we should come straight to the point.'

'I'm glad they've sent someone at last.' She looked out of her depth and had lost her original poise. 'Were you OK with the teaching?'

'The rust shows. But I'm trying. So what's really been going on here?'

'It's been dreadful, largely because management refused to believe me.'

'And by management you mean the late Dr Griff and the current Miss Weinstock? There doesn't seem to be anyone else effectively in charge here.'

'There never has been.' She handed Soames his sherry.

'You've told Mason everything you can?'

'Of course.'

'You won't discuss my role with anyone else, of course.'

'I haven't even mentioned it to my husband. Presumably he counts as anyone?'

'I gather you're separated.'

'We have been for the last year. We've just grown apart over the years. I suppose he has his career and I have mine. Our personal life suddenly seemed irrelevant. In fact, in the end it hardly existed.' She seemed excessively frank, but Soames also wondered what she was leaving out.

'And your husband's a senior army officer?' he interrupted, deliberately matter-of-fact.

'The *most* senior. He's the commanding officer of the Royal Rangers base at Bantry Bay.'

'Does he have any other relationship?'

'He wouldn't have time,' she said drily. 'Edward is too busy being a soldier.'

'How long has he been at Bantry Bay?'

'Ten years, but in a variety of different capacities. He's had this

48

commission with the peace-keeping force for a couple of years.'

'And how long have you been at St Clouds?'

'Exactly ten years. Edward was posted from Catterick and I grabbed the opportunity here.'

'Do you have children?'

'No.' She was abrupt and Soames hurried on, all too conscious of hitting the raw nerve.

'Are you happy here?'

'I was.'

'Despite Miss Weinstock –'

'I can see you've been talking to Noel Bundy. He's very embittered at the way he's been treated, and I really wouldn't place too much importance on what he says. I'm devastated by Dr Griff's death. He was a lovely man and really understood the children, despite the fact he didn't teach. He was due to retire at the end of term.'

'And Miss Weinstock?'

'They were very sweet together. I often wondered if they'd marry. In the holidays they went on academic cruises, but I'm sure they've never even touched one another. It was all in the mind. Just companionship.'

'I didn't really mean in that capacity.'

'As a Deputy Head she's been very effective. Full of good commonsense authority, and although she's tough with the boys they need her structure desperately. I suppose she *is* a control freak in some ways, but believe you me the boys definitely need control.'

'Do the pupils like her?'

'I'm not sure I'd use the word "like", but she's been a rock. They can always rely on her.'

Soames was sure Gaby was genuine about Miss Weinstock's leadership, but there could be no doubt she felt deeply rejected by her husband. Was that why she was so frank?

'I got a very different version from Noel Bundy.'

'I'm sure you did. They don't like each other, never did and never will.'

'How long have you known about the ring?' asked Soames casually.

49

'There's only been rumours.'

'What rumours?'

'Just talk. Miss Weinstock checked the local youth club out and gave the all clear. That's the only place the boys congregate outside the school.'

'How would she know it was safe?'

'She has faith in the club leader.'

'Do you?'

'He's very authoritarian. A bit like Kate Weinstock.'

'And a born again Christian?'

'I don't hold that against him.'

'What about the army connection? Does your husband know about that?'

'There's an investigation going on.'

'Who's in charge?'

'Edward.'

'So he *is* taking it seriously.'

'Of course.'

'Do you still see each other?'

Gaby looked irritated now. 'Edward and I are on good terms. We just don't see the point of living together, that's all. We need space.'

'And this allegation?'

'It was made by one of the boys. Bernie Lofts.'

'Who to?'

'Me.'

'So he trusts you.'

'I've taught him for three years.'

'What's he like?'

'There's been abuse at home. But Bernie's made progress here. He's much more stable, although I have to say that he's made false allegations – sexual allegations – against members of staff, but that was when he was much younger.'

'And now he's doing it again?'

'I'm sure it's not like that. I know him.'

'So you believe his allegation?'

She paused, as if for further consideration. 'Yes. I listened carefully to what he said and found him convincing.'

'Tell me more about him.'

'Bernie is seventeen and a prefect. He's talented and creative, but very insecure.'

'Does he go to this club?'

'Yes. There's a training programme being run there.'

'Who by?'

'The army.'

'What part does he play in the training programme?'

'Bernie's particularly keen on athletics. The programme at the club – it's called Ballard Youth Club – is a precursor to a more intensive course at Bantry Bay.'

'Could the idea be seen as a public relations exercise by the army?'

Gaby Darrington shrugged as if she didn't want to commit herself either way. 'The course has proved very popular and is extremely well organised, both at Ballard and Bantry Bay. We've had glowing reports from the boys.'

'There've been no other allegations?'

She shook her head.

'Except for Lofts.'

'That's right.'

'Mr Bundy also confirmed he'd made sexual allegations before '

'Three years have passed since then.' She sounded impatient.

'Even so.' Soames was doubtful.

'I *know* Bernie. He wouldn't have made this up. Not now he's so much more positive.'

'Do you ever see him alone?'

'He has private English tutorials with me.'

'What exactly did Lofts tell you?'

'That he was sexually assaulted.'

'Who by?'

'Someone at Bantry Bay.'

'A soldier?'

She nodded.

'Why didn't Lofts give you more detail?'

'He was too upset.'

'When did this alleged incident occur?'

'The previous night.'

'So why wasn't it reported to the police?'

'He didn't want what happened made public.'

'Can you remember exactly what he said?'

'Usually the boys stay overnight, getting a taste of army life. That evening there was a run with the NCOs. One of them told Bernie he wanted him to help check something out and took him away from the others.'

'This is all very vague.'

'Bernie was very upset.'

'Did he give you any description?'

'No.'

Soames frowned, not sure whether to believe her or not.

'Bernie was led into an empty hut by this man and – the assault happened there.'

'According to Lofts.'

Gaby shrugged.

There's something very surface about her, thought Soames.

'So what happened then?'

'When it was over, Bernie rejoined the other boys.'

'Why did his assailant let him do that? He could have given him away at once.'

'Bernie was threatened.'

'So he was interfered with, threatened and then rejoined the others and got on with the course.'

'Don't you believe me?'

'It's all so unlikely that I suppose I do,' Soames conceded.

'Bernie promised me he'd tell me more the next morning. Suddenly he seemed very anxious to get away. Perhaps it was because I kept begging him to go to Miss Weinstock.'

'I thought Noel Bundy was in charge of pastoral care.'

'I couldn't afford to take that risk.' Gaby was uneasy.

'Why?'

'Weinstock is so much better at dealing with the boys. Bundy blunders.'

'Go on.'

'Next morning, Bernie came to see me again and confessed he'd made up the allegation. I told him I didn't believe him, but he was adamant. I asked why, and he said he'd just been seeking attention.'

'Sounds a little too glib.' Like you, Mrs Darrington, Soames thought. 'So he withdrew everything?'

'Mostly everything. He said it hadn't happened to him, but *had* happened to other boys on other occasions. He told me certain boys were known as "Prits". They got taken to Bantry Bay for training and were abused.'

'Did he use that exact term?'

'Abused? Yes, I believe he did. I can't be exactly sure though.'

Who's a pretty boy then? asked Hamlet in Soames's mind. 'So someone warned Lofts off?'

'I'm sure of it. Bernie hasn't been the same since. He's lost a lot of the confidence he'd built up.'

'That the school had fostered in him?'

'Yes.'

'You eventually told Miss Weinstock?'

'After I'd contacted the police.'

'Don't you think contacting them was premature? Shouldn't you have gone straight to Miss Weinstock?'

'Of course. I was in a flap. She was furious with me.'

'What did Miss Weinstock do?'

'She interviewed Bernie – and then told me he *was* attention-seeking.'

'Weren't you – didn't you probe a little further?'

'I tried, but she was certain Bernie was fabricating everything. Like he had before . . .' Gaby Darrington paused and then brought out the words in a rush. 'He once told Miss Weinstock he'd killed his mother.'

'And . . .?'

'Bernie's mother answered the phone when Miss Weinstock called her. Mrs Lofts seemed quite chirpy until she was told what her son had said. Miss Weinstock's never forgotten the way Bernie lied.'

'So there's hard evidence about him being a fantasy merchant then, as well as making sexual allegations about staff. So why do *you* believe him?'

'I know him, warts and all. This time I was *sure* he was telling the truth.'

'Have you approached him again?'

'He dropped the tutorials. But Bernie still comes here because we run the debating society together.'

'Do you think Rowland Griff's murder could be linked to a pederast ring?'

'I just don't know.'

'What about your husband? Did you confide in him?'

'Mason asked me that too. The fact is I didn't tell Edward because I was afraid we'd have a row.'

'What about?'

'I'd already told him I thought his internal investigation could turn out to be a whitewash. If I started making unsubstantiated allegations against his men I don't know what he'd do.'

'You felt he'd be angry, or wouldn't take you seriously?'

'I didn't know how he'd react. That's why we separated. I felt I didn't know Edward any longer.'

'And you haven't got any *facts* at all?'

'None.'

'But you still believe Lofts?'

'Yes.'

There was a long silence.

'Is there anything else you want to ask?' said Gaby Darrington awkwardly.

'I'd like to know more about the school.'

'Can we do that over lunch?'

As Soames washed his hands, he wondered about Gaby Darrington, trying to work out what her motives had been for calling him in. He had the unsettling feeling that he was only looking at one detail in an overall picture – without being able to see the actual picture itself.

As he turned off the taps, Soames came to a sudden realisation. He had expected a school in trauma – and in mourning – but what he had seen was a school still locked into apprehension and expectation.

We've had quite a few parents phone,' said Gaby. 'They want to take their sons away. Some for a week or so – others for good.'

She had made a clear soup with garlic croutons followed by crisp whitebait with lemon and salad and new rye bread. Gaby ate steadily, while Soames relished every mouthful, realising how long he had lived off junk food.

'That's not very supportive of them,' he said.

'Word has got round.'

'About the ring?'

'Isn't Dr Griff's murder enough?'

'I suppose Mason has seen Lofts?'

'He's with him now.'

'Maybe he'll convince him.'

'Bernie's very stubborn.'

'And being frightened off by someone?' Soames persisted. 'His assailant, or someone else – someone here at the school?'

'I'm sorry to keep sounding so negative, but I just don't know.'

'There's no one here at the school you'd even have the slightest suspicion of?'

'No. I promise you I'm not concealing anything – or shielding anyone.' She looked down at her plate and Soames wondered if Gaby was doing just that.

'You'd be very unwise if you *were* concealing something.'

'Don't you mean just plain stupid?'

'I suppose I do.'

'Well, I'm not. I care very much for the boys and I love my job. I don't want to lose it, and I don't want them harmed.' Gaby paused. 'Surely you can do better than Mason?' she asked.

'It's early days. I need to be accepted. Once I start taking too many risks I'll only create suspicion.'

Gaby nodded reluctantly. 'I just don't think we have much time.'

'Until . . .?'

'Something else happens.'

6

Just as Soames was leaving, a black Daimler glided almost soundlessly up the drive with an army flag and a uniformed chauffeur.

'Edward's here,' said Gaby. She seemed agitated.

'Has he visited you since Dr Griff's death?'

'No. But he phoned. He was very alarmed by – by this development.' She glanced down at her watch and then too deliberately changed the subject. 'I don't think Edward's ever accepted that I've got anything to do or that I work to a time-table. He once referred to my teaching career as "her little job".' Gaby gave Soames an ironic smile but it was tinged with bitterness.

Colonel Darrington was tall with close-cropped fair hair. He wore fatigues and highly polished boots. He was the only man Soames had ever seen who could honestly be described as having 'steely blue' eyes. Yet there was more to him than the stereotyping seemed to demand. Darrington looked slightly awkward, as if paying this visit was difficult and he would be much happier elsewhere. So this was what growing apart felt like, thought Soames. He wondered what had caused the anger. Did she feel sidelined? The little lady at home with a job that didn't matter?

'This is Alan Soames. He's come to join the department on a temporary basis to cover for Mr Blenheim.'

'Oh yes – the poor chap with the heart condition.' Edward Darrington sounded dismissive, but his voice gave him distinction and there was no doubt he had considerable charisma.

'The poor chap with the heart condition,' thought Soames. Would he describe Dr Griff as 'the poor chap who had his throat cut'?

'Good to meet you.' Darrington pumped his hand. 'God awful business about Griff,' he said, and Soames realised he had done him an injustice. He seemed genuinely upset and, unless he was very much mistaken, deeply shocked. 'I can't imagine who'd want to do such a terrible thing.' He glanced at his wife. 'What do the police say? Did he disturb an intruder?'

'No one seems to know,' said Soames and Darrington turned to him in surprise, as if he had spoken out of turn.

'I expect you've heard the other allegations? About the pederast ring?' Darrington enunciated the words slowly and with considerable distaste.

Soames wondered if he had underestimated Darrington. He would have to be more careful.

'Filthy business, but it's difficult to assess its veracity, and now the police are talking about army involvement.' Darrington looked concerned. 'Anyway, I've put an investigation in hand. We're a tight community, a bit like St Clouds, and if there's a rotten apple, we'll find him.'

Slightly disarmed, Soames glanced at Gaby and saw that she had become even more agitated.

'Pederasts are apparently very cunning – or at least that's what I'm told,' said Colonel Darrington. 'They move in.'

'To the army?' said Gaby, to Soames's surprise. If she believed Lofts's allegations – as she said she did – why on earth was she querying that?

'Why *not* the army? They seem to have infiltrated other professions.'

There was a short, unyielding silence.

'I would have thought the security screening was too tight,' said Gaby lamely.

'If there haven't been any previous convictions, what the hell can we do? Anyway, I'm fast-tracking the enquiry.' He paused. 'Naturally I'm praying that no one in the regiment will be held responsible for any of this.'

'Did you want something, Edward?' asked Gaby awkwardly while Soames tried to work out whether he should leave or not.

'Just some papers from the study.'

'I'll have to go,' said Gaby, calmer now. 'Can you lock up after you?'

'I always do, don't I?' Darrington was smiling, but there was a hint of irritation. 'I know where the papers are. Why don't

I just run up and get them? I shan't be more than a couple of minutes and then you can lock up yourself.'

'I haven't got a couple of minutes,' snapped Gaby. 'I've got a class.'

'Then you must be on your way.' Edward Darrington turned to Soames. 'Good to meet you, Alan. I'm so sorry you had to arrive at such a terrible time.' They shook hands again, this time rather more self-consciously as if both were aware of the friction.

As his class worked quietly and the afternoon sunlight filtered through the latticed windows, Soames sat at his desk wondering about Gaby Darrington. There had been something decidedly glib about the conversation they had had at lunch-time and underneath all that easy capability he was sure there was considerable bitterness. But what about? *Just* a failed marriage? Or was there something more? Lofts had claimed he was assaulted and had then recanted. Was someone leaning on him? And could Griff's murder really be linked to a ring of pederasts, or had he simply surprised a burglar? Was Gaby Darrington holding out on him despite the fact that she was his own 'insider'?

The bell rang for the end of afternoon school and the class began to pack up their books.

'Can I speak to you, sir?' asked one of the boys, and Soames, light years away, looked up in surprise.

'Sorry?'

'Can I speak to you?'

'Of course.'

'When the others have gone.'

Soames was suddenly alert. 'OK.'

The boy hung back, pretending to be searching for something amongst his books, and when one of his friends came up and whispered he gave an impatient shrug.

Finally, the others went, their glances curious, but now they were alone the boy seemed hesitant, as if he was regretting an impulse that had been made on the spur of the moment.

'Well?' Soames tried to keep his tone as neutral as possible. 'I'm sorry, I don't know your name yet.'

'Simon Grace.' He was tall, with classic good looks, but he was obviously very unsure of himself.

'How can I help you?' asked Soames affably and he hoped reassuringly.

'You're new here, sir.'

'That's right.'

'All the other teachers have been here for ages.'

'So?'

'They're set in their ways.'

'You make them sound like bits of furniture.' Soames laughed, wanting to make the boy feel at ease, realising he could put him off at any moment.

Simon Grace didn't reply.

'So what is it you want to talk to me about?' Soames asked even more gently.

'I'm afraid –'

'Why?'

'Because of what's happening.'

'This dreadful murder?'

'That – and other things too.'

'What other things?'

'I can't say.'

'Come on, Simon. You said you wanted to talk to me.'

He was silent again.

'Do you have friends?' asked Soames.

'I've got good friends.'

'Look –' Soames decided to take a risk – 'is there something that's – frightening you?'

Again, Grace didn't reply. Then he gabbled, 'I don't want to go up to the army base,' and Soames felt a rush of adrenalin. At last, here was some more corroboration.

'Do you have to?'

'I signed up for the course weeks ago. But now I don't want to go.'

'Why not?'

'I just don't want to.' He sounded childish and sulky and Soames knew he was going to have to work hard.

'Do you want me to get you off it?'

59

'Can you do that, sir?' Immediately Simon Grace's eyes lit up, and he was obviously clinging to unexpected hope.

'I don't know. Who do I speak to?'

'Bernie Lofts, sir.'

'Who is he?'

'He's a prefect, sir. He organises – helps to organise – stuff with the army.'

'What stuff?'

'Physical training courses, sir.'

'Isn't there a teacher involved?'

'Just the youth club leader.'

That's odd, thought Soames. 'What's his name?'

'Mr Hinton.'

'So why can't you tell Lofts and Mr Hinton yourself?'

'Because they'll make me go. Now I've signed up.'

'They can't *make* you do anything. This is a voluntary activity and not part of the curriculum.'

'They can, sir. That's why I've come to you. Because you're new.'

'I still don't get it. You could go to any of the teachers here. If you don't want to do something, surely no one's going to force you, are they?'

'The school rule is that if you put your name down you can't back off. You have to honour your word – unless you're sick or something.'

'Whose rule *is* this?'

'Miss Weinstock's, sir.'

'I'll speak to Miss Weinstock. I can't liaise with another pupil I don't know – and I've never met Mr Hinton either.'

Grace gazed at him uncertainly. 'You'll have to work hard on her, sir. She's as tough as they are.'

'Don't tell me what to do.'

'No, sir. Sorry, sir.'

'Tell me why you're afraid of going up to Bantry Bay.' He had the feeling he was still losing an argument.

'It's too tough, sir.'

'You're no coward.'

'I am. Something could happen to me.'

'What?' Soames asked sympathetically.

60

'I might break a leg. And anyway ...' Grace paused as if searching for inspiration. 'I get vertigo – you know, sir, the fear of heights.'

'I know what vertigo is.' Soames paused and then decided to take the ultimate risk. 'But I honestly don't think you're telling me the truth.'

'I am, sir.' Grace was feebly indignant.

'There's something else.'

'No.'

'There must be.'

'Why?' Simon Grace was desperate now, his fingers twitching.

'You can tell me,' said Soames. 'That's why you came to me, wasn't it? Because I'm new?'

'I just have, sir. I've told you everything.'

Soames sighed. 'I'll see Miss Weinstock and discuss the problem with her.' He paused again, wanting to keep the boy's confidence. 'I'll do my best for you.'

'Thank you, sir.'

'I can't say more than that.'

'No, sir.'

Soames was conscious that Grace was gazing at him pleadingly.

He knocked apprehensively on Kate Weinstock's door, wondering if he had really thought this through.

'Come.'

He opened the door and stood on the threshold.

'Can I have a quick word?'

'Of course. Do sit down.' She was writing at her desk and didn't look up. Soames watched her from the depths of an armchair, still wondering if he was pushing his luck.

Eventually Kate Weinstock was ready.

'How can I help you?' She smiled without warmth.

'I've been approached by a boy called Simon Grace.'

'Yes?'

'About a visit to Bantry Bay.'

She nodded enthusiastically. 'We have an excellent relationship with the Royal Rangers. They've set up a physical training scheme for the boys linked to Ballard Youth Club in Swanage. It's a wonderful opportunity for us – and of course our students will be mixing with boys from the town. An excellent arrangement.' She swept on. 'I've been most impressed by Mr Hinton who leads the club, and I'm thinking of inviting him to start some youth activities here.'

'Simon Grace has a bit of a problem with the scheme.'

'Which is?' She suddenly looked hostile.

'He's scared of going. Seriously scared. He wants out.'

'Didn't you refer him to Noel Bundy? Noel is in charge of pastoral care here.'

'I didn't know that.'

'I thought I explained his role at your interview.'

Soames inwardly cursed. He *should* have thought this through much more carefully.

'This isn't your province?' he asked feebly.

'Not at all.'

'I'm sorry.' Soames rose to his feet.

'But if it was –' Kate Weinstock looked up at him dismissively – 'I would say this – I know Grace of old. He's a procrastinator. He'll put anything off if he possibly can. Grace is always signing himself on and never committing, never delivering. This is a golden opportunity for Simon to actually see something through.'

'He seemed very upset.' Soames was not prepared to give in just like that, but he knew he had lost.

'I quite understand why he came to you. You're new – and if you don't mind me saying so, he thought he could use you – so that's why I'm very glad we're having this little chat. You can't remember all our procedures in one day, Alan, so please don't blame yourself. I'll see Simon personally – it's about time we had one of our little talks.' Kate Weinstock smiled up at him again and Soames realised yet again what a formidable opponent she was.

'I'll get on then.' He felt defeated.

'How are you coping with our boys?' There was a hint of patronage in her voice.

'I had a very successful afternoon.'

'I'm so glad. I saw your two miscreants.'

'They were afraid they were going to be caned.' Soames thrust back, but she wasn't in the least embarrassed.

'I save that for grave offences and carry out the punishments myself, on very rare occasions. Dr Griff had angina so I couldn't let him take the risk, and we preferred not to let other members of staff take on such a difficult task.' She paused. 'I realise it's not the done thing to cane nowadays, but here at St Clouds we've retained the right to corporal punishment in extreme cases. What else can you do with boys with these problems? They desperately need structure and we provide a clearly defined regime. But we have to be vigilant, Alan. We're trying to restore damaged human beings.' She ended her speech with the same bland smile as she had begun, leaving Soames in some confusion. 'You may not agree with me, Alan, but I can promise you I'm consistent.'

Soames frowned. He found her 'frankness' as contrived as Gaby Darrington's. It was as if he was banging his head against shatter-proof glass.

'I'd better be getting on then,' he said, rising slowly to his feet.

'If you ever want to have a talk – please come and see me. I try to keep my door open to staff as well as boys.'

Was she ever so slightly thrown? Soames decided to capitalise on the possibility. 'Thank you. Are there any developments in the murder enquiry yet?'

'I'm afraid not. Who *would* want to hurt Dr Griff?' Her shoulders shook. 'He was such a good man. A gentle, good man.'

To Soames's surprise Kate Weinstock's voice broke and she looked down at her desk.

'He must have surprised an intruder. Surely that's the most likely explanation?'

Soames said nothing and she buried her face in her hands, her shoulders shaking again. He didn't know whether to comfort her or not and felt thoroughly disconcerted.

Then Miss Weinstock looked up and he could see the hostility in her eyes. 'Would you mind?'

'Sorry?'

'Leaving me alone.'

63

'Of course. I just wondered if there was anything I could do.'

'There's nothing. Please go.'

Conscious that he had appeared insensitive, Soames left the room torn between concern and dislike.

The mellow warmth was comforting as Soames walked back through the cloisters to what must once have been the old coach house that housed his own modest flat.

'Sir?' Simon Grace was standing outside, all too obviously waiting for him. 'Did you have any luck?'

Soames sighed. 'You shouldn't have come here.'

'I know where you live, sir.'

'That's obvious. I've got to have *some* privacy. You should have waited until I contacted you.'

'I'm sorry, sir.' Grace obviously wasn't in the least apologetic. 'Have you seen Miss Weinstock?'

'She's going to have a chat with you herself.'

'But you know what I mean . . .'

'Sorry?'

'Have you got me off going to Bantry Bay?'

'Miss Weinstock will talk to you.'

'You've *got* to tell me, sir.' Simon Grace was desperate and pleading and fatalistic all at the same time.

'She wants you to go.' Soames spoke as gently as possible.

'I *won't*.' Soames was suddenly appalled by the intensity of his fear. 'No one can make me go.'

'I'm sure it won't be –'

'So bad when I get there?' Grace's voice rose hysterically. 'That I'll have a lot of fun?'

'She didn't say that.'

'What *did* she say?'

'I can't remember the whole conversation.' Soames suddenly felt incredibly guilty, as if he had been discovered consorting with the enemy. Why was this kid making him feel like a traitor?

'You never stood a chance,' Grace was saying bitterly. 'She's a fucking monster.'

'You mustn't speak like that.'

'Look, sir.' Grace was wheedling now. 'I'll do anything.'

'What?'

'I'll do anything for you. Anything you like. Whatever you want.'

It was Soames's turn to be shocked as he realised how grossly he had underestimated the situation.

'Shut up and calm down.' Trying to subdue his rising panic, Soames knew he had to use the opportunity. 'If you want me to help you – anyone to help you – I advise you to come clean.'

'What about?' Simon Grace suddenly switched to the defensive.

'The camp. Bantry Bay. What *are* you afraid of? It's more than getting hurt, isn't it? It's more than being scared of heights. So what is it? What's really bugging you?'

7

'Bugging?' Simon Grace began to laugh. 'You don't mean buggering, do you, sir?' He looked as if he was literally aching with mirth, bending double, hands clasped over his stomach, gasping and laughing until the laughter became a series of gulps that led to hard, dry sobs. Soames grabbed Grace's shoulders and shook him, looking around, praying no one had seen them.

Slowly, Grace became calmer, gazing up at him, his mouth half open, looking idiotic and pathetic at the same time.

'Now,' said Soames. 'Now talk to me quietly and properly.' He suddenly felt a rush of pain, for this was the way he had talked to Rik when he had had his own temper tantrums. 'Talk to me quietly. Talk to me properly.'

'What about?'

'What's this buggery business?'

'Sorry?'

'You said, "You don't mean buggering, do you?"'

There was a short, sharp silence.

'I don't get you,' said Grace eventually.

'You do.'

'What do you mean?'

'What are you really afraid of at Bantry Bay?'

'I told you.'

'There's something more, isn't there?'

'I'm afraid.'

'I know. But what of?'

'I've got to go now, sir, or I'll be late for prep.' But still Grace didn't move.

'What are you afraid of? It may be hard, but it'll be much better in the end if you tell me.'

They gazed at each other, and Soames felt the glass wall again.

'The assault course, sir. I'm afraid of heights. I could fall and break a –'

'You'd better go then,' snapped Soames.

Grace turned and began to run back to the cloisters.

The flat was depressing in the extreme and comprised two small rooms, one with a view over the road that ran round the school, serviceable and sterile with dull furnishings, dominated by a wide-screen TV and empty bookshelves.

The bedroom was worse, with flock wallpaper that was peeling and ragged-looking curtains with a pattern of marigolds. The colour clashes were enough to give Soames a migraine and he hurried into the narrow, carbolic-smelling kitchen and took two Disprin from the packet he had providentially brought with him. He ran water into a glass that smelt of whisky he hadn't had – but the previous owner presumably had needed before he was invalided out.

Soames returned to the living-room and lay on the sofa, turning on the TV but not the sound.

Soames felt more depressed than he had even felt at home. St Clouds was permeated by a dispiriting, unenlightened regime which was getting to him. Yet, in some ways, he had to acknowledge Weinstock could be right about the boys and their need for structure, although he was sure she was wrong about her use of the cane. Soames felt her attitude to Simon Grace, however, had been inflexible.

Very much to his surprise, he found himself longing for the lonely but comfortable house in Croydon, with its trim garden and heart-breaking memories. Here, this dreary little flat seemed to say it all. Life was functional: the paint might be off-white and the wallpaper flocked, but the roof didn't leak, the taps worked, the electricity could be switched on and off and the toilet could be flushed. That was it. That was all one should expect.

Soames dragged his thoughts back to the staff he had met so far. Even if he cared for the students, Bundy was clearly no more than a cynical whinger while Weinstock and Griff had been far too long at the helm for their own good, and anyone else's come to that.

Gaby Darrington was another matter. There was something curiously plausible about her. Too plausible.

As to Griff's murder . . .

The doorbell rang and Soames felt apprehensive. What the hell was the matter with him? This wretched school was really undermining him. The bell buzzed again and as he slowly got up Soames found himself worrying that Simon Grace was going to be on the doorstep again. Christ – the boy had all but propositioned him.

A short, slightly belligerent-looking red-headed man in his late forties stood on the threshold. He had a rather untidy reddish beard and a small, well-trimmed moustache, as if this was the only item of personal adornment on which he really lavished his attention.

'Mr Soames?'

'Yes.'

'DI Mason. Could I have a word?'

'Of course.' Soames was grateful that contact had come at last as he led the way upstairs.

'You're new to the school?'

'Today.'

'Settling in?' Mason looked askance at the drab room.

'It's not exactly a home from home.'

'You're right there.' Then Mason lowered his voice. 'But then, with a bit of luck, you might not be here long.'

'That's a cheering thought.'

'But you need that bit of luck.'

'I'm working on it.'

'I think you and I should have a session elsewhere. I live near the jetty – at the end of the town. Fourteen The Strand. Would you like to drop round at about eight tonight? Have some supper.'

'I think that's too risky.'

'What about The Cutter? There's an upstairs room we could use. That's near the jetty too. You can't miss it.' Mason paused. 'Have you come to any conclusions I might need to think over?'

'I'm concerned about the youth club, and its possible connection with the ring. And I've just had a worrying conversation with a pupil here.'

'Worrying in what way?'

'His name's Simon Grace and he's terrified of going to Bantry this weekend.'

'Did he say why?'

'Went on about being afraid of heights, but I know he's lying. He wouldn't tell me what he's really afraid of, but he even lay in wait for me here.'

'Lofts denied everything too. Said he'd been winding Mrs Darrington up and apologised. He's a fairly odd character – one of many, I suspect.'

'That's the nature of the school,' said Soames abruptly.

'The place has always had a weird reputation among the locals.'

'It would.'

'You sound sceptical.'

'I am. Some of the boys just come from broken homes, that's all. They're not freaks or psychos. There haven't been any major incidents in the past, have there?'

'No.'

'There you are then.'

Mason gave him a dubious look. 'How are you getting on here?'

'It's challenging. I met Colonel Darrington too. Briefly. You know he's separated from his wife?'

'No wonder.'

'Why do you say that?'

'Gets too close to the boys, doesn't she?'

'Does she? I hadn't heard that.'

'I have.'

'But if she does, wouldn't Miss Weinstock have got rid of her? Who's your source?'

'Common knowledge.'

'Did Lofts tell you?'

'He said they were friends, but that could be wishful thinking on his part.'

'If Gaby Darrington is behaving unprofessionally, wouldn't Weinstock have dealt with her long ago?'

'Maybe she didn't take it all in. I mean, Weinstock's not exactly the perceptive type, is she? I can't make her out.'

'And you don't like people you can't make out?' asked Soames.

'That's right.' Mason grinned at him, relaxing a little.

'So you wouldn't like enigmatic foreign movies?' Soames was beginning to like Mason, not for his orthodoxy, which seemed to run to blimpishness, but for his honesty. What you see is what you get, thought Soames, and that, in the present situation, was refreshing.

'Hate 'em.'

'Or ambiguous endings?'

'Can't be doing with those either.'

'So we know where we both stand.'

'You done this job before?'

'Once.'

'What rank did you hold in the Met?' asked Mason hesitantly.

'DI.'

'One of us then. Must be a funny sort of job you're doing now.'

'Bit ambiguous,' agreed Soames.

'Better be going.' Mason went to the door and threw it open. 'Well – no little boys lurking this time.' Then he came in and closed the door again. 'If you can't beat 'em, join 'em,' he whispered. 'You really prepared to do that?'

'If I have to.'

'Could be a bit on the murky side, couldn't it?'

'I'll try not to make it a hands-on experience.'

Mason seemed disconcerted. 'See you later then.'

Soames strolled down the cliff path, noticing that Dr Griff's house was marked off with police tape. As he passed, he wondered what had happened to the parrot. Had Hamlet been put down, or was Weinstock caring for the thing? Somehow he rather hoped that she had been forced to do just that.

The evening sunshine was still warm and the sea glinted below, the tide on the ebb, the chalk white of the Old Harry Rocks bright and luminous. Now he was away from the claustrophobia of the school, Soames felt more liberated, more able to think clearly.

The steep path began to wind down the cliff towards the town and Soames stumbled, grabbing a scrubby bush to steady himself, realising again how unfit he had become. Shouldn't he be running up and down this path twice a day? The idea was not attractive.

As Soames looked down at the line of white surf, he felt a strong desire to stay outside in the great outdoors as long as he could. At St Clouds, jealousy, rivalry and secrecy seemed the natural order. Once again the idea of his lonely house in Croydon, the endless days of nothingness, the ritual walks in the park, seemed a painful freedom that he'd lost, somewhere where he could breathe.

Swanage was surprisingly old-fashioned in a particularly comforting way, with beach huts along the front facing a narrow strip of sand and a rather genteel promenade which straggled for at least half a mile around the bay. Tall Victorian buildings surrounded the seaweed-draped rocks, and in the distance there was a lighthouse.

A wooden jetty thrust out into the sea and Soames wondered if the locals fished there as they had in the seaside towns of his youth. Passing some billboards he saw that a small theatre

70

played old-fashioned music-hall and felt a stab of nostalgia that had more to do with his grandparents than himself. Then another stab came, this time of loss and deep regret. It would have been so wonderful to take Rik and Mary here when they were younger to have a bucket and spade holiday. He'd love to take them back in time. But Soames knew he couldn't take them anywhere now and that was the hell of it.

Soames found The Cutter, and walked upstairs to a small Victorian room with dark panelling and dramatic oil paintings of sea rescues. One of them depicted a girl kneeling on a pebble beach, over what he took to be the body of her drowned father.

Ted Mason sat under the painting, a pint of beer in front of him.

'I arranged for some food to be brought up in about half an hour. They do fresh fish and chips. Would you like a drink? I can ring down to the bar from here.'

Soames sat down opposite him. 'I'll have a pint of bitter.'

When Mason had placed the order he said, 'I've been in Swanage for a long time. I think I'm trusted.'

'I'm sure you are.'

'We won't be disturbed here, but we must make sure we leave separately and go out the back way. In your job I'm sure you do that all the time.' He leant back, with a slightly mocking smile.

'You see him here,' Soames improvised. 'You see him there. You think you see him everywhere. So do you cast Kate Weinstock as some kind of scarlet woman? Or is that role reserved for Gaby Darrington?'

'I told you. I can't really make out either of them.'

'Why don't you brief me? After all, as you say, you've been here a long time. What have you picked up on the wider grapevine? The school seems divided into two camps. Kate Weinstock and the rest.'

'That's where I'm not going to be of much help to you. The school isn't part of the local community. It's on its own, and so far the investigation seems to have ground to a halt. Everyone we've interviewed wants to subscribe to the intruder theory.'

'Do you?'

'It's too convenient.'

'What about the ring?'

'All I've got is Bernie Lofts and all you've got is Simon Grace.'

'So why is Colonel Darrington taking all this so seriously?'

'Because he wants the regiment squeaky clean. He's got to follow it up.'

'Even if the ring gets into the press?'

'He wouldn't want that. But Darrington's right to make a stand, especially as Lofts is his wife's protégé.'

'Did forensic come up with anything else?'

'Not a lot. There was no sign of a struggle, nothing on Griff's clothing and no fingerprints.'

'Not an outside chance of suicide?'

'The murder weapon went in at the wrong angle for that.'

'What kind of weapon are we talking about?'

'Something sharper than a kitchen knife.'

'Not a spontaneous act?'

'If he'd surprised someone, maybe. If he'd found something or seen something, then it could well have been premeditated.'

'Whatever Dr Griff found or saw would have had to be very incriminating.'

'I'm sure you're right.'

'So if we rule out the intruder, then we're almost certainly talking about the ring.'

'There've been some rumours in the town. Nothing specific unfortunately. Ballard Youth Club doesn't just arrange for St Clouds pupils to visit the base. The scheme's for anyone who belongs to the club and wants to apply.'

'Do you know of any local boys who've spent time at Bantry?'

'We've checked them out, but drawn a complete blank. Our best bet's still Lofts.'

'I haven't seen him yet.'

'Make the boy a priority.'

'I'll have to be careful,' said Soames.

'Don't you teach him?'

'Unfortunately not.'

'Can't you arrange to do so?'

'No.' Mason obviously had little experience of schools. 'What did Lofts actually say to you?' asked Soames.

'That his allegations were a deliberate wind-up of Gaby Darrington. Lofts claimed he wanted to hurt her, although he didn't give me a reason. It doesn't seem to make a lot of sense.'

'It might,' said Soames, 'but only if they have a close relationship. Too close.'

'You think she's got something going with him?' asked Mason.

'It's possible.'

'So why did she contact the police? Why didn't she just keep quiet?'

Soames shrugged.

'Tell me something else,' asked Mason. 'Do you know who dragged you into this?'

'Maybe Colonel Darrington was involved.'

'Wouldn't you have been told?'

'Not if Creighton thought the knowledge could be compromising. If you go undercover you have to be overwhelmed by your new identity.' But in this case Boyd knew he was lying. Alan Soames's personality was still like a badly fitted suit.

'I've been left out on a limb,' grumbled Mason.

'I promise I'm levelling with you,' said Soames. 'What about you?'

'There's nothing *I've* left out.' Mason was defensive now. 'What are you going to do next?'

'Check out the youth club, after I've talked to Lofts.'

'We need to break one of these kids,' said Mason as a waiter brought in their fish supper. 'And break him fast.'

8

Soames returned to his dismal flat at about ten. Ted Mason had become less disgruntled and they had had several more pints. But now his temporary feeling of well-being had faded as he stood outside his front door with a sense of something wrong. Then he had an alarming revelation. Soames realised that he had locked himself out. Why had he been so stupid? Had he imagined that he was leaving home in Croydon, slamming the Yale locked door with the key safely in his pocket? Both keys to Blenheim's flat were on one ring and Soames knew he should have separated them. Instead he must have left them on the table in the living-room.

What the hell was he going to do? The downstairs flat was in darkness, but Gaby Darrington's house had a light behind the closed curtains in the front room.

Soames rang the bell, but no one came. He waited and then rang again. Then the door was abruptly swung open by a boy of about seventeen, short, stocky and blond with broad shoulders and a tanned, but acne-pitted complexion. It was his only flaw. Otherwise he seemed perfect. Too perfect, like an old-fashioned Charles Atlas advertisement, a body builder who had been let down by his hormones.

'Mrs Darrington around?'

'She's not available.' The voice was deep and brown.

'I need to see her.'

'I'm afraid she's busy.'

'The name's Soames.'

'The new teacher?' The boy seemed dismissive and Soames's temper flared. He wasn't going to be made to look a fool by this arrogant little sod.

'That's right. I'm sorry. I need to see Mrs Darrington urgently.'

'Can I help?'

'I'm afraid not. What's she doing?'

'Some paperwork.'

'What paperwork?'

'In connection with the debating society. We've just had a meeting.'

'The two of you?'

'The committee's been here. I was just doing a bit of washing up for her.'

'That's nice of you.' Soames was feeling increasingly embarrassed. How could he admit that he had locked himself out?

'Mrs Darrington works very hard for us.'

'What's the – what's the debate?'

'This house believes that sexual discrimination in the UK is increasing.'

There was an awkward silence.

'Look. I've lost my keys,' he finally admitted.

'Yes?'

'Well – not lost exactly. I've locked myself out. I was wondering if Mrs Darrington could help. Would you ask her?'

'I really can't disturb her at the moment.'

'Why on earth not?'

'She's just running off some posters.'

'At home?'

'She's got a machine in her office upstairs.'

'How long will she be?' snapped Soames.

'Not long. Can you come back?'

'Come back?' Soames was furious. 'I'm locked out.' He paused. 'What's your name?'

'Lofts. Bernie Lofts.'

Soames realised that he had put himself at an even greater disadvantage and wondered if Lofts guessed he'd been drinking. Then he realised he'd been breathing beer all over him.

'Get Mrs Darrington down here immediately,' he said, trying to pull himself together, seeking assertion and not sure he'd found the right level.

'I'll see if she's finished.'

'Finished or not.'

'What shall I tell her? That you lost your keys?' There was a slight, deeply irritating smile playing on Lofts's lips.

75

'I haven't lost them,' rapped Soames. 'I locked myself out. In other words I left the keys inside the flat.'

'OK, sir.' Disconcertingly, Lofts suddenly reverted to the obedient schoolboy.

With an athletic stride he ran up the stairs, reached the landing and hurried off to the right, opening a door and closing it behind him.

A few seconds later Gaby Darrington emerged, looking flustered and slightly confused, while the sound of a machine clacked away behind her.

'Alan?' she called, and then began to hurry down. 'Is there something the matter?'

'I've been a fool and locked myself out. You can't think of a solution, can you?'

'Both keys?'

'I'm afraid so.'

With that mocking half smile, Bernie Lofts was slowly descending the stairs behind her, feline, sinuous, his pitted features catching the light, the pockmarks standing out against the tan. Ruined angel, Soames thought and then substituted ruined demon.

'Are you talking about miracles?' Gaby was smiling. 'I'm your Wonder Woman. I've got another set of keys. Tommy – that's the cook – he's been away for the holidays. I've got an emergency set for the flats.'

'Thank God. I'm really sorry.'

'Don't go. Unless you're too tired to talk. Why don't you come in for a nightcap?'

'That would be nice.' Soames noticed that Bernie Lofts looked surly now and much younger as he waited to be dismissed.

'We've been having a meeting about the debating society. It's very popular here. A major debate each term, and Bernie's on the committee. He was doing the washing up while I was running off some posters.'

'He was telling me,' said Soames flatly.

'OK, Bernie – thanks again.' She seemed falsely bright and self-conscious. 'You'd better be getting back to your room.'

Without a glance at either of them, he went out into the darkness.

76

'The sixth form have flats in the new block,' Gaby explained to cover Bernie's abrupt departure. 'They're small but nicely decorated – and modern.'

'Unlike my own quarters,' said Soames ruefully.

'Perhaps that's why you locked yourself out – as a protest.'

'Anyone else here?' he asked as she led the way into the sitting-room.

'I'm not running a male harem, you know.'

Soames felt uncomfortable as he sat down, attempting to laugh off his gaffe while Gaby went to the drinks cabinet.

'I'm sure they'd all like to be your courtiers.' Soames was appalled. What on earth had made him say something so idiotic. He *must* not drink.

'You're really wondering if it's wise to have the boys in my home – especially late at night.'

'Yes.'

'At least you're honest. Would you like scotch?'

'Thanks. I would.'

She poured them both large scotches and added ice.

'Where have you been – if that's not prying?'

'Not in the least. I've had a meeting with Mason. Isn't it a bit dangerous to have boys here so late?'

'I always have done, though obviously Edward was around then. Occasionally. But now he's gone I don't like to break with tradition and I'm not the only one. Other members of staff have the older boys in once or twice a week. We find it breaks down barriers.' Soames noticed that she didn't seem in the least defensive.

'Lofts is a curious guy.'

'He certainly is.'

'A control freak?'

'He wears that on his sleeve.'

'A bit like Miss Weinstock?'

'That's unfair. She has to be strong. The boys would never respect her if she wasn't.'

'Fair enough. Lofts seemed very at home here,' he probed.

'Bernie's been coming to the house for three years now. He seems to relate better to adults than to his own peer group.'

'What's his background?'

'Father was an army officer and they were posted all over the world. Bernie was permanently changing schools until he came here.'

'You must have been sympathetic to the problem. After all, you've experienced that kind of life yourself.'

'That wasn't the half of it. His father abused him and when it all came out he committed suicide. Bernie adored him.'

'What about the mother?'

'She couldn't bear the sight of him when she found out what had been going on. He was an only child.'

'He sees you as a mother figure?'

'Always has done, and can I fill in the next question for you? It's a *mother* figure we're talking about. He doesn't see me as anything else. Not as a sexual object, and before you say "Are you sure?", I've really searched my conscience. He's never touched me.'

'And you – not even a motherly kiss?'

'Hardly. The only thing is . . .'

'He's possessive.'

'Increasingly so and that's beginning to worry me.'

'Have you talked to anyone on the staff about the problem?'

'Would you?'

Soames thought of the personalities he had met so far and realised that he wouldn't. 'Have you spoken to anyone else?'

'Edward.'

'Was he unhelpful?'

'No. Oddly enough, he wasn't. I've often misjudged him. He said that I should be very consistent with Bernie – and that's what I'm trying to be. He's leaving at the end of term and I need to see it through.'

'Where's he going?'

'To read History at Cambridge.'

'So he's clever.'

'Very.'

'So he could have told you he was sexually assaulted to get a reaction. To draw you closer to him.'

'Everyone except me thinks that's the most likely explanation.'

'Was he afraid when he told you?'

'Very.'

'If it was true, was he warned off?'

'We've had this discussion before.'

'We need to have it again.' There was increasing tension between them now.

'Yes, I know he was telling the truth, so he must have been warned off.'

'And you're *sure* you don't know who by –'

'Look, Alan. I wouldn't have gone to the police if I wanted to hold anything back. Or do you think I'm trying to work some kind of double blind?'

'No. It's just that this place is such a tight little community, you've all been together for so long, the barriers are hard to penetrate. I need to ask some hard questions.'

'I know you do.' She sounded much less defensive now and Soames thought he was getting through at last – or at least some of the way through.

'Bernie seems quite dangerous. He *does* enjoy winding people up. He just did the same to me.'

'He must have seen you as a threat.' She looked uneasy.

'That's not my intention,' said Soames.

'So you think I've been encouraging him in the wrong way?'

Why can't she make up her mind? wondered Soames. 'I just don't know enough about him,' he replied.

'Or me,' Gaby said with a determined honesty. 'I know Bernie regards me with affection, but that's all.'

She still wasn't entirely convincing, thought Soames. And that's because she wasn't convinced herself. Had everything run out of control? Or had she just made a big mistake?

'I'd better be going,' he said, draining his glass.

She stood up. 'Tomorrow's youth club night. I think it would be a good opportunity if you took the boys down in the minibus. It's my turn, but you could say I'm not feeling well.'

'Can I stay on at the club?'

'Of course. You'll be in a supervisory capacity – and be paid for your time.'

'I appreciate your help.'

'Do you think you stand a chance of clearing up this business quickly?' She suddenly seemed dependent.

'Only if I get some breaks.'

'I suppose you would have told me if Mason had any new leads.'

'Of course.'

'You're not holding anything back?'

'No. He's not moving forward at all.' Soames paused. 'Before I go, tell me one last thing and please consider it carefully.'

'What is it?' She was anxious again.

'When you and your husband separated, what was Lofts's reaction?'

'I think he was pleased.'

'Do you remember what he actually said?'

'He asked if I was all right.'

'Is he afraid you'll get back together again?'

'There's no chance of that.'

'That's not my question.'

Gaby paused and considered. 'I think he might be. Edward's a very dominating influence in the house.'

'Thanks for your help.' Soames decided to stop leaning on her, at least for the moment. 'What time do I take the kids down?'

'They meet outside the gym after tea. You can drive a minibus?'

'Yes – but what about a test?'

'There isn't one. Not here anyway.'

They shook hands rather awkwardly and Soames had to ask her for the keys.

When she had found them, Gaby said, 'I'm sure the caretaker can make your flat a little more welcoming.'

'I'm hoping I won't be here long enough for that,' he replied.

'Does St Clouds get to you that much?'

'Don't you find it too small a world? Too oppressive?'

She seemed to think about that carefully. Then she said, 'Personally, I rather like it this way.'

Soames knew he wasn't going to be able to sleep and for a long time didn't, tossing and turning on the hard bed in the stuffy room. He had already pushed the window up as far as possible, but the night air seemed just as suffocating as his room.

He couldn't stop thinking about the nature of pederast rings. Were they former victims, clinging together, moving in, like a pride of lions, waiting patiently for the kill, waiting for months or even years? Stoically determined, did they stalk until the moment of weakness was shown?

Eventually Soames slipped into a light and restless sleep.

He woke at dawn, sweating and with a grinding headache, and at the thought of the coming day his sense of claustrophobia increased. The St Clouds community now forcibly reminded him of the Met, where camaraderie had been the order of the day and communal breakfasts, lunches, coffees, teas and suppers were part of the culture. But he had never really gone along with all that and always hated the levelling down, the pecking order and the resultant narrowness. The talk, the complaints, the inter-necine warfare, the tirades against management who never sat with the plebs, except on special occasions when hair was offi-cially let down.

Boyd had always hopefully regarded himself as something of a renegade, deliberately going out of his way to avoid the camaraderie, taking meals out on his own and having the temer-ity to refuse to join the police sports clubs. As a result, he had been regarded with slight suspicion, as an odd-ball who might be grudgingly respected but not entirely understood.

As he walked down to breakfast, Soames condemned himself for thinking of Boyd. With his last job he had renounced his identity, delving deeper and deeper into his alias. Here, at St Clouds, he was having difficulty keeping Soames alive.

PART TWO

9

The refectory next door to the hall had once been a ballroom with a high raftered ceiling, wood panelling and a couple of chandeliers. The chandeliers were still there, but the panelling was stained and scored and there was an all-pervasive smell of meat that had been roasted a long time ago.

The tables were laid out in long rows behind which the boys were seated. The staff table was broader, with leather banquettes.

Soames sat down and then realised he would have to get up again to go to the kitchen counter and pick up his breakfast tray. The noise in the echoing space was penetrating and once he had queued up and returned with his tray his hangover was worse. To his irritation he found he was sitting next to Noel Bundy.

'I'm sorry I didn't refer Simon Grace to you,' he said, wanting to placate.

'Don't worry,' replied Bundy magnanimously. 'Weinstock passed the problem on in her usual style. I could never accuse her of finding delegation hard.'

He was back in his usual mode and Soames's migraine pounded, his mouth dry and stale as he gazed down at his congealed bacon, egg and fried bread with distaste. There was a huge teapot on the table and a slopped jug of milk. The atmosphere reminded him of Wormwood Scrubs.

'Do you think Grace is genuine?'

'Yes. But I'm trying to encourage him to have more confidence and not to always back out.'

'Because he put his name down?' Soames risked.

'That would be the Weinstock view.'

'What's yours?'

'I just think he's got to face up to these fears. Craig Johnson and Andy Day, two of our staff you'll meet later, are going up to Bantry Bay. They'll keep an eye on him.'

'I suppose he manipulated me.'

'There's no great harm done.' Bundy didn't want to hear Soames's remorse.

'He got very worked up after I'd seen Miss Weinstock and lay in wait for me outside the flat.' Soames decided to press on, cutting up the bacon that was slippery with fat.

'That's par for the course.'

'Attention-seeking?'

'He's a real hysteric. We've all had our fair share of that. But otherwise he's an interesting, talented lad. I wouldn't *force* him, but because Craig and Andy are going I reckon he'll be OK. I think he'll calm down.'

'So what's he decided to do?'

'He's thinking it over. Don't let Weinstock fool you. I may have a softly, softly approach but it works.'

'I'm surprised you've managed to put up with her all these years.'

'I'm a prisoner of conscience, as I told you before. So what was your impression of her?' Bundy suddenly turned to him with a social smile, unexpectedly putting him on the spot.

'She seems to have a power thing,' Soames replied cautiously, and an image of Bernie Lofts flashed across his mind.

'You can say that again.'

'She says she likes the boys.'

'Weinstock doesn't like any of us. She was set on Dr Griff and that's where her affections began and ended.'

'She almost wept while I was with her.' Soames decided to see what effect the information would have on Bundy. It had none.

'Dr Griff's death has made Weinstock twice as stubborn. She'll continue running the school as it's always been run. She's fanatical.'

Soames decided to change the subject before Bundy could get back on his soapbox. 'Mrs Darrington – Gaby – asked me if I'd take on her youth club run tonight. She's not feeling so good. Is that OK?'

'Of course it is. Give you a sighting of Hinton. I don't like him either. Creepy bastard. I'll fight tooth and nail to stop him getting a foothold here. He's a mealy-mouthed little Jesus freak.'

Noel Bundy tucked into his similarly congealed egg and bacon with relish.

'I gather he co-ordinates this army link. How does it work exactly?'

Bundy didn't reply directly. 'Bantry Bay need some decent PR round here.'

'Are the soldiers unpopular?'

'Very. There've been a lot of incidents in the pubs. Brawling and drunkenness, that kind of thing. Swanage is, as you may have noticed, a decent sort of town. I've lived here most of my life and the residents won't put up with that kind of crap. In fact it got so bad that the town's been made off limits to the Rangers. A few months ago they decided on this new marketing exercise, in association with the school and Ballard Youth Club. The army has got a very superior assault course on the cliffs at Bantry Bay.'

'Is the project popular?'

'The kids love it.'

'And the mixing of town and gown?'

'Doesn't seem to have produced any problems.'

'Aren't you worried about this ring?'

Bundy shrugged. 'As I said before, there's no evidence, just gossip and rumours. I need to see some hard facts.'

'They might come when it's too late.'

'I'm not starting scare-mongering.' He sounded aggressive.

Soames wondered if he'd pushed him too far and hastened to make amends. 'Have you been up to Bantry?'

'Thoroughly enjoyed it,' Bundy replied through a mouthful of bacon. Then he returned to the theme, his aggression more muted. 'Look, I'm not unaware of the problems we could be up against. You probably know some boys are being withdrawn by their parents, but so far only a handful. We need to sit tight and show we aren't rattled. DI Mason seems an intelligent chap and I hope he'll get a result soon. As far as Dr Griff is concerned, I still think we're talking about an intruder.'

'Maybe you're right.'

Soames's voice contained enough doubt to make Bundy look uneasy and he hurriedly attracted the attention of a couple of his colleagues across the table. 'By the way, I don't think you've met

Alan Soames. Alan, this is Chris Bayliss and Harry Mott. Both scientists, of course, so we don't know how to talk to them. But I gather they've got hearts – artificial of course, probably computer driven.' The rest of his ribbing was drowned by hearty male laughter.

The day, however, was not to pass so blandly and during the last period of the morning Soames made a major blunder with his GCSE set.

They were studying D. H. Lawrence's *The Plumed Serpent* and one of the boys commented that he'd have thought Shaw would be more at home in the desert than Lawrence and his wife Frieda.

'Don't be so stupid, Stapleton,' said Soames. 'Shaw never went to the desert in his life.'

Stapleton and a sharp-featured boy called Hodge exchanged glances.

'Stapleton didn't mean Bernard Shaw, sir,' explained Hodge patiently. 'He means *Aircraftman* Shaw – *T.E.* Lawrence, sir.'

For a fateful second Soames hesitated, staring at Hodge in silence, aware that he had been led into a trap, and Hodge stared back at him inscrutably.

'Didn't you know that, sir?'

'I made a slip. We can all do that.'

'It was a bit of a clanger though, sir.'

There was a pregnant silence, followed by explosive giggling.

'No need to be rude, Hodge,' said Soames. Did he detect a malicious gleam of derision in Hodge's eyes, or was he overreacting?

Suddenly Soames had run out of control again, panicky and sweating, fearing ritual humiliation as he stood before this smug group of fifteen-year-olds.

'I'm not being rude, sir,' protested Julian Hodge. 'I just don't understand.'

'Understand what?'

'Why you didn't know. After all, you're the teacher, sir.'

There was protracted sniggering from the class.

88

'I told you – it was a werbal –'

There was a shout of laughter.

'I mean a verbal slip. We all have them. We all make them – have lapses – lapses of memory I mean.'

His obvious confusion brought the house down and Soames, now crimson in the face, fought for control. He couldn't let them hound him like this but he felt dangerously close to angry, humiliating tears.

'Now listen, you lot. Just shut up and keep quiet. If you don't, you go straight to Miss Weinstock.'

There was a sudden down-scaling of the merriment.

'Perhaps you'd like to go, Hodge? I'm sure Miss Weinstock would enjoy your puerile humour. Would you like to go and see her now? This very minute?' Soames was sure his voice was ridiculously shrill.

Hodge was silent.

'I'm waiting for an answer.'

'No, sir.'

'Don't you think you need to apologise to me? For being so rude?'

'I'm very sorry, sir.'

'You mean that?'

'Yes, sir. I was rude and insensitive – and I'm very sorry.'

'OK,' Soames snapped. 'As this is a first offence I accept the apology.' He gazed round at the rest of the class, beginning to recover himself, the colour in his cheeks dying away. It had been a close-run thing. 'A lot of students in this school profess themselves to be extremely sensitive. I accept that, and would wish to help where I can – in a genuine and non-patronising way. But the trouble with people who are sensitive is that they are often very *in*sensitive to others. This happens all the time and you must recognise that.'

There was silence.

'Has anyone got anything to say?'

The silence continued.

'Very well,' said Soames. 'Let's carry on, shall we?'

He allowed himself a precious moment of heady triumph. Once again, they had almost broken him but he had come back fighting. That should teach the little bastards a thing or two. But would it?

Soames was feeling less pleased with himself as he sat behind the wheel of the minibus. He'd made a major blunder, and if he wasn't careful he could make others. What the hell was the matter with him?

Ten students between thirteen and seventeen had joined him and one of them asked if he could sit in the front. He was Asian, short and sturdy with gelled black hair and a round, handsome face.

Soames agreed grudgingly, for he was in no mood for chatter.

'Are you going to stay at the club tonight, sir?' He seemed confident, very sure of himself.

'I might.'

'My name's Shafiq. Will you give me a game of table tennis?'

'OK, Shafiq.' Soames leapt at the chance, for this would give him a chance to hang around in a less obvious way. 'I might be a bit rusty. But I used to play for the –' He paused, horrified. He had been about to say that he had played for the Met. Was he completely cracking up? 'For the Malayans,' he finished quickly, plunging himself in too ludicrously deep. Why did these boys throw him so much? They seemed to have only one instinctive objective – to expose him.

'You mean Malaya, sir?'

'Yes. I was out there for a couple of years and I got into a team that represented the country.'

'You must have been pretty good, sir.' Shafiq was enthusiastic and admiring, but Soames was terrified. He knew he was heading for another humiliation.

'I wasn't bad then, but now – as I say – I'm pretty rusty. How about you?'

'I'm in the school team, sir. Not exactly playing for my country yet.'

'Malaya wasn't *my* country.'

'No, sir.' Shafiq looked at him speculatively. 'But it'll be good

90

to challenge a crack player. I can beat all the boys at school – and the staff too.'

Soames felt that sinking sensation. How was he going to get away with this one? But he knew there *was* no getting away.

'I'm going to have my work cut out then,' he said ruefully.

'Not if you've played for Malaya, sir.'

'I told you, Shafiq,' began Soames, irritable now, 'it was a long time ago.'

'Even so, sir . . .' Shafiq turned back to his companions and shouted, 'Mr Soames used to play table tennis for Malaya.'

There was a hushed and respectful silence as Soames drove slowly down the esplanade.

'Are you going to beat him, Shafiq?' asked one of the boys.

'He's going to give me a match directly we get to the club.'

'Not directly,' snapped Soames, willing himself to keep calm. 'I have to see the youth leader first.'

'Do you mean Ray Hinton?'

'The very man,' replied Soames with a hideous attempt at joviality that surprised even himself.

'He's a wanker,' came a disembodied voice and there was a burst of uneasy laughter.

'Who said that?'

'Me, sir.'

'Who's me?'

'Guy Downing.'

'Do you think it's clever to use language like that?' Soames decided to be admonishing, anything to put aside the dread subject of table tennis.

'No, sir.'

'That's an appalling thing to say about Mr Hinton – after all he does for you.'

'Sorry, sir.' Guy Downing sounded unashamed.

'The trouble is,' said another voice in the back, 'that he really *is* a wanker.'

'Who's that?'

'Mr Hinton, sir.'

'No, you idiot. Who are *you*?'

'Doug Cass, sir.'

'What's the problem with this guy? This Hinton?' Soames

91

wanted to take advantage of the opening, but knew he had to come across as only peripherally interested.

'He grasses everyone up.'

'Mr Hinton's in charge. Sometimes you have to report people if you're in authority.'

'OK, sir – but it's not just that,' said Doug Cass slowly. 'He's a hypocrite, sir.'

'Aren't most of us?'

'He's religious. Hinton should be setting an example.'

'He's an evangelist, isn't he?'

'He says he's always spreading the good news, sir,' said Cass. 'He once asked me, "Have you heard the good news?" and when I asked *what* good news, he said. "Have you heard the good news that Jesus Christ died for you?"'

'Well – that's his faith talking, isn't it?'

'And then he'll pick on people – if their face doesn't fit.'

'Give me some examples. You can't make accusations without substantiating them.'

'I'd rather not.'

There were cheers, derogatory comments and hoots of derision.

'What do you think, Shafiq?' asked Soames curiously.

'I think a man should stand up for his religion, sir. My father does. He goes to the mosque every day.'

'Do you go – when you can?'

'I never go, sir,' said Shafiq. 'I don't have any faith.'

'Doesn't that upset your father?'

'I think he's got over it now, sir. But I agree with Doug that Hinton's a hypocrite.'

'No one seems able to tell me why.'

'Take our word for it, sir. You'll find out for yourself one day. Maybe you'll suss him out right away – and when you have, we can have our game of table tennis, can't we, sir?'

'Can I watch?' asked Doug Cass, and the others began to clamour to do the same.

Soames felt trapped. Why had he been such a fool as to play into their hands again? The world of childhood had never seemed darker. He remembered the crowd of boys who had been whispering by the lockers in the corridor yesterday and how they had turned to watch him – the alien adult.

Ballard Youth Club was run-down to the extreme. The building had once been a Methodist church and the stone exterior seemed solid enough. The interior, however, was squalid and needed painting. In the centre of the tawdry space was a motley collection of battered table tennis and snooker tables, while a number of pinball machines had been crowded into a corner. Raucous music blared, but above the heavy rock came a harsh squawking sound.

'Who's a pretty boy then?'

Soames whipped round, comically surprised. 'What's that?'

'Who's a pretty boy then?'

Soames spotted the parrot in a glass-fronted office at the entrance to the club where a young man in a Fair Isle sweater was sitting behind a desk at a computer. He had thinning curly brown hair and an oval face. He wore a denim jacket and jeans.

'That's Mr Hinton, sir,' said Shafiq. 'I'll go and book a table.'

Soames wished Shafiq would disappear in a puff of smoke. 'I didn't realise he had a parrot.'

'That's Dr Griff's.'

'What's it doing here?'

'Didn't you know, sir? Miss Weinstock gave Hamlet to Mr Hinton, sir. She didn't like Hamlet being around after what happened. At least, that's what she says. But I know the truth, sir.'

'What *is* the truth?' asked Soames doubtfully.

'She could never stand Hamlet. I think she hated him.'

'How do you know that?'

'It's common knowledge, sir.'

'Or just a rumour?'

Shafiq looked hurt. 'Honestly, sir. I can tell you it's true.' He paused and then asked, 'What's it like, sir?'

'Now what are you on about?'

93

'Coming to a school just after the Head has had his throat cut.'

'A bit of a shock. Now why don't you go and set up your table?'

Soames watched Shafiq's stocky frame stride purposefully down the long, shabby hall, looking heroic. Apart from the St Clouds pupils there were a few local teenage boys and girls who seemed surly, as if although they had nowhere else to go they still resented being where they were.

'Don't be long, sir,' called Shafiq and Soames turned his back on him, knocking at Hinton's door with some relief. He needed sanctuary.

'Come in.' Hinton was taller than Soames had imagined and with a much stronger personality than his looks and clothes conveyed. In fact he had considerable authority. 'How can I help you?'

'I'm Alan Soames. I've brought some of the St Clouds boys over. Mrs Darrington isn't feeling well and she asked me to step into the breach.' He spoke lightly, with a joviality that seemed necessary to the aura of the club.

'I'm sorry to hear Gaby's not well,' said Hinton flatly.

'Who's a pretty boy then?' squawked the parrot.

'I gather the parrot's a present.'

'That's right.' The smile was suddenly warmer. 'Hamlet's got a rather limited vocabulary.'

'Is that *all* he can say?'

'I'm afraid so. It grinds me down a bit, but I wanted to help Miss Weinstock out. She was obviously deeply distressed and it's the least I can do in such terrible circumstances.' He paused. 'I gather you're new to the school.'

'Does it show?'

Hinton laughed emptily. 'How are you getting on with the boys?'

'They need a lot of structure.'

'And that's Miss Weinstock's greatest strength.' Hinton turned to look at the group outside. 'The kids seem to enjoy coming down here – just for a break – although there's not really much we can offer them. As you can see, we're grossly under-equipped and underfunded. But at least there's the adventure training now. Would you like a coffee?' He spoke casually, although complacently. Why couldn't he get a working party together, wondered Soames, and slap some paint on the walls? At least it would be some kind of start.

Knowing how appalling the coffee would be, Soames almost refused. Then he caught sight of Shafiq impatiently waiting for him and hurriedly agreed.

'Why are you so underfunded?' asked Soames. 'I thought the club was run by the council.'

'Cutbacks,' said Hinton and took a swig of coffee.

'As you say, at least they get up to Bantry Bay,' said Soames, wanting to avoid a diatribe.

'Thank God for army PR – and I really mean that. They've offered the club a good deal and for that we thank the Lord.' The phrase jarred in the context of what he had said, but Soames noticed that Hinton spoke unselfconsciously.

'Who's your contact? Colonel Darrington?'

'No. He's the boss. We liaise with Sergeant Joe Billings who's the physical training instructor – at least, one of them. The assault course is pretty hairy. You must try it sometime. It nearly finished me off.' His laughter was noticeably self-deprecating.

'I gather you mix town and gown.'

'Absolutely. St Clouds and town youth have got a lot to learn from each other.'

Samuel Smiles, thought Soames. He was irritated by the smug philosophy.

'And do they?'

'Sorry?'

'Do they learn from each other?'

'I'm always hopeful.' Hinton seemed slightly deflated.

'So all the action's at Bantry Bay. What do the boys actually do up there?'

'They do PE sessions here first, and then go on the assault course. There's also sports coaching and night survival training.'

'Character-building?'

95

'I like to think so.' Hinton shrugged, guessing he was talking to the unconverted.

'And members of staff go with the group? Or is all the care side left to the army?'

'Some of it. They have excellent facilities. I go with the groups as much as I can, and so do my voluntary workers. There are staff from the school as well,' he added, making them sound like hangers-on.

Soames realised he was asking too many questions. 'I'm very keen on that kind of thing. I wonder if I can worm my way in,' he said too smoothly.

'I'm sure you'd be very welcome. I know how enthusiastic Miss Weinstock is about the project.'

'Was Dr Griff?'

'A hundred per cent.'

Soames was getting tired of Hinton's muscular Christianity and decided to provoke him. 'I'll be absolutely straight with you. I know I'm probably speaking out of turn, but I've heard these rumours about a pederast ring and it really concerns me.'

'So have I.' Hinton spoke seriously and his expression changed to one of concern.

'What do you think?' Soames was surprised. Somehow he hadn't expected such a straightforward reaction.

'There's never smoke without fire,' he said. 'But I can assure you I've been vigilant both here and at Bantry Bay.'

Hinton was making more eye contact. Looking at him, Soames wondered why he'd been so influenced by the boys' prejudices. It must be tough being a Christian, he thought, and then cursed himself for the cliché.

'You heard about Bernie Lofts?' Hinton's voice dropped as he glanced at the door.

'His confession?'

'And his retraction. I felt he was leant on.'

'Do you know Lofts?' asked Soames.

'Yes.'

'What's your assessment of him?'

'A main chancer.' Hinton sounded almost comfortingly professional.

'So the ring could have permeated St Clouds?'

96

'You've left out my youth club as another possibility.'

There was an uncomfortable silence.

'Who told you about the Lofts problem?' Hinton asked.

'Gaby Darrington.'

'She confided in you?'

'She's desperately worried.'

'Yes.' Hinton gazed at him thoughtfully. 'She needs a confidant. The school is very split and now, with the current tragedy, the split's widened.'

'I hear you might be working with us,' said Soames.

'Miss Weinstock wants to employ me and I'd like to head up a youth wing. A Christian youth wing, of course, but I don't want to thrust the Lord's work down the pupils' throats – or the staff's come to that.'

'Of course not. But what would happen down here?'

'I'd like to site the club in the youth wing but that might put off the locals. I don't think they'd be willing to make the trip to St Clouds. So it's all a bit of a dilemma.'

'Is the wing going to be purpose built?' His questions were deliberately safer now.

'I don't know yet. Nowhere could be much worse than here, could it?'

Soames decided that it couldn't.

'Is that kid waiting for you?'

He turned to see Shafiq staring through the glass.

'He wants to play table tennis.'

'He's a fine boy, Shafiq – if a little over-serious.'

'And persistent.' Soames got up and waved Shafiq away. 'This ring – do you reckon the school's really got something to worry about?' he asked, hoping he would still sound like a concerned and perhaps rather over-intense new teacher.

'I'm sure it has, but Miss Weinstock seems to have a blind spot. At least Colonel Darrington's taking the situation seriously though.' Hinton paused and then spoke clearly, directly, with a passion he hadn't shown before. 'There's nothing more disgusting than pederasty. That men – even women sometimes – should prey on vulnerable boys is beyond my understanding.' He paused, gazing ahead, his mind elsewhere, not really seeing Soames at all now. 'But these rings are hard to crack. They're

97

very subtle and move into position well before a strike is made. Believe me, Alan, I know. I've been a youth worker for a long time – mainly in Southampton – and I've been up against a ring before.'

'Did you have any success?'

'None. It's still intact and as voracious as ever.'

'You liaised with the police?'

'Of course. But most of the ring were untouchable.'

'Why was that?'

'They *were* the police.'

For a moment Soames was appalled and then realised how naïve he was being.

'There's a kind of freemasonry to it all,' said Hinton. 'Safety in numbers, safety under the umbrella of authority.'

'What about other social agencies?'

'The caring professions are riddled with pederasts. It's like a cancer. They scent victims and have easy access to them. The last experience was terrible, but if I *have* got another ring on my hands, as I'm sure I have, I'm determined to stop them and at least I know I've got the good Lord on my side.'

'I'm with you all the way,' said Soames. Except he didn't think the good Lord was going to be much help. But maybe he was wrong about that, for despite Hinton's evangelism, his determination was refreshing after the complacent evasion at St Clouds. 'Now I'd better go and get beaten at table tennis.'

'Don't throw the match away,' advised Hinton.

Soames opened the door only to face an eager and impatient Shafiq. Fleetingly, he wondered if Hinton believed in thunderbolts for those who practised to deceive. He had a horrible feeling Shafiq was going to be his thunderbolt.

10

Fortunately, Soames held his own, only losing in the third game by which time he was totally exhausted, particularly as the match had been watched by the entire club, cheering on the participants, fortunately not favouring either.

When Shafiq won the final point, they shook hands a little awkwardly but with mutual respect.

'Can I give you a game, sir?' demanded another of the St Clouds pupils.

'No way,' said Soames hurriedly, trying not to gasp for breath too much. 'Well done, Shafiq. You're good – more than good,' he conceded genuinely.

'Do you think I could play for the country one day? Like you did for Malaya, sir?' Shafiq had all the enthusiastic generosity of the victor.

'Why not?' Soames glimpsed another boy in Hinton's glassed-in office and heard Hamlet squawking.

The boy was tall and thin and vaguely familiar.

'Who's that in there with Mr Hinton?'

'Don't you recognise him, sir? That's Doug Cass. He was in the van with us. He's the one who thinks Mr Hinton's a –'

'Thank you, Shafiq,' said Soames hastily. 'No need to say any more.' He paused. 'Is Cass a prefect?'

'Yes, sir. He's also Captain of Games.'

'Nice guy?'

'He's terrific, sir.' Shafiq's enthusiasm switched to Cass. 'You ought to see him on the rugby field, sir.'

'Right now,' muttered Soames, 'he seems a little over-wrought.'

Then Douglas Cass erupted.

'You bastard!' He was standing very near to Hinton's desk, almost leaning on it. 'You total wanker!'

The atmosphere in the club became electric. Hinton said something inaudible and his audience froze, anxious not to miss a single moment of this unexpected confrontation. Soames glanced around him, but there seemed to be no other youth workers around.

'Fuck off!' said Cass, striding to the door.

Somebody whispered and there was an intake of breath.

'Who's a pretty boy then?' contributed Hamlet, the harsh squawk covering something that Hinton had been saying.

Why doesn't someone strangle that fucking parrot? thought Soames.

Cass was slamming the door behind him now, rattling the glass.

Hinton rose to his feet and then noticed his audience. Shrugging, as if disclaiming responsibility, he returned to his desk.

Cass ran out on to the street. No one seemed prepared to follow him and a buzz of excited conversation broke out.

'I'd better go and speak to Hinton,' said Soames.

'Shall I come with you, sir?' asked Shafiq hopefully.

'Of course you can't. If you want to help, why don't you get after Cass?'

Shafiq stayed where he was. He looked uneasy, and when Soames glanced round at the others he could see that they, too, seemed reluctant to follow Cass. Why? he wondered, as he strode towards Hinton's office.

'Can I help?'

Hinton was sitting behind his desk, hands folded, eyes shut. Was he praying, Soames wondered, as he saw his lips moving.

'Are you all right?'

'Yes.' Hinton opened his eyes and shrugged. 'I'm OK.'

'What happened?'

'I seem to have become the Father Confessor they all learn to hate. You can go off adolescents.'

'Why?' asked Soames inadequately, knowing he felt much the same.

'Doug accused me of interfering with his girlfriend – in a theoretical sort of way, if you see what I mean.'

They glanced at each other and suddenly laughed. Soames warmed to him. He might be a Holy Joe, but at least he had a sense of humour which was more than he'd expected.

Then Hinton continued. 'They had a row down here last week which was very disruptive to everyone. So I had them in the office and tried to sort things out. I didn't, of course. But I called Miss Weinstock and told her what had happened so I thought I'd

100

at least done my duty, and that's all the thanks I got for it.' He sounded partly indignant, partly hurt.

'What exactly was the row about?'

'Cass is a very dominating guy, too dominating for Susie's taste, and she wasn't – isn't – prepared to obey the Captain of Games's every command.'

'He'll apologise.'

'Don't compel him. I'd rather have something genuine.'

'Wouldn't we all,' said Soames. 'But what am I going to do? I'm meant to be taking them all back in the minibus.' He glanced at his watch. 'We've only got twenty minutes left and he's run off.'

'I'll go,' said Hinton.

Soames hurriedly intervened, not wanting to let the opportunity slip. 'Let me. Perhaps I can talk to him.'

'I'd rather go myself.' Hinton was beginning to be insistent. But just as they were about to continue the debate, a couple of soldiers in fatigues arrived, opening the door of the office without knocking.

'Joe,' said Hinton, looking relieved, as if the cavalry had just arrived. He turned to Soames. 'Alan – meet Sergeant Joe Billings. He's in charge of the adventure training project at the base, and this is Lance Corporal George Repton, his two-in-c.'

They all shook hands. Billings was broadly built with short legs and a square face fringed by greying brown hair. Repton was younger, tall and lanky, prematurely balding.

'Who's a pretty boy then?' squawked Hamlet.

Billings and Repton looked startled.

'That parrot wasn't here last week,' said Billings. 'Was it an offer you couldn't refuse?'

'Something like that,' said Hinton with a weary smile. 'Look, we've got a bit of a crisis on. Could you give me ten minutes before the meeting?'

'Can we help?'

'Not really,' said Soames firmly. 'One of our boys has thrown a bit of a tantrum. I think I'll go and check him out. He's done a runner.' Soames saw Hinton and Billings exchange a glance.

'OK,' said Hinton, backing down. 'Maybe you're right. He's your pupil, after all.'

101

'Any idea where he might have gone?'

Hinton shrugged. 'Maybe he's darkly brooding on the promenade.'

'Ray's got a tough job,' said Billings supportively.

'You have your meeting,' suggested Soames. 'I'll find my lost sheep.'

Soames stepped out into yet another glorious sunset as the crimson ball plunged into an iridescent sea. The promenade was almost empty despite the fact that it was only just after nine. There were a few fishermen on the jetty and someone was scrubbing down the hull of a motorboat drawn up on the quayside. The pub looked full inside, but only a few customers had spilled out on to the pebbles.

A light aircraft from a flying club buzzed over the sea and then began to drone like a circling insect. Soames could smell tar and fish and weed as he hurried down a flight of stone steps to a narrow strip of beach. Here the smell of the seaweed became even more intense, a rotting aroma, attracting a small cloud of flies. There was no sign of Cass.

Soames looked at his watch. Ten minutes to deadline. Had the wretched boy decided to brood somewhere else, or was he determined to miss the bus? He swore, sure it was the latter. Well, let Cass play the prima donna then. But how could Soames possibly justify taking the minibus back without him?

He searched the seafront for a while longer and then decided to check the arcade of shops that was next door to the youth club. Maybe he'd missed him. Or Cass might have been sulkily hiding there. But there was no sign of him amongst the cheap, run-down little shops.

Returning to the club and checking that Cass hadn't turned up, Soames's temper began to boil. He had achieved nothing and had now been overtaken by yet more adolescent angst. Where the hell was Cass?

Back on the street, Soames noticed a narrow alley running between the club and the next building, a garage with a Ford dealership. At the end of the alley was a small yard with rubbish piled up behind some dustbins and a pile of broken furniture. A high, close-mesh wire fence bolted to concrete posts separated the club yard from the garage.

Soames dimly saw that one of the concrete posts was stained with some kind of substance that was still fresh and damp-looking. Had some idiot been throwing paint about? Could this be Cass's vandalistic revenge on Ray Hinton? But where had he got the paint?

Soames went over to the dustbins and saw more of the stuff, smeared over an old mattress. He gazed at it for a long time as an impossible thought struck him and he put out a finger, touching another crimson stain on a plastic dustbin and then returning to the fence post to check again. The stuff was identical.

Soames then noticed a section of the fence was slightly buckled, as if a heavy weight had rested against it or someone had tried to climb. Climb? Why should they do that?

Soames grabbed a couple of solid-looking packing cases and piled them up, one on top of the other. Steadying himself by grabbing the fence, Soames clambered up and found they were bearing his weight.

Shakily he peered over the wire and saw something lying on a tarpaulin covering the open back of a truck in the garage yard. Presentiment filled him, and his mind seemed to bluster, trying to block out the idea. A game was being played. It didn't have any importance, did it? But Soames knew he was only fooling himself.

Letting go of the wire, which was hurting his fingers, he jumped off the packing cases, feeling nauseous. Whatever was lying on the tarpaulin hadn't moved and there was more, much more, of the dark stain saturating the canvas. Soames climbed back up and forced himself to look again.

Soames paused for a moment in the doorway of Ballard Youth Club, out of breath and wondering how he was going to handle the situation.

'Want another game, sir?' asked Shafiq.

'Not now.'

'Did you find Doug?'

Soames turned away from Shafiq, pushing open the door of Hinton's office. Billings, Repton and Hinton were sitting around a coffee table.

'Something's happened,' he said.

They looked up casually. 'Now what?' Hinton asked. 'Is Cass still playing up?'

'He's next door – in the yard at the back of the garage. He must have climbed over the fence.' Soames's voice was slow and neutral, entirely without expression.

'Why?' said Hinton, looking puzzled.

'Someone was after him.'

Billings looked puzzled, Repton slightly alarmed and Hinton uncertain.

'There's blood on the dustbins and on the side of the fence.'

'For Christ's sake –' began Repton.

'*Where* is he?' demanded Hinton.

'I told you. In the yard, lying on top of a tarpaulin on the back of a truck. He's not moving.'

'Stay here.' Joe Billings took charge with quiet authority. He was a soldier. He was behaving like a soldier should behave and he gave them confidence. 'No one is to leave the club.'

'What are you going to do?' asked Soames, still trying to imitate the reactions of a shocked schoolteacher.

'Scale the fence. You'd better come with me.'

'Is there no other way in?'

'No,' said Hinton. 'It's all sealed off with security gates and razor wire on top.'

'There's no razor wire on the fence,' said Soames.

'I suppose they thought it was too high.' Billings gazed at him impatiently. 'Cass's hurt himself then?'

Billings stood on the crates and peered over the fence into the back of the truck. The twilight was deepening now and Cass had been reduced to a dark, sodden-looking shadow.

'He's not moving.'

'Can you get over there?'

'Yes.' Billings began to climb hand over hand up the wire, seeming to get finger and footholds out of nowhere.

104

Reaching the top, he hauled himself up and jumped on to the roof of the truck. Then Billings knelt and gazed down at the body on the tarpaulin. He examined Cass carefully and didn't speak for a long time.

But Soames knew Douglas Cass was dead.

'His throat's been cut.'

Just like Dr Griff, thought Soames. Then he asked, almost academically, 'You mean he scaled the fence, bleeding from a throat wound?'

'He's got cuts on his arms and chest as well, but nothing so lethal as the injury to his neck. I reckon that was done after he'd scaled the fence. You'd better call the police. The pathologist will be able to establish the exact cause of death, although it's pretty damned obvious.' Billings kept talking, but his voice was shaking. 'God, man, don't just stand there! Go and call the police. Now!'

Stumbling, Soames began to run back down the alley.

Hinton and Repton were standing anxiously outside the door of the club, above which Soames could still make out the faded lettering 'Swanage Methodist Church'.

'It's bad,' he told them.

'What's happened?' Hinton's hands were clasped.

'Cass is dead.'

'*Dead?*' Hinton looked at him unbelievingly. His mouth opened and shut but no sound came out.

'I'll call the police.' Repton assumed some of Billings's authority. He hurried back inside, and before he slammed the door, Soames could hear Shafiq asking questions.

'Was there an accident?' asked Hinton. 'Did he get knocked down by a car?' He seemed unable to come to grips with any other possibility.

Soames hastened to put him right. 'Someone attacked him at the back of the club. He managed to get over the fence next door, but he was pursued. His throat was cut very deeply – just like Dr Griff's.'

Hinton stared, his mouth slightly open, looking incredulous. Then he said, 'There must be some maniac on the loose.'

'Or maybe it's someone who wants to keep a secret.' Soames

decided to sharpen up. Surely his shocked teacher role would allow a little initiative?

'Whoever it is,' began Hinton, 'is psychotic.'

Soames held back, and then decided he should push things a little further. 'I've been very concerned since I first came to St Clouds.'

Lance Corporal Repton saved him from saying any more, shutting the door of the club behind him. 'The police are on their way – and the boys are in a hell of a state, particularly the St Clouds students.'

'Do they know what's happened?'

'I didn't think it was my place to tell them.' Repton sounded as if the boys' anxiety was Soames's fault.

'Shall I?' asked Hinton. 'I'm quite prepared to –'

'No,' said Soames decisively. 'I'll speak to them.'

The pupils looked younger, more vulnerable now, gathered silently behind one of the table tennis tables as if they needed a barrier between them and harsh reality.

'I'm sorry. Doug Cass is dead.'

As if they wanted to distance themselves, the half-dozen boys and girls from the town were sprawled on one of the judo mats that had been pushed back into a corner.

A pupil from St Clouds gave a half sob and another boy began to weep silently. No one spoke. Not even Shafiq.

'You'll have to wait here while I phone the school. I expect the police will want to talk to you.'

Knowing he should have been more reassuring, Soames hurried back into the office and dialled the St Clouds number, which rang for a long time until it was finally answered. He didn't recognise the voice.

'Who's that?'

'Len Chaplin. I'm one of the care workers. Can I help?'

'It's Alan Soames. There's an emergency. I need to speak to Miss Weinstock very urgently.'

'It's a little late.'

'It's extremely urgent.'

Chaplin went away and Soames could hear him making a call

106

on an internal phone. After an agonising delay he eventually returned. 'I'm going to give you another number to ring. Miss Weinstock's home number. I'm afraid the phone system at St Clouds is a bit antiquated.'

'Please hurry.'

'Is there something wrong?'

'For God's sake – I've told you it's an emergency.' Soames's voice rose.'

'OK. It's 963471.'

Soames slammed down the receiver and dialled again.

Kate Weinstock answered immediately.

'It's Soames. I'm at the youth club. Douglas Cass has been murdered.'

As he spoke, Soames wondered what Cass had known. Then he remembered what he had said in the back of the minibus. *Hinton's a hypocrite, sir.*

Kate Weinstock surprised him by her decisiveness.

'What happened?'

'His throat was cut.'

There was a short silence, but she was still calm when she said, 'Have the police been called?'

'Of course.'

'Who could have done this?'

'God knows. Maybe Dr Griff didn't surprise an intruder after all.'

'Did any of the boys see what happened?'

'Fortunately not.'

'Who found the body?'

'I did. Cass had run out of the club after an argument with Ray Hinton. Something about a girl. I searched and eventually found him in the yard of the garage next door. The police will need to talk to everyone so I'll bring the boys back as soon as I can.'

'I'm coming down now. No one is to do *anything* until I get there.'

Soames began to have a new respect for her.

PART THREE

11

The tension in the club was reaching breaking point. The boys from St Clouds were still behind their table tennis table barrier, looked at askance by the town as if they were behaving stupidly. Most of the boys were staring ahead, but a few wept silently. They all looked incredibly defenceless, numbed at first, but with the shock slowly surfacing.

Billings, Repton and Hinton had joined Soames in the office. The two soldiers were calm and restrained but Hinton had deteriorated badly and was now in tears, sitting at his desk, hands over his eyes. Soames put a hand on his shoulder, not knowing what to say.

Hinton's emotion seemed to have embarrassed Billings and Repton, and they stood around self-consciously. The enforced waiting was getting to them.

'I should have handled this better.' Hinton wiped his eyes with his fists, like a child who knew he was in trouble but didn't know the extent.

But how *did* you handle it? wondered Soames. Again, Cass's voice rang in his mind. *He's a hypocrite, sir.*

'Kate Weinstock's on her way,' said Soames.

Hinton looked up eagerly. Was she some kind of mother figure to him, like Gaby was to Lofts? wondered Soames, appalled at the ludicrous nature of the idea.

'Thank God for that.'

The sound of sirens slowly drew nearer and the tension began to unwind a little.

'I haven't covered him up or anything,' said Billings. 'I couldn't find anything for a start and anyway the police will want Cass left exactly as we found him.'

'Of course,' Soames agreed.

'I could – should have done more,' said Hinton.

'What more *could* you have done?' Billings sounded impatient.

111

'Been more sympathetic.'

'Weren't you?'

'Some of these boys are very demanding. They need a great deal of attention and that can get to you. The town boys may be rough, but they're more self-contained.'

'I know what you mean,' said Soames appeasingly.

Then Mason arrived, looking grim, with a group of police officers, flooding into the club like a black tide.

'What happened?' Mason ignored Soames.

Billings became spokesman. 'Doug Cass – one of the St Clouds pupils – has been murdered. He was attacked with a knife and his body's lying on a truck in the yard of the garage next door. It looks as if someone chased him over the fence and cut his throat. I'm Sergeant Joe Billings and my colleague is Lance Corporal George Repton. This is the youth club leader, Ray Hinton – and a member of St Clouds staff, Alan Soames.'

'I know Hinton,' said Mason brusquely. He turned to his team. 'Let's take a look.'

'You'll have to force the security gate of the garage. It's on the right next door,' said Billings.

Mason left a couple of officers with the boys and they stood silently, trying not to catch anyone's eye.

'What are we going to do, sir?' asked Shafiq. 'Is there a deranged killer out there?'

'We don't know what's happened.' Soames paused by the door of the office and then walked back to the boys. 'You're going to have to hang around, maybe for a long while. Would you like some cans of drink?'

No one replied.

'Miss Weinstock should be here soon.'

Like Hinton, they obviously found her impending arrival comforting. Had he completely misunderstood the woman? Was she really the bedrock they all needed?

'How did Cass die?' asked someone.

'I can't tell you that now. What's your name?'

'Palmer, sir. Why not, sir?'

'The police need to talk to you.'

112

'To question us?'

'They'll have to question everyone here.' Soames tried to keep the exhaustion out of his voice but failed.

Palmer continued to cross-examine him. 'Was he murdered, sir?'

'I told you – I can't tell you anything now.'

'He *was* murdered, wasn't he, sir?'

'Shut up,' said Shafiq and there was a buzz of agreement from the others.

But Soames decided to go a little softer on Palmer. Did he have something to say that was important?

'Why are you so sure about that?'

'About what, sir?'

'You just said Cass was murdered.'

'Maybe it was the same person who killed Dr Griff,' continued Palmer. 'Someone in the school? On the staff? Maybe in the army?'

'Army? Why should you say that?' asked Soames gently.

'I don't know, sir.' Palmer held his gaze for a moment and then looked away.

'Have you got anything to tell the police?'

'No, sir.'

'Are you sure?'

'Quite sure, sir.'

'Palmer's a very morbid person,' explained Shafiq, perhaps put out that he'd been overshadowed. 'He's in love with death.'

'Don't be melodramatic, Shafiq.'

'He is, sir. Isn't he, Jack?' he asked, turning to a slight, fair-haired boy standing beside him.

'He dreams about graveyards,' said Jack.

Palmer looked away.

Soames lost his temper. 'Look, we've got enough problems without this sort of idiocy. Can't you show some respect for –' He paused, seeing the sweat pouring down Jack's face and his sudden pallor. Why hadn't he realised the boy hadn't been joking? He looked round at the others, aware of how badly he was handling the situation. 'It's OK, Jack,' he said, trying to back off.

'Sorry, sir.'

'I understand.' Soames patted the boy's shoulder while Shafiq looked on disapprovingly. 'It's been the most appalling shock for us all.' He turned away, making for the office, and ran straight into Kate Weinstock.

'Alan. Thank you for holding the fort. Let me talk to the boys.'

'I already have,' he said. 'They're very upset.'

'I'm hardly surprised.' She pushed past him, heading towards her pupils like an angry mother hen.

Mason returned just as Soames had sought refuge in the office again with Hinton, who appeared to have got more of a grip on himself. Billings and Repton had gone over to the drinks machine in the foyer.

'I've never seen such a savage attack.' Mason looked ashen as he glanced at Hinton. 'You know these boys. Can you help me with this?'

'I'd like to. But they won't talk to me.'

'You appreciate the direct link with Dr Griff's death?'

'Of course. So who are we dealing with?' asked Soames, knowing he had to contribute. 'Somebody who's disturbed?'

'Or just desperate,' Hinton said uncertainly.

'Desperate to keep a secret?' suggested Mason. 'Or to protect someone?'

'Someone's panicking.' Hinton seemed more resilient now and Soames wondered why the boys disliked him so much.

'Have you any idea who this person might be?' asked Mason.

'No.'

'You're quite sure?'

'Absolutely sure.'

'What about you, Mr Soames?'

'I haven't any idea at all.'

'Could Griff and Cass have known the identity of a member of this pederast ring?' asked Mason.

'God knows,' said Hinton, his authority gone. 'This kind of slaughter is almost like an act of terrorism.'

'There certainly seems reason to believe we could be dealing with a paedophile ring,' persisted Mason. 'And now it looks as if the ring is vulnerable.'

'I've seen a ring in action before when I was in Southampton,' Hinton said. 'But they move in imperceptibly, and nothing happens for the hell of a long time. Then one of them pounces.'

Mason seemed interested. 'The members of the ring know each other?'

'Not all.'

'Groups who don't connect?'

'Some connect.'

'So the rings are concentric and overlapping.'

'Something like that,' said Hinton.

'And yet you don't suspect anyone?'

'No.'

'Or have the slightest suspicion?'

'If I had, I'd have told someone.'

'OK.' Ted Mason turned back to Soames. 'I'd like to talk to the boys.'

'You'll have to check with Miss Weinstock.'

Mason nodded impatiently. 'You make her sound as if *she's* the investigating officer.'

'Of course you must talk to them, Inspector Mason.' Kate Weinstock was instantly co-operative.

The boys were sitting on the floor now, grouped around her, looking up at her trustingly, much more relaxed, bathing in her quiet authority.

Soames watched Mason frown. Kate Weinstock would be only too delighted to do the job for him. It was a natural instinct.

'Look.' Mason was awkward and too brusque as he addressed her pupils. 'One of your – school friends – Douglas Cass, has been murdered.'

There was a long silence as the boys turned to Kate Weinstock as if they were waiting for permission to speak, or even think.

She nodded slightly and Shafiq asked, 'How was he murdered?'

'His throat was cut,' said Mason.

115

'Do you know who did it?'

'We believe he was attacked by the same person who murdered your Headmaster, Dr Griff.'

'But do you know *who* did it?' persisted Shafiq.

'No,' said Mason. 'We don't know yet, but we're going to find out, and you may be able to help us. You may all be able to help us. Can someone tell me if Doug Cass had been frightened of anyone you know? Or saw?'

There was no response. Soames watched Kate Weinstock's face, but she gave nothing away.

'Or had he been threatened by someone you might know?'

The wall of silence seemed to thicken.

Mason changed tack. 'Who was Cass's best friend?'

Still the silence.

'Did anyone know him well?' Mason half turned to Kate Weinstock.

'You must help the Inspector,' she said admonishingly, magisterially. 'We must all help him. There's nothing to be afraid of.'

But they *are* afraid, thought Soames.

'He didn't make friends,' said Shafiq woodenly.

'Surely everyone makes friends.' Mason was obviously even more irritated by the stubborn assertion.

'He didn't.'

'Why not?'

'I don't know, sir.' Shafiq was sullen.

'Surely someone can help me?'

More silence. Then Kate Weinstock intervened. 'Douglas didn't make many friends,' she said. 'What they're telling you is the truth.'

'Let me be the judge of that, Miss Weinstock.' Mason deliberately flouted her authority. 'We shall need to talk to each boy individually,' he said.

Soames saw the sharply hostile look in Kate Weinstock's eyes.

'There's been this talk,' said Shafiq suddenly.

'What talk?' asked Mason more gently while Kate Weinstock watched Shafiq intently.

'We go on a course with the army – up at Bantry Bay.'

116

'When you say "we",' said Mason slowly, 'do you mean you've personally experienced this course?'

'Yes, sir.'

'What do you do?'

'Adventure training, sir.'

'Go on.'

'There's been this talk. About men. Who do things to you.'

Soames watched Kate Weinstock watching Shafiq. She seemed slightly mesmerised.

'Who did things to *you*?'

'No, sir.'

'Then how do you know?'

'Cass told me.'

'They did things to him?'

'He didn't say.'

'What *did* he say?'

'That a man did something to his friend.'

'I thought he didn't have any friends,' snapped Mason.

'He doesn't, sir. Not that he ever told me – us – about.' Shafiq turned to the rest of the group for corroboration, but the other boys had their eyes on the floor. One or two shuffled. Another cleared his throat.

'Who was this friend?'

'I don't know, sir.'

'He told you without naming him?'

'Yes, sir.'

'Weren't you curious? Didn't you ask who the friend was?'

'Yes, sir.'

'What did he say?'

'He said he wouldn't tell me.'

'So why try to confide in you in the first place?'

Shafiq shrugged, but Soames was convinced he was telling the truth.

'Was he desperate?'

'About what, sir?'

'Desperately needing to confide.'

'Not really.' Shafiq sounded as if he was backing off.

'Where did this conversation take place?'

117

'In the changing rooms, sir.' For the first time he looked worried.

All the boys were staring at Shafiq now. Were they willing him to stop talking, or to continue?

'He told you in the changing rooms?' repeated Mason.

'Yes, sir.'

'What were you doing there?'

'Dressing, sir. It was after cricket practice.' Shafiq sounded worried.

'Strange that he chose to tell you. You weren't a friend of his?'

'But I wasn't *unfriendly* to him,' protested Shafiq.

'Why did Cass choose you to confide in?' Mason persisted.

Shafiq seemed to think hard. 'People tell me things,' he said eventually. 'I guess they think they can trust me.'

'Don't be afraid, Shafiq,' urged Kate Weinstock.

Now her authority had been undermined by Mason, she sounded trite.

'Just tell me the truth,' said Mason. 'It's the only way we can solve this.'

'He only told me – this man did something to a friend.'

'What kind of something?'

'He wouldn't say.'

'How did the conversation begin?' asked Mason, trying another tack.

'Cass just came out with it.'

'Can you remember his exact words?'

'He said – something like – have you been up to the base, and I said yes, and then Cass said one of these guys did something to his friend and I asked what something and what friend, but he didn't want to tell me any more,' Shafiq finished in a rush.

'Did you ask him again?'

'Yes.'

'Did he say any more?'

'No, sir.'

'What did he do next?'

'He finished dressing and walked out.'

'Did you follow him?'

'No.'

118

'No one came to interrupt you?'

'We were alone all the time.'

'So that was the sum total of what Cass said to you?'

'He did speak to other boys. Later.'

'No one here?'

'No, sir.' The reply was too fast, too glib.

'What did he say to the other boys?'

'The same.'

'Was this before or after Cass spoke to you?'

'After.'

'So he was desperate?'

'I suppose so.'

'Why did he go around telling everyone the same thing?'

'Maybe he hoped we could help.'

'And did you?'

'No, sir.'

'Why not?'

'I was scared, sir.'

Mason looked as if he was searching for words. 'Why didn't you tell someone in authority?'

'In the end I decided Cass was making it up, sir.' Shafiq sounded defensive.

'Did he often make things up?'

'No, sir.'

'So why should you think that he was then?'

'I was scared,' Shafiq repeated.

You're scared now, thought Soames. But what of?

'When he said "man", what kind of man did you think he meant?'

'I'm not sure, sir.'

'A soldier?' prompted Mason.

'A man.'

'He didn't say a soldier?'

'He said a man, sir.'

'I think –' began Miss Weinstock.

Mason frowned and continued. 'And Douglas Cass never mentioned the episode again?'

'Not to me, sir.'

'And you didn't question him again?'

'No.'

'Did it ever enter your mind that Cass might have been talking about himself?'

'I don't get you, sir.'

Mason sighed and it was Kate Weinstock's turn to frown. 'When Douglas said a man had done something to his friend – could he actually have meant that a man did something to *him*?' She sounded as if she was finding the words hard to get out.

Shafiq didn't reply and Mason repeated the question sharply, but Shafiq only stared at him as if he was being stupid. Then he said woodenly, 'I don't think so, sir.' He paused. 'I don't *know*, sir.'

'Detective Inspector Mason,' began Miss Weinstock, 'are the other boys to be questioned tonight?'

'I'm afraid so.'

'Can this be done at St Clouds? They're very tired, and they'll need some refreshment. I quite understand why you wish to see the students immediately, but is it possible for you and your colleagues to conduct the interviews at the school?' Suddenly she was no longer imperious, but almost pleading.

It was a remarkable change of attitude, and Mason seemed thrown, agreeing to the request at once. 'Of course. I need to speak to the adults here and then I'll come up with some of my colleagues.' He paused. 'I take it *you'll* be informing Cass's parents?'

'Of course.'

Mason drew Kate Weinstock aside and said in a low voice, 'You'll tell his parents to liaise with me. Mr Soames has made formal identification –'

Kate Weinstock glanced at Soames. 'I'd have liked to do that myself.'

'I'm sorry,' Soames protested mildly. 'Unfortunately I found him . . .'

'I know.' She began to relent. 'It was a dreadful experience for you.' Then she turned back to Mason. 'Do you mind if I go and see Douglas? On my own. Now?'

Mason paused fractionally. Then he said, 'Of course. Forensic are with him at the moment, but I know you won't touch –'

'Of course I won't.' She turned back to the boys. 'Mr Soames will run you back to school and see you all have something to eat and drink. I'll be along as soon as I can. When you've finished, I suggest you all come over to my house where the police can question you. As I said before, I can't begin to tell you how horrified I am by what's happened, but I know the police are doing everything in their power to – to deal with the situation.' Kate Weinstock turned back to Mason. 'Can you take me to him?'

He took her arm and led her away. As she went with Mason, Shafiq began to cry for the first time. Soames went over to him but for some instinctive reason glanced back – only to see Billings, Repton and Hinton by the office, having some kind of whispered disagreement. Again Soames was reminded of the group of boys in the corridor at the school. It was as if he was living on two different planes.

12

Soames drove the boys back to St Clouds in silence. He could sense the numbing cocoon of their shock and wondered how they could ever be convinced they might trust an adult now. He felt in shock himself, not able to get out of his mind the broken, bloodied thing that had once been a seventeen-year-old who knew something he shouldn't.

The savagery of the attack, the terrible wounds, the ferocity of the mind that carried out the killing were incredible. What kind of person could be driven to do that, and to take the enormous risk that had been taken? While the table tennis balls had pinged their way from bat to bat, while snooker cues clicked and the pop music blared, Cass had been climbing for his life.

Soames knew he had to take the initiative. However much Mason stepped up the investigation, he was sure that the killer was being protected by that glass wall that was so impenetrable. The efficient barbarity and the uncontrolled lust *were* like terrorism. A network of cells that made up a ring. If only he could get into one cell then there was the possibility of penetrating others.

To achieve this, Soames was sure he had to get into Bantry Bay. Somehow he had to get closer to those in charge of the boys' adventure training. Starting with Billings and Repton. Could he offer to drive the boys up to Bantry? Could Gaby Darrington be his fixer again?

As Soames slowed down the minibus he saw Kate Weinstock's car parked in the main drive at St Clouds, next to the incident caravan. He wondered how she had got there without passing them.

'She must have gone down Bagman's Lane, sir,' said Shafiq. He obviously wanted to talk now, wanted to blot it all out.

'Is that a short cut?'

'Sort of. The road fords the river and Dr Griff didn't like the minibus being driven through the water.'

'I expect she wanted to get back before us,' said Soames, bringing the minibus to a slow halt.

'How do you feel, sir?' asked Shafiq with surprising consideration. 'After all, you found the –'

'I'm OK,' interrupted Soames hurriedly. He turned back to the others. 'If anyone does know anything, please come and talk to me immediately. I hope you realise I can be trusted.' Then he saw Kate Weinstock emerging from her car, heading purposefully towards him. He wound down the window.

'Feed and water them,' she said. 'And then go home and get some rest.'

'I expect DI Mason will want to see me.'

'I'm sure he'll ring you. I gave him the number at the flat.'

Soames resented her ability to put him in his place.

'Do you want me to sit in on the questioning?'

'No,' she said firmly. 'Absolutely no need for that.'

Miss Weinstock went round to the back of the minibus and began to count heads.

'Is there anything more you'd like to tell me?' Soames asked Shafiq.

'I've said all I can, sir.' He sounded reproachful.

'Are you sure?'

'I can't *remember* anything else.' Shafiq seemed on the verge of tears again, and Soames was quick to reassure him.

'I'm sorry.'

'That's all right, sir.' Shafiq paused, half in and half out of the minibus. 'I expect there's quite a few boys who would like to get stuff off their chests, sir.'

Soames gazed at him, riveted. Was he being given an unexpected last chance? Was he up to dealing with it? 'Are you one of those boys?' he asked gently.

'No, sir.'

'If you were, would you talk to an adult?'

'I don't think so.'

'Why not?'

'You wouldn't know who that adult was, would you, sir?'

'I'm not with you.'

Shafiq paused again, looking impatient, as if there was some obvious truth that Soames was obtusely unable to see. 'You wouldn't know who you were talking to, would you?'

'You can trust me,' said Soames.

Shafiq looked at him with a mixture of hope and suspicion. 'How?'

Suddenly Kate Weinstock was back by the front passenger window again.

'Come on, Shafiq,' she said briskly. 'No more talk now.' She looked up at Soames. 'They're getting very tired,' she said sharply. 'Enough is enough.'

Soames paused by the front door of the flats and looked down at his watch. It was just after eleven and there were no lights showing in Gaby Darrington's house.

Glancing around to make sure he was unobserved, Soames knocked gently on her door. For a long while there was no response and he was just about to knock again when he heard movement.

A chain was detached, the Yale lock clicked up and the door opened to reveal Gaby in a dressing-gown, looking dishevelled, her studied hair-style tangled and her face puffy and pale, with dark bags under her eyes.

'I've got bad news,' he said baldly.

She said nothing, gazing up at him in bewilderment.

'Douglas Cass. He's had his throat cut. I found him near the youth club.'

Gaby continued to stare at him, not seeming to take it in. 'If you want to talk, we'll go into Edward's study. The light won't show from there and the room faces the back garden.'

Soames followed her through the dark hall and into a small book-lined room. When she switched on a table lamp he could see a comprehensive collection of military history in the bookshelves. A large desk was placed to one side of the room, crowded with carefully dusted photographs depicting rows of soldiers, some seated, others standing. To relieve the monotony, there were some equally formal wedding photographs and a few small military artifacts, including some medals and an assortment of medallions.

They sat down opposite each other in a couple of armchairs that faced an empty fireplace, the desk behind them. The room smelt of leather and book-bindings and polish.

'What happened?' asked Gaby. She looked drained and defenceless, as if all the veneer had been wiped off. Soames wondered if there was now a chance of a less schematic conversation.

'He had a row with Hinton. Something about a girlfriend.'

'He did have this girl. She's very clever.'

'Not in the school?'

'He met her at the youth club.'

'Hinton says Douglas ordered her about and she didn't like it.'

'He's probably right. Douglas tried to dominate everyone. He was a loner – this girl was an exception. He never seemed to make friends and the other kids were in awe of him. He was too much of a cynic.' Like Shafiq, she wanted to talk – and not to think of what had happened to Cass.

'What about Cass's home background?'

'Father left home when Douglas was six, but he had a good relationship with his mother.'

'Too close?'

'No. Just right, I would say – for an only child.'

'Was Douglas behind at school?' asked Soames.

'He was another special needs pupil. I would say he was mildly dyslexic.'

'Any other problems?'

'No. He was talented at sport and of course he was Captain of Games.'

'Did he go to Bantry Bay?'

'He loved the adventure training.'

'Billings didn't seem to know him well.'

'Well – there are other instructors. Billings is only in charge of the programme.'

'Do you know Billings?'

'I know *of* him. I've driven the boys up there a couple of times, but never actually met him.'

'Your husband knows him well?'

'Of course.'

'So why –'

'You don't understand army protocol. Billings isn't high-ranking enough for us to entertain him – when we *were* entertaining.' She paused, the finality of it all beginning to reach her. 'Was Cass alive when you found him?'

'No.'

'So what happened after the row with Hinton?'

'Cass ran off in what appeared to be a fit of pique. Was he like that?'

'No. He was normally very laid back.'

'I offered to go and look for him, and eventually found him lying on a tarpaulin over the back of a truck in the yard of the garage next door to the youth club. His throat had been cut, but he had other injuries – as if he'd been attacked and then chased over the fence.'

Gaby Darrington bent forward, covering her face with her hands. 'Why?' She began to weep.

'Because he knew something? Or was going to reveal something? Just like Dr Griff. The boys are being questioned now.'

'Where?'

'Kate Weinstock's house. I called her right away, and she came down to the club.'

'And took charge?'

125

'It was necessary.'

Looking up at him, Gaby said, 'No one really knows what's going on, do they?'

'I'm sure the boys do – or at least some of them. But they're all too afraid to talk, especially after what's happened. There's a real conspiracy of silence which is very hard to break.'

'That's because of the ring, isn't it? They won't trust adults.'

'Exactly.'

'At least the ring's vulnerable.'

'I'm not sure about that,' said Soames, remembering his conversation with Shafiq, but not prepared to divulge the content. Just as the boys couldn't trust adults, he wasn't sure he could trust Gaby Darrington, although he couldn't think why. It was simply a feeling, probably irrational. She had gone to the police, done the right thing. And now she seemed genuinely distraught. 'They're still able to enforce silence. The boys are united in their anxiety – and yet alone as well.'

'How many pupils do you think *are* involved?' asked Gaby.

'No way of telling.' Soames paused and then asked, 'What do you think of Shafiq?'

'The school lawyer? He doesn't come in the special needs class. His father *is* a lawyer. He's been advising Griff and Weinstock for years.'

'A stable home?'

'Very much so.'

'How do you rate Shafiq?'

'I like him, but he's cheeky and wearisomely persistent.'

'That was my impression. He's also afraid. He told Mason some long and very convoluted story about Cass confiding in him about a friend being abused at the base.'

'Typical of Shafiq.'

'He also spoke to me privately, saying he couldn't trust adults, but Weinstock came up and interrupted us.'

'Do you think you might get him to talk to you?' she asked urgently.

'Is Shafiq trustworthy?'

'I think so.'

'Suppose I tell him who I am?' said Soames, wanting to test her out.

126

Gaby gazed at him.

'That might make him trust me.'

'Would he believe you?'

'If Mason came in on the act. But he could also blow my cover wide open.'

'Even if Shafiq knew the truth, why should he trust you?' asked Gaby, looking agitated. 'Couldn't an undercover policeman be in the ring too?'

'At a stretch of the imagination.'

'Not to a child. All adults are suspect.'

He nodded, sure that she was right, but still far from sure about her.

'I'm still concerned about Bernie,' she said. 'He's in a very vulnerable position.'

'I'll speak to Mason.'

'Can he be given protection?'

'I'm sure they'll keep an eye on him.'

'That doesn't sound very reassuring.'

'I know it doesn't, but that's all Mason could do.' He paused. 'There's something I want you to do for me. I need to go to Bantry Bay.'

Gaby hesitated for a moment. 'I'm sure I can arrange that,' she said eventually.

'You sound doubtful.'

'No. I just don't think any of the boys should go up there after this.'

'If they don't, I'll have less of a chance.'

'You can't use them as decoys.'

'I'll be with the kids. All the time. And it's not just a question of Bantry Bay, is it? They're not safe anywhere – as Cass's murder has just proved.'

'I know,' said Gaby. 'But to use our pupils like this. It's terribly irresponsible.'

'I'm sorry,' said Soames. 'It's a risk we've got to take.'

She was silent. Then Gaby spoke so fast she gabbled her words out.

'I've got a rota of drivers but no one wants their Saturdays cluttered up. I believe it's Andy Day's turn. He's a history teacher – but he spends most of his weekends mugging up for a PhD. I'm sure he'd be only too pleased to swap with you.'

'Do you need Weinstock's permission?'

'No. But we've got to be very careful. I'm not sure that –'

'And one last question,' Soames swept on. 'Does the driver usually get to stay, or even take part?'

'Most people don't stay, and certainly wouldn't want to take part. The assault course looks formidable. But a few of the staff watch for a while, particularly if they're living-in at school and they've got nothing else to do. You'll have to ask Sergeant Billings's permission to stay overnight. For God's sake, Alan, be careful with them.' Gaby Darrington repeated. 'Do you know much about children?'

'I've got two of them at home.' The lie was painful.

'Could you confide in them – give them as much responsibility as you're proposing to load on Shafiq?'

'They'd be silent as the grave,' said Soames quietly.

'I'm not sure about Shafiq.'

'It's only a thought, and I won't lean on him until I really have to.' Soames had only made the proposal so he could gauge her reaction and she had definitely seemed genuinely concerned. So what was so worrying about her?

'Do you mean you think there are going to be more of these attacks?'

'Depends on the boys. Those who know what's really happening are still too afraid to own up – just like Lofts.'

'But Dr Griff and Douglas were made of sterner stuff. Is that what you're saying?'

'We're up against raw fear. Once one of these kids breaks the silence they'll move in.'

'As in Cass's case?'

'Yes.'

'So it's deadlock?'

'I want it to stay that way,' said Soames. 'For a while.'

128

13

That night, after hours of lying awake and running over the events of the evening, Soames drifted into light and uneasy sleep, dreaming of entwined serpents with venomous tongues, whose sinuous coils had St Clouds in their writhing, crushing and ever-tightening grip.

Soames woke sweating, trying to work out where he was, the pale morning light just visible in the gap between the ill-fitting curtains. Then the burden of it all returned and he realised how puny he was in the face of the serpent. He slept again, but only dreamt of the boys sheltering behind the table tennis table in Ballard Youth Club while Cass lay dead on the darkly stained tarpaulin. Then Kate Weinstock arrived, and stood guard over her waifs and strays. Good versus evil, Soames wondered as he woke for the second time, or just a season in hell with Weinstock as the boys' controller with the ring winding itself around her stout legs?

The phone rang and Soames clutched at the receiver uneasily.

'How are you, Alan?' Kate Weinstock's voice was warmer than usual.

'I didn't get much sleep.'

'I don't think many of us at Clouds slept last night.'

'Have there been more developments?'

'DI Mason was most thorough. He and his team closely questioned each boy without bullying them, but none of them could help. Has he spoken to you?'

'Yes,' said Soames. 'He called me early this morning.' Too late he realised that Mason would have told him about any developments. Had she picked up on that? 'Did Shafiq repeat what Cass had told him – about a man doing something to a friend?' he said quickly, hoping she hadn't.

'Yes. But that's all he said.'

'So we're no further forward.'

'Not at all. I went down to the newsagent to get the early

morning papers. Unfortunately, we have front-page coverage in every edition and the switchboard is buzzing with parents wanting to take their boys away.' She should have sounded beaten but Kate Weinstock spoke buoyantly, as if marshalling her troops against the impossible odds of a long seige.

'If there's an immediate withdrawal, that will make the police's job even more difficult.'

'I'm sure it will.' Kate Weinstock paused. 'What are you doing this morning?'

'I'd volunteered to drive the boys on the adventure training course up to Bantry Bay. I swapped with Andy Day.' Soames tried to sound casual, knowing that Weinstock would explode. This was a very risky moment and he wasn't surprised when he got the predictable reaction.

'Is that wise? After all the horrors of last night?' She was astounded.

'I was going to get permission to stay with them all the time.'

'You're not conducting your own one-man investigation, are you, Alan?'

Soames froze. Had everything backfired on him? Desperately he tried to seize the initiative. 'I'm just very concerned.'

'You don't think enough is being done?'

'I certainly don't think the boys should continue the course unless there's someone with them.'

'You imagine I hadn't thought of that?' she asked angrily, almost menacingly.

'Of course –'

'But you seized the opportunity. Without the slightest reference to me.'

Suddenly, Soames knew why the boys feared her. He felt eleven years old, put firmly in the wrong.

'I'm as exhausted as –'

'I am.'

'I'm sorry. I wasn't thinking.'

'I'm sorry, too, Alan.' He was amazed at the climb-down. 'We're both drained. Maybe you're right and we should carry on as normal. Perhaps that would discourage the parents from taking the students away. But you mustn't let the pupils out of your sight – not for a moment – and if the army don't agree to that then you must bring the boys back.'

Why was she trusting him? Soames wondered. 'Of course.' He felt a great surge of relief.

There was a momentary pause and then Kate Weinstock continued. 'I wondered if you might be available to counsel one of the boys. He's going up to Bantry Bay this morning, but I'd be obliged if you would have a talk with him before he goes. His name is Peter Dawson.'

'What exactly do you want me to talk to him about?'

'Peter's in quite a state.' She sounded hesitant.

'He wasn't at the club last night.'

'No. Peter says he doesn't want to go up to Bantry Bay. He's a confident boy and not one to look for excuses.'

'You should ring Mason.' What the hell was she playing at? wondered Soames. First she hadn't put up any real protests at the trip. Now she was dropping him in the deep end. He could be anyone. He could be a nonce.

'I've made that suggestion, but Peter refuses to speak to anyone. Even me. But I thought there might be some point in you having a try. After all, you took the initiative and you have the boys' interests at heart, just as much as we have. But maybe a fresh face . . . I've got to go down to the police station and talk to Mason again. Can you help me out?' She paused. 'I'm rather reliant on your fresh face. I don't trust anyone else.'

'How can you trust me?'

'I'm not sure. It's as if – as if you've been sent. The objective stranger.'

'I could be anyone.'

'Well – you're not. Mason told me he'd checked you out.'

'I see.' But was that enough? Why was she behaving so strangely? But Soames knew he had to take advantage of her odd behaviour. There was no time to do anything else. 'What do you want me to do?'

'Can you see Peter in the interview room?'

'Will he turn up?'

'If I tell him to.' She seemed surprised he could ask such a question.

'There's something else . . .'

131

'Well?' Kate Weinstock was impatient.

'Last time one of the boys spoke to me personally, you told me I should have sent him to Noel Bundy. This situation seems very similar. Shouldn't Bundy be handling it?'

'He's away for the weekend, although I'm sure he'll be returning when he sees the television or picks up a newspaper. But until then we've got no way of contacting him, I'm afraid.' She was brisk. 'I'd like you to have a go.'

'I'll see him,' said Soames. The opportunity, however risky, couldn't be wasted.

'Peter will be in the interview room in forty minutes then, or will that be too soon?'

'Not at all.'

'See what you can make of him. And by the way, I'll send the *Telegraph* down with him in a large envelope. The newspapers aren't available to the boys unless they go to the library and Miss Baxter doesn't open till ten.' She sounded conspiratorial. 'You'll keep me in touch then, Alan?'

When Weinstock had rung off, Soames wondered yet again exactly why she had singled him out to see Peter Dawson. And, more importantly, why *had* she agreed to the trip at a time like this? *You can't use the boys as decoys*, Gaby had said last night. But could Weinstock be doing exactly that?

The questions drummed in his mind over breakfast, which he took alone in his room, and continued to nag at him as he washed up his cup and plate. Then he got out his mobile, checked his watch and saw that he had a quarter of an hour before he had to see Dawson, and an hour before he was due to leave for Bantry Bay.

'Thank God you're there,' said Soames when he got through to Mason. 'I've told Weinstock we've already talked.'

'She's coming over to see me. The boys are scared shitless and we're now going to have to interview every pupil in the whole damned school.'

'A lot of parents are withdrawing their sons.'

'That's all we need!'

'Have the Cass parents turned up?'

'Just his mother. She's in shock. They were obviously very close.'

'I'm still going to take a group of boys up to Bantry Bay this morning and stick with them. I'll get permission to stay the night, and I've cleared the trip with Weinstock.'

'Doesn't she feel you've acted on your own initiative once too often?'

'I know she does. But I've got to take the risk. And now she's asked me to counsel one of the boys, which I find very odd.'

'Who is he?'

'Peter Dawson, who's due to join the adventure training course at Bantry Bay this weekend – and won't go. Weinstock has asked me to see him.'

'Alone?'

'Yes.'

'You shouldn't see any boy alone.'

'I'm going to have to risk it. I might get something out of him.'

'Why is she asking you to do this? You've only just arrived. What about the care staff? What about anyone else but you?'

'That's what I've been wondering. Apparently the Head of Pastoral Care, Noel Bundy, is off for the weekend.'

'There must be more experienced staff around.' Mason was perturbed. More than perturbed. 'I don't like it.'

'Neither do I.'

'Then back off.'

'It's too late. I've agreed. Suppose she thinks I'm a member of the ring?'

'For God's sake –'

'Why not? I've taken a year out, I could come at short notice, she knows I've got close to the boys – and I was down at the youth club last night. Now I'm off to Bantry Bay today – and, of course, I found Cass's body.'

'Too obvious?'

'Maybe not to her. Anyway, she says you checked me out. Did you tell her that?'

'I did.'

'I'm sure she's playing games. But I've got to grab the opportunity.'

133

'Maybe all she cares about is the school,' said Mason doubt-fully. 'As far as I can see, she's obsessed with the place. The school's her life. Perhaps she would do anything to keep it going.'

'She won't have a school left if she's not careful. She's running scared, like the boys. She could be trying to set me up.' Soames suddenly felt indecisive.

'Then don't speak to Dawson.'

'It's a risk I'm going to have to take.'

The interview room was surprisingly welcoming, with posters on the walls and photographs of school trips as well as an unmatching collection of chairs and a central table with an un-tidy heap of books and comics. The walls were painted a Van Gogh yellow and early morning sunlight was filtering in shafts on to the carpet.

Peter Dawson, a small, overweight, owl-like boy with glasses, was already sitting in one of the chairs with a large envelope on his lap, looking wary. He jumped to his feet when Soames came into the room.

'Peter Dawson?'

'Yes, sir.'

'I'm Mr Soames. Do sit down and I'll come straight to the point. Miss Weinstock asked me to talk to you about Bantry Bay. I'm driving the group up there this morning.'

'I don't want to go, sir.'

'You're not the only one. Another boy I talked to didn't want to go either, but I gather he's coming with us.'

'Who's that, sir?' The boy seemed too eager to know. Was it just because he wanted other people to be in the same plight?

'I can't tell you. It wouldn't be fair.'

'No, sir.' Soames was conscious of the boy's eyes on his, pleadingly.

'Why don't you want to go?'

'I'm scared, sir.'

'What of?'

There was a silence. Are we going to have vertigo all over again? wondered Soames in frustration.

134

'This man. He did things to my friend.'

Soames gazed at Peter Dawson in amazement. That was the exact wording that Douglas Cass was alleged to have used when apparently confiding in Shafiq. Was he in with a chance at last?

'Why didn't you tell Miss Weinstock?'

'I couldn't, sir. She's a woman, sir.'

'That's a bit old-fashioned, isn't it?'

Peter Dawson stared at him.

'OK. Who was this man?'

'A man at the base.'

Breakthrough! The word echoed through Soames's mind like an exploding star. But he had to be careful. He'd been on the edge before and thrown it all away.

'Can you identify him?'

'No, sir.'

'Why not?'

'This man at the base did things to my friend.'

Soames paused, knowing that one wrong move could wreck any more progress.

'What things?'

'Dirty.' Peter Dawson looked away, his face crimson.

'Was your friend hurt?'

'Yes.'

'What kind of hurt?'

The boy wasn't looking at him now, but staring down at the floor.

'Sore hurt.'

'Sore –'

'The man . . .'

'Yes?'

'He went in behind with his thing.'

'His penis?'

'Yes, sir.' Dawson was still looking down, trembling slightly.

'OK. Try and relax.' The advice seemed ludicrous. 'Where did this take place?'

'In his behind, sir.' Dawson looked up, puzzled.

'I'm sorry. I didn't mean that.' It was Soames's turn to feel acutely embarrassed. 'I meant in what part of the base? Was it daytime or –'

'At night, sir.'

'Whereabouts?'

'In a hut.'

'Where is this hut?'

'On the cliffs.'

Soames felt a surge of adrenalin. The hut again. 'This man. Could your friend remember what he looked like?'

'No, sir.'

'Why?'

'I don't know, sir.'

'Can't he describe him at all?'

'He was a big man, sir.'

'Has this happened to other boys?'

'Yes.'

'Who?'

'I can't say.'

'Many?'

'Some.'

'Why won't they talk about it? Why aren't they brave, like you?'

'They're scared, sir.'

'What of?'

'They were told they'd be hurt, sir. Hurt badly.'

'Like Doug Cass?'

Peter was staring down at the floor again. 'Like Cass, sir,' he muttered.

'No wonder they're afraid. Did Cass – do you think Cass could have identified the man who – who did those things to him?'

'I don't know, sir.'

'He did do things to him, didn't he?'

Peter was silent.

'If you're so scared, why are you telling me?'

'I don't want to go to Bantry Bay, sir.'

'No one should have to go,' said Soames. 'But I'm taking you this morning – and I'll be with you all the time.' The statement didn't seem to reassure Dawson at all, and he carried on as if Soames hadn't spoken.

'Not all the boys get picked on.'

'No?'

'It's not – everyone.'

'Will you trust me?' Soames asked quietly.

'Trust you to do what, sir?'

'To do something about this.'

'What are you going to do?' He was pleading again now.

'Sort it out. But to do that I have to ask you something else.'

'I've got nothing else to say, sir.'

'Just one more question.'

'What is it?' Peter asked grudgingly.

'There's no friend, is there? The things were done to you, weren't they, Peter?'

'No, sir,' he replied stubbornly. 'They happened to my friend.'

'Who's your friend?'

'I don't know. I mean, I can't say.' He was flustered now, his eyes darting around the room, increasingly incoherent. 'There *is* a friend. He's too upset. He made me promise.'

'Come on, Peter,' said Soames. 'You know there isn't a friend. You know you're making that friend up. You know you're talking about yourself. You must be able to tell me who assaulted you.'

Peter half nodded and then his features contorted in childish fury. 'You've no right,' he stuttered.

'No right to do what?'

'To touch me.'

'Sorry?' A sudden cold chill swept through Soames. What the hell was this?

'To put your thing in me.' Peter's eyes were slightly glazed. He blinked in his owlish way through his spectacles which had become slightly misted up.

Soames saw the abyss opening up before him. After all, Mason had warned him. Why hadn't he listened?

'*What* did you say?'

'A man touched me.'

'It wasn't me.'

'I shall tell.'

'There's nothing *to* tell.'

'How will they know? It's my word against yours.' Peter Dawson's voice was high and shrill, the sweat was pouring into his eyes and he kept clenching and unclenching his fists.

Soames struggled to keep calm. 'Look, Peter, Miss Weinstock wanted me to talk to you, to try to help you.'

'Instead you helped yourself.'

'What do you mean?'

'You helped yourself to me.' Peter giggled.

'For God's sake –'

'You stuck your –'

'Shut up!' Soames was beside himself with anxiety.

'Why should I? You asked me to tell the truth.'

'It's not the truth,' Soames said quietly, trying to keep control. 'We both know you're lying.'

'No one will believe you. You were alone with me.' Peter Dawson's grin was fixed, almost a rictus.

14

'Try to relax,' Soames exhorted him, the panic rising just as it had done when he had been facing the Lower Fourth. But this was much more serious.

'You've got to get me off going to Bantry Bay.'

'Because you'll be interfered with?'

There was only silence now. Then Peter repeated, 'You've got to get me off going to Bantry Bay.' It was like a litany.

Soames got up and walked to the door, determined to blast Weinstock to hell and back for this. Had she really set him up with this crazy boy to trap him?

He turned back to Dawson. 'Unless you withdraw your false accusations, all of which I'm repeating to Miss Weinstock, you'll be expelled.'

'I want to be expelled,' said Dawson truculently.

'And your parents will be told what you've been saying.'

'I'm not responsible.'

138

'What?'

There was a gleam of cunning in Peter's eyes. 'I'm not responsible, sir. I'm under a psychiatrist.'

Soames had a sudden, impulsive and all-consuming desire to laugh and go on laughing. At the same time he had never felt more terrified. Somehow he managed to control himself. 'I'm going to speak to Miss Weinstock. Do you have anything else to say?'

Peter shook his head.

Soames made a hurried departure.

He met Noel Bundy in the corridor, looking highly agitated, heading in the direction of the staff room.

'You've heard what's happened? And seen the press? I just can't believe what's going on. There's a serial killer out there, for Christ's sake. What are the police doing? What's Weinstock doing? The kids should have been gated, not allowed anywhere near that fucking youth club.'

Realising he was about to take another group into the lions' den, Soames decided not to start the conversation with that piece of information. He already felt frantic with worry and what he didn't want was another major confrontation. Peter Dawson was enough for one day.

'Whoever the killer is,' said Soames, 'could get in here just as easily.' Then he realised he'd left Miss Weinstock's neatly packaged newspaper in the interview room. 'I'll be back.'

Soames hurried down the corridor and threw open the door, only to find Peter Dawson avidly reading the front page of the *Telegraph* which bore the headline: MAYHEM AT SPECIAL SCHOOL.

Soames snatched the paper out of his hands. 'That wasn't meant for you.'

'I found it, sir.' He sounded mockingly indignant.

'You opened the envelope.'

'Sorry, sir.'

'Remember what I said.'

Dawson looked at him in some confusion. 'What *did* you say, sir?'

'Never mind.'

For the second time Soames abruptly left the room.

Noel Bundy was waiting for him in the corridor. Soames laid out the *Telegraph* on a window sill and together they gazed down at the front page.

MAYHEM AT SPECIAL SCHOOL

A serial killer is thought to be on the rampage in Swanage. Less than a fortnight ago, Dr Rowland Griff, the Headmaster of St Clouds School, was found dead in his study. His throat had been cut. Yesterday, seventeen-year-old Douglas Cass – a pupil at the school – was discovered with his throat cut in a garage yard behind a youth club. Cass had also been wounded in the chest and arm.

DI Ted Mason of Swanage CID made a statement late last night. 'We are confident of making an arrest within the next few days and would advise anyone against walking alone in the Swanage area for the moment.'

There was more detail inside, with pictures of the school as well as pupils in the grounds which Soames knew must have been taken with a telescopic lens.

'We're finished,' said Bundy with gloomy relish, but Soames could see that he was broken-hearted. Despite his undeclared war with Weinstock, the school was everything to him, as it was to her. But at least Bundy cared about the pupils.

'I thought you were away for the weekend,' said Soames, trying to gather his thoughts.

'I came back immediately I heard. I gather you discovered Cass's body. That must have been the most dreadful experience.'

'It was. But I've got another problem . . .'

Soames began to relate what had happened between Peter Dawson and himself, and by the time he had finished, Bundy was furious, but fortunately not with Soames. That was to come, he thought.

'Why the hell didn't Weinstock tell you never to be alone with *any* of the boys? She knows what little sods they are.'

'I'll tell her.'

'So shall I,' snapped Bundy. 'Where the hell *is* she?'

'With the CID at the police station. What shall I do about Dawson?'

'Leave him to me.'

'What are you going to do?'

'Scare the shit out of him!'

'Is that wise?'

'You certainly weren't. How could you be so naïve? But the extraordinary thing is why did she let you see him alone? Weinstock's always on at the staff about –'

'I gather the older boys are encouraged into people's homes. Staff homes.'

'That's only when they're trusted, and much older. Even then we have to have the whole family unit present and correct.'

Soames thought of Gaby Darrington and made no comment. Then he plunged reluctantly on to what he was sure was going to be a bad confrontation. 'I'm supposed to be driving the boys up to Bantry Bay in a minute.'

'You're what?' Bundy looked almost comically apoplectic.

'I'll be there with them all the time. I shan't take my eyes off them.'

'You're sleeping there?'

'If I can get permission.'

'And if not?'

'I'm bringing the boys back.'

'Does Weinstock know?'

'Yes.'

'God Almighty!'

'I know what you're thinking.'

'So you go in for mind reading as well as risk taking?'

'You're thinking – suppose he's a pederast too . . .'

'Steady on.' Bundy looked horrified.

'I'm sure Miss Weinstock does. That's why she put temptation my way.'

'Dawson?'

Soames suddenly realised he'd said exactly the right thing. He nodded.

'She always uses the boys. To Weinstock, they're pawns in her power games.'

Divide and rule, thought Soames. He reckoned he had done just that.

'Whatever game she's playing,' said Bundy, 'count me out. I think you're a man with considerable initiative. Good luck to you.'

'You mean you trust me with the kids?'

'Of course I do.'

'You sure you shouldn't come with me?'

'No,' said Bundy. 'I may not know you that well, but I do trust you.'

Soames was sickened. He didn't think Bundy trusted him at all and guessed the only reason he was allowing Soames to take the boys was because he wanted to score off Miss Weinstock.

He returned to the original problem. 'What the hell's the matter with Dawson?'

'Leave him to me – and I *mean* leave him to me. I'll soon sort Dawson out and I'll be making sure I have another staff member with me. You should have been more careful.'

'I know. I didn't think. So much has happened. Maybe that was Weinstock's problem too.' In fact, he was still sure she'd set him up. And was Bundy about to do the same with Bantry Bay?

Bundy nodded impatiently, dismissing further explanation. 'Suppose the whole idea of a ring is a monster red herring?'

'What other motives could there be for Griff and Cass's killings?'

'I can only –'

They both swung round as they heard the rapping of shoes on the stone floor of the corridor and Kate Weinstock came into view. She was wearing a well-cut dark green suit but her face was grey with fatigue and she hardly glanced at either of them.

'Any developments?' asked Bundy.

Soames had known he would never confront her. She was too powerful for him at close range.

'Nothing. But Mason seems sure this ring's responsible.' Her voice shook. 'Surely no one could ...' She didn't finish her sentence. 'There's no chance for St Clouds now, is there?'

'There might be if an arrest is made,' said Noel Bundy, clutching at straws. When Weinstock didn't reply, he continued, 'Alan's had some problems with Peter Dawson. Serious problems. He should never have been allowed to be alone with him.'

Soames was surprised. So Bundy *was* confronting her. Was this because she had just demonstrated weakness?

'I know,' said Kate Weinstock with sudden humility. 'I'm terribly sorry, Alan. It's all my fault.'

Both Bundy and Soames were taken aback.

'I should have reminded you to take a colleague in there with you. Peter is one of our more disturbed boys and could make any accusation that comes into his head.' Just like Bernie Lofts, thought Soames, still amazed by her acquiescence. 'I'll go and see Peter and deal with him.'

'I was just going to save you the trouble,' put in Bundy.

'It's no trouble.' Kate Weinstock gave him a forced smile.

Soames had never seen her like this before and the climb-down made him uneasy. How are the mighty fallen – at least on a temporary basis. He almost felt sorry for her, but when he glanced at Bundy he saw his delight.

'The whole business has brought me to my knees,' Kate Weinstock admitted. 'I just don't know what I'm doing any longer. I can't make judgements.' She paused, perhaps realising how much Bundy was enjoying her lack of grip, and struggled to pull herself together. 'I shall have a rest and then I'll be quite back to my old self. Where *is* Peter?'

'Still in the interview room,' said Soames.

She looked worried. 'What's he been doing?'

'He was reading this paper. I'm sorry. I was in such a flap that I left it behind,' said Soames apologetically.

Bundy sighed.

'I'll go and see him,' said Weinstock. 'And by the way, thank you so much for returning so promptly, Noel.'

'It was the least I could do.'

'Of course.'

'I'll go and fetch my tracksuit,' said Soames. 'I thought it might be a good idea if I stayed with the boys overnight at Bantry Bay. Took a bit of a look round.' Although she had

143

already given him permission, Soames wanted her to repeat her willingness in front of Bundy. It seemed rather a neat touch.

'I'm still not sure –' began Bundy, as if he was firing the necessary warning shot and needed a witness.

Weinstock swept him aside. 'I think that's a very good idea, Alan. But what happens if the army refuses permission?'

'I don't think they will. It wouldn't look good.'

'I'm sure you're right,' said Kate Weinstock. 'But if you're not allowed to stay, I want you to bring the boys home.' They were both repeating themselves now. 'I've been very impressed by Alan's relationship with the boys and I trust him with them.'

'After a few days?' Bundy burst out. She'd stolen all his thunder and Soames tried not to show his amusement.

'He's achieved more in a few days than you have in years. The police are equally useless. If we're going to track down this – this maniac, then Alan staying the night at the base could produce results that Mason can't.' She paused, trying to calm down but not really succeeding. 'I'm not saying the source of all this is the army, the club or the school. But we've got to *do* something.'

For someone who had tried to ignore the existence of a ring from the start, Weinstock was a bit of a late starter, thought Soames. Then he realised that she was doing it again, that she was plunging him into what might turn out to be a very compromising situation.

She hurried away towards the interview room.

'For Christ's sake –' began Bundy.

But Soames also hurried away. 'I haven't got time for this,' he said. 'Do you always change your mind so quickly?'

'I'm sorry. The shock of all this . . .' he began feebly.

For the sake of expediency, Soames let him off the hook. 'I understand. I can see the strain you're under – that we're all under – but I must get going. The kids will be waiting.'

'No hard feelings?'

'Of course not.' Do you really think I'm a nonce too? wondered Soames as he ran towards his flat.

Tracksuited and with a change of clothes in a duffel bag, Soames discovered only six boys standing by the minibus.

'I thought there were going to be twelve of you,' he said to Shafiq, who was clearly delighted to see him.

'The others have gone home,' Shafiq replied. 'And I don't think they're coming back.'

Soames checked the list. Shafiq Abnar, Graham Joyce, Tim Penman, Tristan Hardy, Harry Tate and Paul Malling.

'I'm glad you're prepared to keep going with the course,' he said to them. 'It's important to you. I'm going to spend the night up there too – so I'll be able to keep an eye on you.' As he gazed round at them he couldn't detect any visible signs of relief.

'It's our last weekend,' said Penman. 'It's been great so far. We don't want to miss out on our certificates.'

'What do you have to do?'

'Try and break a record over the assault course and then there's a night survival exercise. We've got to build bivouacs, light a fire and scavenge food off the beach.'

'All together?'

'In pairs, sir,' said Shafiq.

'Have any other members of staff ever shared the experience with you?'

'Not on our course, sir,' said Shafiq. 'But it's a bit different now, isn't it?' He looked relieved. 'I'm glad you want to keep an eye on us.'

The boys were wearing jeans and T-shirts and carrying rucksacks. There was a rather pathetic determination to them that Soames found touching.

'Do you know what you're letting yourself in for, sir?' asked Tate.

'Probably not,' replied Soames briskly.

'Have the police found the murderer?' Tristan Hardy was tall and slender with sleek blond hair.

'Not yet. But they soon will,' he added with determined, but what he was sure was inadequate, reassurance.

There was an uneasy silence.

'Tell me – did you lot volunteer?'

'There were too many volunteers at first,' said Shafiq.

'So who made the final selection?'

'Mr Hinton and Bernie Lofts.'

'So some people were disappointed?'

145

'Yes, sir.'

'What skills do you have to have?'

Shafiq looked blank. 'I think they just drew names out of a hat. Something like that.'

Something like that? Soames didn't think so. 'Who's a pretty boy then?' Hamlet rasped.

The day was rain-washed, grey clouds racing against a background of pale blue sky with the sun occasionally breaking through.

The atmosphere in the minibus was leaden and flat. Even Shafiq seemed subdued and hadn't chosen to sit in the front with him. Soames was relieved, hoping to take the opportunity to clarify his thoughts which had become circular. The school. The club. The army. The school. The club. The army . . .

Soames drove through Swanage, taking a route that didn't pass the youth club, although none of the boys, except Shafiq, had been with him last night. He wondered how the horror of Cass's death had affected him deep down, for on the surface Shafiq seemed bland, all too well contained.

From Swanage, Soames drove on to Corfe Castle and then Lulworth until he drew up at the Royal Rangers base. The gates were picked out in red and gold, with a military crest, and fronted by smooth verdant lawns. There were manned sentry boxes, each of the soldiers with a rifle over his shoulder.

The gates were open, but there was an automatic barrier and a guard house just inside. The large mansion beyond had turrets and pediments which were also picked out in red and gold, and there was a huge tarmac surround on which were parked rows of military vehicles. The flagstaff bore a Union Jack that flapped in the breeze and grey-painted huts stretched beyond the tarmac in serried ranks.

Soames drew up at the control point, only to find another bus in front of him bearing the name Ballard Youth Club on the rear doors.

A soldier poked his head out of the guard house, wearing fatigues and a red beret. 'You'll be for Sergeant Billings too, will you, sir?'

'That's right.'

'As you can see, Mr Hinton is here. I believe Colonel Darrington's coming down to see you all himself. Would you mind following Mr Hinton into the visitors' car-park and the Colonel will join you.'

Soames nodded as the youth club minibus pulled away. He drove behind it, following the vehicle to the car-park that was just to the left-hand side of the house and opposite a volley ball court.

They waited. Neither Soames nor Hinton got out. It was like a challenge, Soames fancied, to see who would attempt to communicate first.

Then there was the slamming of a door and Hinton walked over towards him, looking apprehensive. 'What kind of nutter are we dealing with?'

'I'm not sure the person could be classified as a nutter,' said Soames.

'You think we're up against someone who is *sane*?'

'It's possible some of the pupils know who we're up against.' Soames lowered his voice.

Hinton shrugged. 'God knows how we're going to squeeze it out of them.'

'I've decided to stay up here if I can get permission. What about you?'

'I can't. I've got to open the club tonight.'

'Have you ever stayed over?'

'Oh yes. A couple of times. Gave me an insight into how claustrophobic barrack life can be.'

'You didn't enjoy the experience?'

'I nearly went stir crazy.'

'And that parrot will probably finish the job!'

Hinton gave him a humourless grin. 'Actually, I'm getting rather fond of him.'

'So you reckon I'll get permission to stay?'

'They might allow you. You want to try to get the boys to confide in you – or just keep an eye on them?'

'Both. I'll do the same for your lot.'

'It won't be as easy as that. There's a survival exercise tonight and the boys will be in pairs.'

147

'What about the squaddies?'

'They go from group to group, so if you want to join in you might end up on your own.' He hesitated. 'Should it really be business as usual?'

'Yes,' said Soames firmly. 'It should be.'

'I'd leave the police to their job.'

'As I said, I'm just here to keep an eye on the kids. *All* the kids.'

'Even so –'

Further discussion was interrupted by the arrival of a black Daimler, flying the regimental pennant on its bonnet, which glided up to the minibuses and stopped, regarded curiously by the boys inside.

'Mr Hinton? Mr Soames?' Colonel Darrington opened the rear door. 'I'm wondering if you'd join me for a coffee? Perhaps the boys would like a kick around.'

While Hinton and Soames nodded acquiescence, Darrington spoke into a mobile and signalled them to join him in the Daimler. More army public relations? wondered Soames, and glanced at Hinton. Was he thinking the same?

The chauffeur drove away, and looking back Soames saw Shafiq staring after them nervously. Was he wondering if he'd been deserted? Well – he had been. After all he had said. But Soames knew he had to seize his opportunity and take the risk.

Colonel Darrington's office was sparse but comfortable, with little furniture except for a large rolltop desk and a computer on a side table.

Darrington gestured towards some leather armchairs in the window.

'I'm sorry to postpone activities for an hour, gentlemen, but I'd very much like a word first.' As he spoke, a corporal came into the room with a tray of coffee, setting it down with smooth dexterity on a small table and pouring with military precision.

Silence reigned during the well-drilled task and Darrington only continued when the corporal had left the room.

'These murders have shaken me as deeply as they must have

148

shaken you. I'm appalled at the wanton brutality of it all.' He spoke with considerable passion. 'You may or may not know that we've been carrying out an investigation up here. The very thought that we could be harbouring some perverted monster is beyond belief.'

'There might be more than one monster,' said Soames.

'A ring? That's already been suggested. Like bees around a honeypot apparently, according to Detective Inspector Mason. So far I've drawn a blank and the same applies to Captain Penrose of the military police. We've interviewed each soldier connected with the adventure training programme and there seems to be nothing in their past or present conduct that might arouse our suspicions or give us a lead. I told Mason this morning that he's welcome to interview *any* of these men.' Darrington paused and turned to Hinton. 'Have you noticed anything out of order?'

'The St Clouds boys are definitely afraid of someone, and I'm certain they're withholding information.'

'What about you, Mr Soames? Can you be more specific?'

'I'm new to the school, which doesn't help, but I agree there's a definite undercurrent of anxiety. Two of the boys have implied that someone is interfering with them – and others. Someone up here. Of course the murders themselves were enough to terrify the students, but there's more to it than that.'

'I'm not new to the boys,' said Hinton. 'I've tried to reach them and I've got nowhere. Usually they confide in me.' He paused. 'I've been up against this kind of thing before, as Mr Soames knows.'

'How does it operate?' Darrington was impassive.

He's strong, thought Soames. As strong as Weinstock.

'They patiently establish credibility and when they eventually attack the victims are too afraid to shop them.'

'In your experience, are the members of the ring in contact with one another?' Darrington sounded as if he was planning a campaign in a battle zone, and Soames found him reassuring. There seemed no question of a cover-up.

'Not necessarily.'

'Do you have an example I could learn from?' asked Darrington.

Hinton looked deeply troubled and Soames had the feeling

that the memory was so painful that he was having trouble delving back into it. 'I was leading a club in Southampton. I was sure that something was going on because the boys were reacting exactly as they are here. Anxiety, fear, inability to communicate, partly because they were concerned about the ramifications, and also because they'd been threatened and made to feel as guilty as their predators. They felt dirty, they felt they'd participated in something horrendous and in some ways it was their *own* fault. I believe in God, Colonel Darrington. I'm a Christian, and yet I've sometimes thought I should kill these bastards with my own bare hands. It's always so hard to bring them to justice because they're very slippery and can prey off their victims for years without being detected.' Hinton was silent, his hands trembling. He clasped them together, looking away, and then unclasped them, quickly draining his coffee.

The silence lengthened like a rubber band, tightly stretched.

'What you say is very convincing,' said Colonel Darrington at last. 'What do you think, Mr Soames?'

'I agree. Mr Hinton exactly describes the situation we're up against. The point is that we seem to be at an impasse.' He paused. 'By the way, I'd like to ask a favour.'

'Ask away,' said Darrington.

'Can I join the adventure course?'

'Of course you can. But I warn you –'

'It's tough. OK, but I'd like to try.'

'Is this because you're afraid to leave your pupils in our care?'

'We don't have any hard evidence the ring is operating here,' said Soames. 'But the boys are definitely anxious so naturally I'd like to stay around.'

'I'll talk to Sergeant Billings.' Colonel Darrington took a discreet look at his watch. 'These barracks have been here in Dorset for over a hundred years, and there's been very little connection with the town, unless you count the odd football or cricket match. When I was asked to take command of the Royal Rangers I decided we should get in touch with the local community. The barracks have never had a particularly good local reputation. Incidents in the town, fights in the pubs, that kind of thing. But I have to create a crack peace-keeping force, and wherever we're sent, we're going to be up against local communities and we've got to interact with them. We've got to run play schemes for kids while we keep sides apart, so we might as well get in some practice in Swanage before we set out for Kosovo. Before all this ghastly stuff blew up, we were doing pretty well, weren't we, Mr Hinton?'

'Absolutely. I've been delighted.'

'Of course, the rotten apples could be anywhere, but I'm reluctant to believe they're here on the base. They could be in the school, or the town for that matter.'

'I hadn't lost sight of that either,' said Hinton.

Soames said nothing and Darrington rose to his feet. 'I'll have you driven back to your charges. I take it you won't be staying, Mr Hinton?'

'I've got to open the club this evening.'

'Then it's just you, Mr Soames,' said Darrington. 'I can assure you we've got nothing to hide.'

When they got back to the volley ball court most of the boys had returned to their individual minibuses. Clearly town and gown had concluded their interaction.

Spotting a toilet, Soames hurried over and stood in a cubicle with the door half open so that he could see if anyone was coming. Then he ran the risk of calling Mason on his mobile.

'I haven't got much time,' said Soames.

'Where are you?' Mason sounded depressed.

'I've decided to stay the night at Bantry Bay, check the place out and keep an eye on my charges.'

'You've got permission?'

'From the horse's mouth.'

'Darrington?' Mason was startled.

'He gave us coffee.'

'Who's us?'

'Hinton and myself. He says the army investigation is still proceeding, and Hinton told us about the ring he was up against in Southampton. He was very convincing about how subtle the waiting game is.'

'Did you have to leave the boys alone?'

151

'Yes. And I might have to do it again.'

'You're taking too much of a risk.'

'I'm certainly taking a risk, but whether it's too much I don't know. I've got to pick up what I can – and at the hell of a pace.'

'What are you going to do now?'

'Join in.'

'God help you!'

'He'll have to.'

'Be careful.' There was an unfamiliar note of concern in Mason's voice but Soames didn't know whether it was for him or the boys.

'I'm going to be. I'll take a look at the army personnel involved in the adventure training.' He heard someone shouting outside. 'I've got to go.'

'Be careful,' repeated Mason.

'Are you going to manage this, sir?' asked Shafiq brightly.

'I shouldn't think so.'

'Can I be your partner? I could give you a hand, sir.'

The boys from St Clouds and Ballard Youth Club were gazing down at a formidable assault course that swept across a small valley.

Sergeant Billings and Lance Corporal Repton were in charge of the operation, with half a dozen squaddies for back-up. Soames surveyed the course with apprehension, contemplating the A frame, the swinging logs high above a pit of muddy water, the big scramble net, the hurdles, the wall, the rope swing, the balancing poles, the death slide, the climbing tower, the high ropes, the even higher ropes and the final A frame in the distance.

'You've done this already?' he asked Shafiq, grimly knowing what the answer would be.

'Three times, sir. But now we've got to make it twice without a break to qualify.'

'My God!'

'Maybe they'll let you off, sir.'

'I don't want to be let off,' muttered Soames.

'Are you sure, sir?' asked Shafiq innocently.

Mercifully the conversation was interrupted by Billings, bellowing at them through an electronic megaphone. 'As you all know, this is a double treat. The whole course – twice – without a break. Each pair will be competing for the fastest time and we'll give you a staggered start.'

'Who's your partner, Shafiq?'

'Ben Harris, sir. But he's not here today.'

'Tristan doesn't seem to have a partner. Why don't you join him?'

'We don't get on that well, so I'm just as happy to –'

'I'll hold you back, Shafiq. Have a go at getting on with Tristan.'

Reluctantly, Shafiq began to amble over to him and they held a hesitant whispered conversation.

Soames stuck his hand up, shivering slightly in the sea breeze, vulnerable in his skimpy tracksuit.

'What is it, Mr Soames?' asked Billings.

'I haven't got a partner, Sergeant.'

'That's easily solved. I'll be your partner.'

'Er . . .'

'Don't you like the idea?'

'No. I'll be . . .'

'Honoured?' asked Billings sarcastically. 'We'll go last. Do you think you can make it twice?'

'We'll soon see,' said Soames unhappily.

'Lance Corporal Repton, will you take over the stop-watch?'

'Sir.'

'Everyone else to your positions.'

There were barked responses as the squaddies ran to various pieces of equipment, no doubt ready to ensure no one came off. Soames wondered what they would do if anyone did.

'Don't worry,' said Billings, as the first pair got ready for the start. 'I'll give you a hand.'

'I'll need it. All the boys look horribly fit to me.'

'They don't know danger at their age,' he said and their eyes met for a moment. 'Any news?'

'Not on the school grapevine.'

'Nothing here either, and I can assure you the Bantry grape-vine is just as sensitive.'

'I'm sure it is,' replied Soames evenly. 'You've seen the press, no doubt?'

'They're talking about a ring, aren't they?' said Billings. 'Those pederast bastards.' He lowered his voice. 'Fucking perverts. If I had my way I'd have them disembowelled and that would only be a beginning.'

'Wouldn't it be difficult for a ring to penetrate the army – of all institutions?'

'They can get in anywhere. Everywhere. I was on a posting to Brunei and there was this play scheme for local kids organised by a long-serving officer. He'd been biding his time.'

'Was he caught?'

'Not by the MPs, but the squaddies beat him to a fucking pulp and broke his arms and both his legs. Later on he made a confession to the Brigadier and now he's in a special unit in the Scrubbs, banged up with the other fuckers. But he'll be out soon, starting on kids again. Sick cunt.'

Soames was getting rather tired of Billings but he knew he had to encourage his vitriol. 'So you think a ring could have spread tentacles into Bantry Bay?'

'It's possible.' Billings was watching the penultimate pair start on a shouted command from Repton. 'Wish we could have got the local kids to pair up with your lot, but they didn't seem to go for the idea.'

'Maybe it's best not to run with a stranger,' said Soames without thinking and then wished he'd kept quiet. For some reason Billings seemed to have clammed up. 'Do *you* have the slightest suspicion of anyone here?' he said abruptly.

'No. Do you?'

'I haven't picked up on anything. But some of the kids are shit scared. They've come to me and other members of staff.'

'And given you names?'

'Not so far.'

'I wonder what the hell Griff and Cass knew. If only there was a clue then we'd be on to something.'

'I'm sure it was something incriminating about the ring.'

'You may be new to the school,' said Billings, 'but you suss

154

things out fast, don't you?' He looked slightly puzzled and Soames knew he'd gone too far.

A whistle shrilled and Billings clapped him on the back with a show of hearty enthusiasm that he couldn't share.

But just like the table tennis match against Shafiq, Soames surprised himself and the adrenalin pumped hard as they scrambled over the A frame, with Billings only a little ahead. Was he saving himself? Being patronising? Being helpful? It was impossible to tell. Like it was impossible to tell if he had blown his cover. *Be careful*, Mason had said. Soames knew he had to stop taking risks.

Soames gathered pace. Now they were approaching the assault wall, climbing up, hand over hand, reaching for the splintered wood, dragging themselves on, straddling the top, turning and jumping.

Then, as his confidence became complacency, Soames slipped, twisted, tried to save himself, failed and fell hard on his shoulder.

He lay on the ground, a dull pain spreading, while Billings sprang down, crouching beside him.

'Where does it hurt?'

'Shoulder.'

Another risk had failed to pay off.

Billings took his shoulder and probed gently. 'I'm afraid it's dislocated.'

'Christ!'

'I can snap it back.'

'You mean I won't have to go to hospital?' Despite the pain, Soames felt a wave of relief. Once again he'd almost wrecked everything.

'No. There's only one problem – it's going to hurt like hell.'

'Don't talk about it,' said Soames. 'Just do it.'

Billings grabbed his shoulder and something clicked. The pain was excruciating.

'Are you all right, sir?' Suddenly Shafiq was standing beside them, spattered with mud.

There were tears of pain in Soames's eyes. 'Not you, Shafiq.'

155

'I was worried, sir. I saw you go over the top and you just didn't –'

'Get back to your partner!' yelled Billings. 'Did I give you permission to come over here?'

'But I –'

'Did I give you permission?'

'No, sir.'

'Then rejoin your partner. At the double!'

Looking indignant, Shafiq began to jog away.

'He's not exactly army material, is he?' muttered Billings.

The pain swelled and then began to ebb. 'Not exactly. But he's interesting.'

'That's what I thought,' said Billings to Soames's surprise. 'I've been impressed by him. I like someone who thinks for himself. But that's not how we train people here.' He paused. 'How do you feel?'

'The pain's subsiding a bit.'

'Can you stand?'

'I think so.'

'Let me help you.' Billings took his arm and Soames managed to stagger to his feet.

'I feel an idiot.'

'Don't talk crap. You did really well. I shall tell the boys.'

'No need –'

'It needs saying. They can learn from that.'

Soames was beginning to like Billings but, he suspected, for the wrong reasons. He was offering him a face-saver and he was grateful.

'Can you walk on your own now?'

Clasping his stiff and sore shoulder, Soames found that he could.

The muddy and bedraggled participants were back where they had started, lying or sitting on the grass, gasping for breath, shoulders heaving.

Billings stood in front of them, hands on hips. 'Not a bad effort,' he said. 'But before we announce the winning pair, I want to talk about Mr Soames, the teacher from St Clouds. He slipped

156

off the wall and dislocated his shoulder. I had to snap it back and that's a very painful process.' Billings sounded genuinely admiring. 'But he took it like the man he is.'

There was ragged cheering, enthusiastically from St Clouds, dutifully from Ballard Youth Club.

'Who won, sir?' asked Shafiq.

'Two of the youth club lads,' said Repton, coming up with a clipboard. 'Joe Hoskins and Dan Charles.'

There was another ragged cheer, this time more muted from St Clouds.

What have I gained? wondered Soames. No insights. No information. No leads. Only pain.

As the boys and soldiers began to walk back to the base, Soames said to Billings, 'Mind if I take a walk round? Or are there restricted areas?' He knew that he was leaving his charges, knew that he was behaving irresponsibly. But guiltily Soames also knew that he had to take the risk.

'Not as long as you stay in the valley,' he replied. 'Once on the cliffs you'll find warning notices. You'd better obey them. If you don't, you could be walking over live ammunition. I don't want you blown away.'

'No,' said Soames. 'I've had my punishment for today.'

With the pain slowly subsiding, he strolled down the sweeping valley. A few windswept trees clung to the brow of the hill and the long wiry grass rustled in the light breeze.

Stopping at the top to get his breath back and to ease the soreness, Soames watched the grasses, listening to the rough salt-caked whispering, and then caught sight of a hut painted in camouflage colours.

Soames began to push his way through the grass, the breeze blowing in his face as he headed towards the hut that was crouched at the bottom of the valley.

Eventually he reached the building, which was rather less tumble-down than he had expected. The place had recently been repaired with strong, stout timber and the roof had been freshly felted. He rattled at the door, expecting it to be locked, but it swung open to reveal a dark interior that smelt of candle grease and sodden woollens. There was a stove, a battered wooden table, a few rickety chairs and a set of bunk beds which took up the whole of one wall.

He sat down heavily, his shoulder hurting, and the chair creaked alarmingly under his weight. Soames shifted to another that didn't. He wanted to think and this seemed the right opportunity.

The boys were fearful, trapped and closing ranks. Weinstock had now swung into action, but against who? Bundy was running scared and Gaby Darrington seemed defensive. Edward Darrington was the only one who had an overview, but then there was the problem of –

Soames started as the door of the hut was swung open and Billings stood on the threshold.

'I thought you might have found your way here.'

'Not off limits, I hope?'

'Of course not. We use it as a rest-up for night exercises. The boys get a taste of regular training, but they couldn't hack what the Rangers have to do.' He paused and then asked, 'Your mobile out of action?'

'It's not switched on.'

'Pity. Your Head's been trying to get in touch. Could you give her a ring?'

'Is there an emergency?'

'She didn't say,' said Billings. 'When you've finished, you might want to make your way back to the canteen. Lunch is in about an hour. I can't guarantee its quality, but there'll be plenty of it.'

Soames nodded, suddenly feeling full of trepidation. Why had Weinstock taken all this trouble to get hold of him?

PART FOUR

15

'Where have you been?' she asked.

'I've been on an exercise with the pupils and –'

'How is it going?' she interrupted.

Soames grew tense. There was an edge to her voice that he hadn't heard before. What was she building up to?

There was a short silence. Then Kate Weinstock said, 'As you know, I've been talking to Peter Dawson, and although he's a very hysterical child and I should never have left you alone with him, certain aspects of the interview *do* worry me.'

'What do you mean?' Again he felt eleven years old, at the mercy of an adult who lived in an untouchable world of power and punishment.

'I'm not prepared to tell you at the moment. I'll be talking to DI Mason.'

'Why the hell won't you tell me?' he said sharply, but she ignored him.

'I've also had occasion to look through some of your classes' English books and I've been listening to some comments from the boys. I'm afraid I'm not satisfied, Mr Soames. Not satisfied at all. Are you sure you've had sufficient teaching experience?'

'Over twenty years,' he replied. Soames's heart was hammering.

'It's not good enough for us. I'm sorry. I acted too hastily and made the wrong appointment. Despite all the dreadful things that have been happening, despite our falling roll, I have to keep our standards high. I can't let those slip as well, can I?'

'Of course not. But I'm sure my work is satisfactory.'

'Not according to what I've seen and heard.'

'I don't understand –'

'I told you – the boys' English books.'

'You were checking –'

'I have every right.' She was slightly indignant, but only slightly.

'Of course,' said Soames soothingly, desperately trying to work out his next move.

'And, as I said, the boys seem unhappy with your teaching methods.'

'Really? Who told you that?'

'I won't name names.'

'How convenient.' Names again. No one wanted to name names at St Clouds.

'I've a right to withhold them.'

'Have you?'

'The boys don't think they're learning.'

'Could that be because of their attitude?'

'I'm talking about the brighter, more motivated sets.' She sighed.

'You were only congratulating me on my achievements a few hours ago, Miss Weinstock. You told me how much you trusted me.'

Had she sprung her carefully planned trap, or was there more to come? She had lured him into the interview with Dawson and she had allowed him to come up here. Was this the moment when she revealed her hand?

'The boys swarm round you – like bees round a honeypot.'

'What are you saying?' The implication was obvious.

'Am I not making myself clear, Mr Soames? Of course you're wonderfully charismatic with the boys and they clearly like you very much. But liking can mask other problems. I'm afraid there's nothing for it. You'll have to go.'

'After less than three days?' Soames was amazed.

'It's equally my fault. I simply made an error of judgement.'

'You saw my references.'

'They seemed excellent. But the proof of the pudding is in the eating, Mr Soames.'

'After less than three days?' he repeated.

'I'm sorry.' She sounded adamant.

'This is unfair dismissal.'

'I've a right to terminate your contract whenever I wish.'

'I have to have a term's notice.'

'Have you checked your contract?'

'I haven't got one yet. I'm on probation.'

162

'There you are then,' she said, but for the first time she sounded slightly uneasy and Soames wondered if she had acted without consultation. If Weinstock had, then he was in with a chance.

But what was she accusing him of? Assaulting Peter Dawson? *The boys swarm round you – like bees round a honeypot.* But he didn't want to challenge her, however grim her implications were. He needed to stay around and Soames knew that he had to create some kind of compromise deadline. How long did he need? A week? A fortnight? At this stage it was impossible to tell.

'Even as a probationer I'd require a month's notice.'

'Rubbish!' she blustered, but Soames guessed she was still unsure of her ground.

'You'll find I'm right.'

'You're being very stubborn, Mr Soames. I make the decisions around here.'

Soames lost his temper. 'Is there some other reason why you want to get rid of me, Miss Weinstock?' he said furiously, unable to prevent himself from challenging her after all.

'Why should there be?'

'We're not really talking about poor work, are we?'

'What *are* we talking about then?'

'I got too involved, didn't I? And you don't like me taking the initiative.'

'Nonsense!'

'Let me explain. I don't have any attachments. I live in the school and I happen to have been in some right places at the right time and you don't like that, do you?'

'There's no need to be abusive. I'm talking about your work as well as your attitude to Dawson. I don't think you fit in here. I want you to leave. Isn't that enough?'

'I'll go when I'm good and ready.'

'I'll give you a couple of days,' she said. 'And no more.'

The sudden concession surprised him and he pulled back.

'During this brief period, I'd prefer you not to teach. We'll have to cope somehow and, of course, I'll start advertising immediately.'

'That's fine by me.'

'And you're not to talk to the boys.'

'I shall talk to whom I damned well please.'

'I hope you're not going to cause trouble, Mr Soames.' Once again she was imperious.

He wanted to ask her what she was going to say to Mason, but decided not to give her the satisfaction of refusing. 'You've already got trouble. By the time I leave you might not have a school left.'

'I can assure you that St Clouds will continue. There's no doubt about that. I've got great confidence in Inspector Mason and his colleagues.' You didn't before, he thought. 'I'd like you to return to your flat, Mr Soames, as soon as possible. It would be quite wrong for you to remain at Bantry Bay in the circumstances.'

'I'll come back when I'm ready,' snapped Soames. 'Your students need protection.'

'I shall be sending Mr Bundy –'

He took considerable pleasure in cutting her off.

A mixture of rage and foreboding filled Soames. How had all this happened so quickly? Or had Weinstock been manipulating all the time? But why? Was she going to tell Mason he was a member of the ring? The thought made him sweat with anxiety.

Soames rang Mason and listened to his mobile ringing for some time until he answered.

'Mason.'

'It's Soames. Where are you?'

'At St Clouds. Interviewing a member of staff.'

'I need to speak to you urgently.'

'I'll call you back.'

A minute later, Mason was on the line again. 'I'm out in the grounds. Where are you?'

'In a hut at Bantry Bay. I've just had a curious experience. With Miss Weinstock.'

'That sounds uncomfortable. Is she with you?' Mason laughed gratingly.

'She sacked me over the phone. She also implied I had some

kind of indecent encounter with that kid Dawson.' He paused. 'On a more academic level she accuses me of incompetent teaching. Either she's sussed me out, or she thinks I've got too involved, or she really does think I'm a pederast. In any case, I'm sure she set me up.'

'This is going to be a problem,' said Mason.

As he began to ask more questions, Soames was gazing absently at the bunk beds. On the lowest there was a dark mass, half protruding from under a pillow.

'Just a minute.'

Soames hurried across the room and knelt down by the bed. The stuff was thick and wiry, flecked with blood.

'What are you doing?' Mason was getting impatient.

'Just give me a second.' Soames was sure he was gazing down at a hank of hair. 'I've found something,' he told Mason, standing up. 'It's a tuft of dark hair, torn out at the roots. There are flecks of blood. Cass's hair was dark. Which mortuary is he in?'

'Local.'

'Can you get someone to check?'

'Got any plastic?'

'I'll find something. Don't worry. I'm not going to mess up forensic after a stroke of luck like this.' Soames was sweating, and not just at the good fortune of a macabre discovery.

'How long have you got left at the school?'

'A couple of days, and I had to fight for that. I'm not allowed to teach and I'm not meant to talk to the pupils. I shall ignore the latter of course.'

'Get that hair to me ASAP.'

'This is a labyrinth,' said Soames.

'Child abuse *is* a labyrinth,' replied Mason and rang off.

Soames glanced down again at the dark tuft of hair and felt a wave of nausea. Had the perpetrator really been so careless? Or was he looking at another set-up? Or even a cry for help? But from who?

Gingerly, Soames scooped the hair into a plastic wallet that had originally contained his driving licence. He then lingered in the hut, torturing himself with images of what might have happened here. Suppose Rik and Mary had been subjected to this? Suppose they'd been victims too?

As Soames continued to gaze down at the bunk obscene images filled his mind and refused to disperse. Nausea welled up again, and this time Soames knew he was really going to be sick. He ran to the door, threw up on the grass outside and seemed to go on vomiting for a very long time until he was only retching, strands of saliva sliding down his chin, the acid smell on the sea breeze.

Looking up, he saw a red flag fluttering on the cliffs. It was midday and the strong sunlight warmed him. Needing fresh air and space after the squalid confines of the hut and his discovery, Soames began to climb through the long grass until he came to the cliff edge, gazing down at the sea breaking over the rocks below, the spray soaring in a fine haze. He had almost forgotten the soreness in his shoulder which sharply returned as he stood on the narrow path above the waves, still looking down, trying to clear the vile images from his mind that wouldn't go away.

As Soames turned his back on the translucent sea, plunging down through the long grass and heading towards the barracks, his mobile began to ring.

'You're right,' said Mason. 'There was a small tuft wrenched out of Cass's hair. Barely noticeable, but a tuft all the same.'

'I can't understand why anyone should be so careless. Why leave it around? Did they *want* us to find it?'

'That's too far-fetched.'

'Is it? Surely the MPs would have checked out this place?'

'What's a small hank of hair? Cass could have pulled it out himself – or the kids could have been rough-housing.'

'I don't see Cass doing anything like that. Have you spoken to Hinton?'

'He talked about this ring in Southampton. I've also interviewed Cass's mother, which was a horrendously painful job and all I really gathered was that he had a bit of a girlfriend problem. I've also spoken to Lofts again, but he sticks to his original story.'

'Do you think Gaby Darrington has too close a relationship with the boys?'

'I don't know. Maybe Lofts got a thing about her and wouldn't let go.'

'I worry about Lofts.'

'In what way?'

'I get this feeling he's dangerous.'

'We've got nothing on him,' said Mason gloomily. 'What are you going to do now?'

'Talk to Billings.'

'I've got this feeling you're standing on the edge of a cess-pit,' said Mason. 'Somebody might just push you into the shit.'

As Soames walked away from the hut and up the other side of the valley, he wondered yet again about the carelessness of leaving Cass's hair on the bunk – even if it had been half-obscured. The more he thought about it, the more he was sure that it was deliberate. As evidence it didn't amount to a great deal, and yet – could there be someone out there who was on the verge of making a confession? Or maybe trying to extract one?

Soames knew that in terms of most investigations he had been on this case a very short time, but there was a terrible volatility here, as if a slow fuse had been lit a very long time ago.

'Sergeant Billings around?' asked Soames when he reached the guard house by the main gates.

'He'll be in his office, sir. Just over there, at the back of the gym.'

Soames hurried over, anxious to catch him before lunch. When he arrived, Billings was reading a newspaper which he slowly put down. 'How's the shoulder?'

Soames ignored the enquiry. 'I found something in the hut.'

'What?'

He showed him the tuft of black hair in the plastic folder.

'Where did you find that?'

'On the bottom bunk.'

'Is it human hair?'

'Yes. It came from Douglas Cass's head.'

167

Billings looked shattered. 'Christ! How do you know?'

'I called the police on my mobile and DI Mason checked and confirmed that the hair most probably belonged to Cass. Obviously, there'll be a proper check.'

Billings still seemed devastated.

'Cass could have been raped up there,' said Soames.

'Cass slept over there with the other boys. They could have been messing about. You know what adolescents are like. It all starts in fun and ends in tears.'

'After what's happened, this needs to be taken seriously, doesn't it?'

Billings looked at him curiously. 'You've got very involved in all this.'

'Cass was a pupil of mine.'

'How long have you been at St Clouds?'

'Time enough to not like what I see.'

Billings didn't reply.

'The kids are terrified.'

'All of them?' asked Billings.

'Too many to be ignored. And the boys who are so afraid seem inevitably to have been on this course.'

'Colonel Darrington is heading up an enquiry.' His tone was cursory. Then he said slowly, 'So you're close to the boys then?' His gaze was steady, only a little pulse beating in his temple giving away Billings's interest. His very strong interest.

There was a silence during which Soames seemed to hear a whisper in his mind that was soft and sibilant, as if a call had come, a tacit understanding, a signal from the depths of a pit. He felt clammy and a sense of revulsion filled him, not for Billings but for the part he had to play. He heard Creighton saying *Only in an emergency*. Now the emergency had come. Soames felt as if he was touching a soft, white serpent. There was no elation, no sense of breakthrough. Only disgust.

'Yes,' he said.

Billings was watching him intently. 'I don't think I understand.'

'I think you do.' There was an ache inside Soames's head that gradually grew worse and an intense feeling of wanting to

168

commit violence. He wanted to hit Billings, to strike him again and again until he was a bloodied pulp.

There was a long silence.

'London has the action,' Soames forced himself to mutter. 'Swanage is over.'

'I still don't get you.'

'It's a pity that someone spoilt the game.'

Billings rose to his feet and moved towards Soames, his hands hanging loosely by his sides. 'You shitting toe-rag. You some kind of fucking pervert?'

Billings hit out and Soames deflected the blow. He came in again and Soames kicked his legs away so hard that he fell on his back, lying on the floor, looking painfully surprised. But the interest – that all-absorbing interest – burnt away in his eyes.

'I'm going to see you off army property.' But Billings showed no sign of getting to his feet.

'What did Griff and Cass know?'

Soames's shoulder was hurting badly and he was out of breath.

Billings stared up at him. 'Who are you?'

There was another long silence. Then Soames said, 'I've never been able to cope with what I want.'

'I don't understand.'

'Someone's lost it, haven't they?'

Billings didn't reply. Then he said, 'You're talking shit.'

'I don't think so.'

'Why did you apply for a job at St Clouds?'

'I was told the fruit was ripe. But it's gone rotten, hasn't it?' Soames paused. 'No point in pushing my luck here. I've got a meat rack in London.'

Billings was watching him again and Soames could detect his interest. How long can I go on wading through this sewage? he wondered.

'You'll have to prove something.'

'What?' asked Soames.

'You're not wired.'

'Check me out then.'

Billings slowly got up and then gave Soames a body search

169

that made him feel like squirming. Just part of the job, Creighton would have said. Eventually, Billings seemed satisfied.

'Who lost it?' asked Soames.

'Are you afraid he'll come knocking on *your* door?' Billings went across to the phone. 'I'll call the MPs, shall I?'

'Why not?'

He hesitated.

'London lights,' said Soames. 'I was thinking about a youth club in Edmonton. Got any leave coming up?'

'I don't know what the fuck you're on about,' said Billings, sitting down and putting his feet on the desk and picking up the newspaper. 'Why don't you just piss off out of it.'

As he spoke, Repton opened the door, pulling out a pile of papers from his briefcase. 'I've got the kids' adventure training certificates. Do you want to sign them?'

'Sure. Mr Soames is just leaving.'

'Shoulder rough?' asked Repton sympathetically.

'It's a bit sore. I'm going back to school. Mr Bundy will be coming up later.'

'We'll see you then,' said Billings.

'You going home, sir?' asked Shafiq who was hanging around outside the canteen.

'It's my shoulder.'

'Are we going to stay up here alone?' He looked suddenly anxious.

'Mr Bundy's coming. I'll wait until he arrives.'

'He'll stay with us?'

'He may take you home.'

'Some of the other guys will be disappointed,' said Shafiq.

Soames thought of the lock of hair he had in his wallet.

'What are you doing this afternoon?'

'Going for a run.'

'All together?'

'Yes, sir.'

Soames found it impossible to even guess at what Shafiq was thinking.

*   *   *

170

When Bundy arrived, Soames simply told him that he'd found something he had to show the police.

'What is it?' asked Bundy suspiciously.

'I can't tell you now,' snapped Soames, determined to keep him in the dark. Bundy would only complicate an already complicated situation. 'Can you and Hinton pile all the boys into the Youth Club minibus? I need this one.'

'There may not be room,' began Bundy.

'I think there is.' Soames was impatient. 'I've done a head-count.'

'All right.' Bundy suddenly gave in.

As Soames left the base in the minibus, he felt deeply concerned on two counts. He shouldn't be leaving the boys. And who was Billings going to alert? Or would he keep Soames's offer to himself?

He shuddered. The afternoon had slowly become overcast and as he drove down past the esplanade he saw a rising wind had whipped up the grey waves, which were beginning to lash at the promenade itself.

'Yes, sir?' Bernie Lofts stood at Gaby Darrington's front door, his acne a grey rash in the muddy light.

'Another committee meeting?' asked Soames.

Lofts smiled, but his stocky body was rigid, his eyes hardening with dislike.

'I was picking up some posters.' He looked down at his hands as if he should have been holding something and then glanced back to the hall table where the pile lay. His bottom lip had been slightly cut. 'I'll go and get Mrs Darrington.' There was no prevarication this time. 'She's upstairs – in the office.'

'Hang on. I'd like a word.'

'I'm in a bit of a hurry.' Lofts looked uneasy.

'I won't keep you long.'

'What do you want?'

'I've been talking to Sergeant Billings.'

Lofts's expression didn't change. 'Billings?'

'Yes – up at the base. The chap in charge of the adventure training.'

'What about him?'

'Some pupils are scared of what's happening at Bantry Bay, aren't they?'

'The course is quite challenging –' began Lofts.

'I'm not talking about that.'

'What *are* you talking about?'

'Why did you retract those allegations of yours?'

'They were a joke in poor taste. I'm sorry. I had a row with Mrs Darrington and I wanted to punish her. I was very stupid.'

'Why did you want to punish her?'

'I don't have much going at home. Maybe I got a bit – dependent on her.' There was a long pause. Then Lofts suddenly began to speak hurriedly, his words tumbling over each other as if he wanted to get them out before he could stop himself. 'She talked about adopting me.'

Soames was taken aback. The last thing he had expected was Lofts to be as open as this and for a moment he floundered. 'I didn't know –' He stopped and tried to recover himself.

Lofts watched his confusion and Soames wondered if the boy had deliberately wrong-footed him.

'Billings believes there's a ring of pederasts operating in Swanage and some of the St Clouds pupils may have been their victims,' he said baldly.

'Christ, that's such a revolting idea,' said Lofts woodenly.

'I agree,' snapped Soames, determined to provoke him. 'I'm trying to get to the bottom of it all.'

Lofts's lips quivered with sudden, silent laughter. 'That's an unfortunate way of putting it, sir.'

Soames was once again forcibly reminded of the Lower Fourth. Why couldn't he cope with these kids without a sensation of rising panic?

'You don't give a damn about your school mates, do you?'

'I do care. Of course I care.' He was far too repentant.

'You know much more than you're letting on, don't you?'

'No.'

Soames paused. The knife-edge was familiar. 'We've had two murders which are connected to the ring. The Head and Cass knew something. What is it?'

'I don't know. Why are you so interested?'

'I'm simply doing my job as a teacher.'

'None of the other teachers keep asking questions.'

'That's a pity.'

'I'm sorry, I couldn't help Mr Mason either. I can't help any-one. I've got to go.' Lofts was becoming agitated and Soames stepped aside, partly because he could hear footsteps on the landing, partly because he felt he'd discomforted Lofts enough.

'Who's there?' asked Gaby.

'It's me,' said Soames as Bernie Lofts grabbed his posters and pushed his way past him.

'What's going on?' She looked wary.

'Just one of those little chats with Lofts. But this one was a tad more productive.' Soames paused and then made his statement as abrupt as possible. 'He tells me you were going to adopt him.'

Gaby Darrington didn't seem in the least fazed. 'That's an ambition – not a fact. God knows what Edward would say. But it's none of his business now and I didn't make the proposal lightly as I'm sure you'll understand. I don't know if I can officially adopt Bernie, and I've tried to make that clear to him and not raise his hopes.' She paused.

'And there's something else.'

Gaby ran a hand through her hair. 'I don't think I can take much more.'

When they were sitting down, Soames told Gaby about Kate Weinstock's telephone call and his discovery of the tuft of dark hair.

She seemed totally bewildered. Then she said, 'Weinstock has to control everyone and keep her finger on everything. And if she can't, she gets rid of them. This has happened time and time again. As to Peter Dawson, I've no idea what kind of weird game she was playing. Weinstock has to win, you see – and she doesn't mind how.' Gaby paused. 'But I think she's also panicking for the first time. She's overwhelmed and she doesn't know what the hell she's saying. I feel much the same. It's all run out of control.'

'Then there's Sergeant Billings.'

'Surely *he's* not mixed up in all this?' She stared at him helplessly.

Soames didn't reply and Gaby was silent.

'How did you find out?' she asked eventually.

'I approached him as a fellow punter.'

There was another long, tense silence.

'That must have been very difficult for you.' Rather than being shocked, she sounded surprisingly sympathetic.

'It was – but he bit. Unfortunately, nothing he said would stand up in court, and there were no witnesses. I still need a pupil to come forward and that's where we stumble at the brink time and time again. I've just spoken to Lofts and come up against the standard impasse.' Soames shrugged. 'I didn't expect any more than I got.'

'So what are you going to do next?'

'Talk to Shafiq. He's my last hope.'

'You haven't identified yourself –'

'Not yet.'

'How many pupils do you need to speak up and be counted?'

'Obviously the more the better. But if one pupil breaks, the others might do the same.'

'Do you think I've been holding out on you over Bernie?'

'I could see how close you were.'

'And you disapprove?'

'Lofts is very damaged.'

'I feel I can offer him more stability than he has now.'

'But only as a single parent.'

'Does that matter?'

'It would with the authorities. Haven't you thought about that?' How could she be so naïve? wondered Soames. Gaby Darrington was behaving like an adolescent herself, desperately seeking a dependant.

'I've thought about that, and I'm sure I can convince them. I want to help Bernie. I want something worthwhile in my life.'

'You're not getting . . .'

'Obsessed? No. I know what I'm doing. I'm quite level-headed, you know.' She gave him a bright, painful smile.

'Bernie isn't. I'm convinced he's got much more to tell me. Aren't you?'

She nodded. 'Yes. Yes, I am. But if I can't get anything out of him . . .'

'Neither will I,' finished Soames.

'Could Dr Griff or Cass have passed on what they knew to anyone else?'

'If they did, and the ring find out, they're dead.' Soames got up. 'I'd better get on.'

She gave him a tentative look. 'Don't you trust me?'

'I trust you as far as I can. Like everyone else in this investigation,' he said frankly.

'But do you think I'm too close to Bernie – that I'm a screwed-up woman who's lost her husband and fancies a disturbed teenager?'

'I didn't say that,' said Soames defensively.

'But you think it,' she said brusquely. 'I'm not ignoring the fact that Bernie is afraid of someone – desperately afraid.' She paused. 'If I find out who it is, I think I'd kill him with my own bare hands.'

'There's no reason to suppose that we're definitely talking about a man,' Soames warned her. 'Women can be involved too.'

As he spoke, he remembered Hinton saying much the same as Gaby. *I'll kill him with my bare hands.*

Soames lay on his bed, staring up at the discoloured ceiling, waiting for Mason to return his call. When he did, Soames told him about Billings.

When he had finished there was a long silence while he waited for Mason to come to the same conclusion as he had.

'That was a lucky strike,' he said finally. 'All hunch and no evidence.'

'Something like that,' admitted Soames.

'Did you sense something about him?'

'Not exactly. I just thought I'd check him out.'

'And then go through the rest of the regiment?'

'We've *got* to get one of those kids to talk.'

175

'I'm working on it.'

'And Billings definitely thinks you're bent?'

'Single schoolteacher gains employment at boys' school.'

'Does he know you've been sacked?'

'Not yet. I expect someone will tell him soon enough.'

'So at least St Clouds is a no-go area for them.'

'Maybe. But as long as the kids know who's involved – they're all in danger. If we don't move fast, there could be another attack. Have you finished interviewing?'

'Yes.'

'Anything to show for it?'

'If there was I'd have told you.' Mason sounded deeply depressed. 'It's a conspiracy of silence. Can't you lean on Lofts?'

'I've tried again with no luck. But he's afraid. Really afraid of someone, and Gaby Darrington can't get anything out of him either.' Soames paused. 'I need to ask you a question about her.'

'What is it then?'

'Does she convince you about her relationship with Lofts?'

'Adoption and all that? Well, she's some kind of idealist, isn't she? But, yes, she does convince me. You don't believe her though, do you?'

'She just seems to be acting in an incredibly naïve way which isn't in character, and I've been wondering if she's protecting him.'

'Why would she do that?'

'Suppose Lofts isn't a victim? Suppose Lofts is in the ring?'

Mason swore. 'Is that really a possibility? Could he be lining up the kids for the nonces?'

'It's a possibility.'

'How did you arrive at it?'

'Once I knew Billings was involved, Bantry Bay *had* to be the base for the ring. But I wondered how the selection process worked.'

'I thought the kids volunteered.'

'They did. But apparently the course was over-subscribed so there had to be some kind of selection. You might have expected names to be drawn from a hat, but I reckon they were sized up.

176

Lofts and Hinton were involved in drawing up the final list apparently.'

'So Lofts *could* have had a different role to play.'

'Maybe I could scare the shit out of him by confronting him with that.'

'Don't underestimate him.'

'I won't,' said Soames. 'Have you spoken to Colonel Darrington about that tuft of hair?'

'Yes.'

'How did he react?'

'He seemed to want to start another World War.'

16

Soames got off the bed and went to the window. It was just after five and the sun had broken through the clouds, casting a faint, rather watery light on the cloisters.

The phone rang and he trudged back into the sitting-room, needing the drink he knew he shouldn't have.

'It's Billings.'

Soames felt as if he had been caught out in a compromising situation.

'Just to say Mr Bundy's arrived.' His voice seemed to carry a threat.

'Thanks for telling me.'

'We're cutting the course short and he's bringing the kids home.'

'That's OK by me.'

'In the circumstances it seems the best thing to do.' Billings paused. 'And by the way, if you're still considering that London trip we'd be interested.'

'*We?*'

'Yes. Me and my mates. But I'll be acting as liaison officer of course. When can you report back?'

'As soon as I can.'

'See you then.' Billings put down the phone and Soames's

elation returned. Then he felt a stab of pain from his still aching shoulder.

The phone rang again a couple of minutes later.

'Soames.'

'It's Gaby.' Her voice was sharp. 'There's a crowd down at the Badlands.'

'Where the hell is that?'

'It's a nickname for the patch of grass behind the stables, at the boundary of the estate just beyond the playing fields. All the fights and feuds take place in the Badlands.' She sounded anxious.

'Aren't there any other members of staff around?'

'You need to get down there fast. It's a chance you mustn't miss.'

'Who told you what's happening?'

'Lofts. But there isn't time for this, Alan. You need to get down there fast.'

Soames's shoulder hurt badly as he ran across the playing fields and down towards the old stable block. A few pupils were also hurrying in the same direction, not running but walking fast, looking expectant. The wind had got up again and was almost gale force, whining in the eaves of the buildings.

Battling against the wind, Soames ran past Shafiq and then slowed up.

'What's going on?' he yelled.

'Probably a fight, sir.'

'So the ghouls are on their way.'

'We want to break it up, sir,' said Shafiq unctuously.

'You do, do you?'

'Sir?' They were jogging together now, nearing the stables, shouting at each other against the wind.

'What is it?'

'Have you been sacked, sir?'

Soames almost came to a halt, but carried on, inwardly cursing. How did Shafiq know? Who'd told him?

'I'm leaving,' he said abruptly.

'Why, sir? You've only been here for a few –'

178

'I don't fit in.'

'That's not fair. You're great.' Shafiq sounded outraged and Soames felt a glow of sudden, unexpected warmth.

'Nice of you to say so.'

'You're different,' continued Shafiq.

'In what way?'

'You don't toe the line, sir.'

'That sounds dodgy.'

'You know what I mean, sir.'

'Maybe I do. But tell me, how do *you* know about me leaving?'

'It's on the grapevine.'

Had Weinstock herself maliciously leaked the information? Soames wondered. He wouldn't put it past her.

'Is there anything else on the grapevine?'

'What do you mean?' said Shafiq, immediately evasive.

'Like who had trouble at Bantry Bay?'

'We don't talk about that.'

'Why not?'

'We can't.'

'That's not a reason.'

'Cass is the reason, sir.' Shafiq cast him a furtive glance.

'You mean – if you talk, then what happened to Cass might happen to you?'

'Any of us.' Shafiq began to slow down, as if he didn't want to arrive and have to stop talking. Was this the moment? Soames wondered. Was he going to get somewhere with Shafiq at last? 'We're all scared.'

'Tell me what you know.'

'I can't, sir.'

'Why can't you trust me?'

'I don't know why you were sacked,' he said, evasive again.

'I was sacked because I took too much interest in this whole ghastly business.'

'Why did you do that, sir?'

'It's my job. It's the job of everyone on the staff. I just happened to be around when Cass was murdered and I tried to help. Miss Weinstock didn't like that. She prefers to handle things herself.'

179

'When are you leaving?'

'Soon. But I shan't be doing any more teaching.'

Shafiq looked at Soames uncertainly. 'Are you on our side, sir?'

'What's that meant to mean?'

'We get fucked, sir.'

They were standing still now, staring at each other, the raw word shocking both of them.

'Who by?' asked Soames at last, trying to react encouragingly.

'I can't say, sir,' Shafiq whispered.

'How many of you?'

'Just Prits.'

'Are you a Prit?'

'Some people think so, sir.' His voice shook.

'Give me a name.'

'I can't, sir. I just can't.' Shafiq was desperate now. 'They'll get me. Like they got Cass.'

'The same happened to him?'

He nodded.

'What about you?'

Shafiq gulped and then nodded again.

'Don't you want it to stop?'

'Yes.' He was almost in tears.

'Then give me a name.'

'I can't, sir. I'm too scared.'

'I'll protect you.'

'You're leaving. How can you?'

'Because it can be over soon – if you give me a name.'

Shafiq didn't reply.

'Trust me.'

'I want to –'

'Just one.'

'I can't.' The circular conversation made Soames want to shake Shafiq.

'One name.'

'No.'

'You'll be protected.'

'How?'

'The police.'

Shafiq shook his head. 'If my dad finds out – he'll know I'm – unclean.' He brought out the word unwillingly.

'What happened isn't your fault, Shafiq. What happened was forced on you. I want to know who did the forcing. But I need your help.'

Shafiq shook his head.

'Your dad will understand. *I'll* tell your dad.'

Again Shafiq shook his head.

'You've *got* to tell me.'

'No chance.' Shafiq was more in control now, more confident of being negative.

'It's not your fault,' Soames entreated.

'My father won't understand.'

With tears in his eyes, Shafiq broke into a run, heading back to the school buildings. Soames knew he couldn't follow and hurried on towards the Badlands, his sense of failure overwhelming.

The stable block was in considerable disrepair. Most of the tiles had fallen off the roof and the yard in front of the low-slung building was piled high with unwanted debris from the school. Old desks and tables were stacked in untidy piles while parts of an ancient oil-fired heating system were rusting away, stacked up against the wall, together with a couple of wrecked cars and a mound of what looked like dismembered bicycles.

Rain spat from the sullen, wind-torn sky on to a group of boys who were surrounding someone who lay face down on the grass, his school uniform muddied and torn. A low murmur swelled as he came nearer and then Soames could finally make out the words.

'Don't tell. Don't tell. Don't tell.' The phrase seemed both absurdly childish and utterly menacing at the same time.

But when Soames burst through and glanced round at the boys, he could see raw agony in their faces.

'What the hell's going on?' he shouted above the wind.

'It's just a game, sir.' Peter Dawson was there, his owl-like face lit with expectation.

Soames knelt down by the boy on the ground, his hand on his shoulder, turning him over on his back. Hunched in their blazers against the increasing rain, the crowd began to move away. Only Dawson remained, silently looking on.

'Shouldn't you be doing prep?' snarled Soames.

'No, sir. It's Saturday, sir.'

'Just push off, you vicious little bastard. Stop watching other people's suffering.'

'You can't speak to me like that,' said Dawson. 'I'll report you to Miss Weinstock.'

'Do what you like!' Soames yelled at him, enjoying the opportunity to vent his frustration on someone, particularly Dawson. 'But clear off. Now!'

Without any further comment, Peter Dawson began to walk slowly away while the victim closed his eyes against it all.

'Tell me your name.'

'Dan Saxton, sir.'

'Have they hurt you?'

'Not really.' He scrambled to his feet, pushing aside Soames's offer of help.

'What did they mean – don't tell?'

'What do you think?' Saxton was short, with glossy black hair and a dark complexion. 'They're all shit-scared, aren't they?'

'Something like that.' Soames felt another spark of hope.

'I'm going to tell.'

'Tell me now.'

'It's raining.'

'Fuck the rain!'

For a minute Saxton grinned at him and then his expression changed. 'I got shagged by this bloke.'

'What's his name?'

'Repton, sir. Lance Corporal Repton.'

Soames sighed with relief. He could barely believe his luck and would be eternally grateful to Gaby Darrington. He had a name at last.

'When?'

'Couple of weeks ago. On a night exercise up at Bantry Bay.'

The truth, thought Soames, was refreshingly simple.

182

'Are you prepared to testify against him?'

Saxton stared up at him. 'I'll shop the bastard.'

'Tell me what happened. Quickly.' They were both shivering in the torrential rain.

'We were on this night exercise and we had to have a partner for orienteering. There were uneven numbers, so I had Lance Corporal Repton. We got to this hut. Then he had me.'

'I know the place,' said Soames quietly.

'I fought back but he was stronger. Repton got me on the floor and –' Saxton's voice shook. 'He kept twisting my arm until I thought it was going to break. I had to let him do what he wanted. I thought he was going to kill me.'

'Will you repeat that to DI Mason?'

'Yes.'

'The others won't.'

'They're scared. And they want it kept quiet in case people think they're poofters too, sir.'

'Wait a minute.' Soames dragged out his mobile and dialled Mason's number, but he only reached a recorded message telling him, 'The mobile number you are calling is not available. Please try later.' 'Shit!' He tried again, but with no luck. 'Shit!' said Soames again. 'Will you come down to the police station with me now?'

'I'll need some dry clothes.'

'I'll come with you. What about the others?'

'They'll try and beat me up again, but I don't give a sod. They don't hurt as much as Repton.'

'We'll have him arrested. Can you give me any more names?'

'The sergeant. What's his name?'

'Billings?'

'That's it – and Holy Hinton. He's up to his neck in the shit too.'

Soames could hardly believe it. Now he had three names. Could it all be over? He thought of Billings. Now *he* would love to kill the bastard with his own bare hands – and Repton too. But he wasn't so sure about Hinton.

'In what way is Holy Joe involved?' he asked.

'I'm not sure, but I'm certain he's got something to do with it.

Maybe he selects kids.' Saxton seemed to think again. 'I'm not sure though.'

'It doesn't matter,' Soames reassured him. 'You've given me a couple of names. That's enough – for the moment.'

'I've never liked Hinton, but I don't want to drop him –'

'What about Bernie Lofts?'

'He's a wanker.'

'But is he involved?'

'He loves it. Can't get enough of it.'

'You're sure?'

'I've seen him with them.'

'Billings and Repton?'

'And some of the others.'

'OK. Let's go now. Where are your dry clothes?'

'In the Senior Dorm, sir.'

'Make it snappy.'

They began to walk back to the school, with Saxton limping badly.

'Do you need any medical attention?' asked Soames reluctantly. He didn't want any delay. Then he saw one coming.

Noel Bundy was hurrying towards them in the teeming rain, umbrella aloft and wearing a pair of green Wellington boots. He had obviously prepared himself for the fray before setting out.

'I thought you were still up at the camp.' Then Soames remembered Shafiq's reappearance.

'I brought them back early. I just don't like . . .' He was gazing at Saxton. 'What's happened?'

'Dan's coming down to the police station with me.'

'What's he done?' Bundy was bewildered now.

'Nothing. He wants to report an assault.'

'By the boys? I'm sure we can clear up –'

'A sexual assault which took place at Bantry Bay. The pupils were trying to intimidate Saxton. I'm just taking him in to change before we set off.'

'I'll do that,' snapped Bundy with sudden, determined authority.

'I was going to –'

'I'll see he gets into some dry clothes.' Bundy was insistent. 'I'll stick with him all the time and we'll meet you at the front

184

door in fifteen minutes. I'll take my car and we'll all go together. There must be a senior member of staff present.' He paused as the rain continued to lash down, not offering either of them the use of his umbrella. 'I'm glad you're going to speak out, Dan. Maybe this will put paid to the whole filthy business at last.'

'Dan's at personal risk,' said Soames.

'I realise that. But just leave him to me. We'll see you at the front door.'

Huddled now under Noel Bundy's umbrella, Saxton half turned to Soames. 'I'll see you, sir.'

'Soon,' said Soames. 'Be careful.' He turned back to Bundy. 'Look. Let me come with –'

'No chance,' snapped Bundy. 'Go and get some dry clothes on. Like now.'

Soames watched them both breaking into a run through the rain, feeling beaten. There was no way he could have insisted on accompanying Dan Saxton unless he had revealed his identity. He knew he was taking a huge risk.

Soon he, too, was sprinting through the summer torrent as the wind began to die back. We're there, he thought. We've *got* to be.

When he had changed, Soames tried to get hold of Mason again. As he punched in the number, he went to the window over-looking the cloisters, only to see Bernie Lofts leave the Darrington house and run towards the school buildings, clad in a plastic mac. The rain still streamed down relentlessly, dark sheets of water beginning to form on the tarmac between the houses and the school.

Soames watched Lofts run with a rising anxiety that seemed quite out of place. Then, on his fifth try, Mason answered.

'Where the hell have you been?'

'I'm in the car. I had a puncture. Had to change a wheel in all this bloody weather. Has something happened?' He sounded thoroughly fed up.

'We've got what we wanted. A confession.'

'Who from?'

'Boy called Dan Saxton. His peer group tried to stop him, but

185

he won through – with a little help from me. We're taking him down to the nick. Can you get there?'

'I'm on my way.'

'Saxton has named Lance Corporal Repton as his assailant, and alleged Billings is involved too. He even suspects Hinton –'

'Does he know who killed Griff and Cass?'

'He hasn't mentioned that.'

'You taking him to the station yourself?'

'With the Second Master.' Soames looked at his watch. 'I'm due to meet them now, so I'll see you down there.'

'Looks like you've cracked it.' Mason was generous. 'Congratulations.'

'We're not there yet,' said Soames.

As he ran through the rain Soames had a sudden presentiment of disaster. Why had he let Saxton go with Bundy so easily? Why had Lofts been running towards the school building at such speed? As he strode through the corridors, Soames wondered if he had just make a major mistake. Stale food smells from the kitchen and refectory wafted towards him as he reached the entrance hall, glancing at his watch which showed he was two minutes late.

The hall was empty.

Were they waiting for him in the car?

Soames pushed open the front door and checked the drive, but there was no sign of a car and the minibus he had parked in its bay was still there, unlit and silent.

So where were they?

Wave after wave of panic swept Soames.

A young teacher, Ben Cassidy, walked across the hall, carrying a squash racket.

'Have you seen Noel Bundy and Dan Saxton?'

'I've seen Noel.'

'Where?'

Cassidy was startled by Soames's abruptness. 'In the staff room. He was having a coffee.'

'Christ!'

'What's up?'

'He's left Saxton alone. He said he wouldn't do that.' The

186

panic intensified. 'Where's the Senior Dorm?' Soames rapped out.

'Upstairs and to the right. Is there something wrong?'

'There might well be.'

'Not again!'

'Why not?' yelled Soames as he took the stairs two at a time.

Dan Saxton was lying on the floor in the middle of the dormitory. He had been beaten yet again but this time much more savagely. Both his eyes were badly swollen, a tooth had been knocked out and one arm was at an awkward, unnatural angle.

'Christ!' said Soames over and over again. 'Oh Christ!'

As he knelt down beside Saxton for the second time that afternoon he cursed Bundy for the fool that he was. Then he began to wonder if he was so much of a fool after all.

'Dan?'

'What –'

'Who did this?'

'Can't say.' The familiar phrase was agonising.

'I'll get you to Casualty. But you'll still talk to the police, won't you? You'll give DI Mason those names? It's essential you do that.'

'I can't say.'

'Where's Mr Bundy?'

'I don't know.'

'Who *did* this? Just tell me.' But Soames already knew that, once again, he had lost out and this time by his own stupidity. Why had he let himself be persuaded? Why hadn't he stayed with Saxton?

'I can't say.'

'Will you still talk to the police?'

'No.'

'You've *got* to.'

'I can't.'

'Who told you not to?'

'I can't say.'

Shafiq walked casually into the Senior Dorm, hands in pockets and then wrenching them out when he saw what had happened, his eyes almost comically wide and staring. *Popping out of his head*, said a banal voice in Soames's head.

Shafiq gazed down at Dan's damaged face. 'Who did it?'

'Don't you know?'

He shook his head, beads of sweat standing out on his forehead.

'Don't give me that!' spat out Soames in disgust. 'It's the usual story, isn't it? Deceit and more deceit. Go and get Mr Bundy. Now!'

Shafiq began to sob. 'I don't know where he is, sir.'

'He's in the staff room, swilling coffee. Get him now.'

Sobbing even harder, Shafiq ran out of the dormitory while a number of other boys pushed past him, crowding in.

'Get out!' yelled Soames. 'All of you.'

They went.

He leant over Dan Saxton again. 'Anything else hurt?' he asked. 'Your arm's broken, but is anything hurting inside?'

'One of them kicked me in the balls, sir, but it's not hurting so much now.'

'Who was it?'

'I can't say.'

Noel Bundy arrived, looking shocked and blustering badly. 'I was only out of the room for a minute.'

'I gather you went for coffee.'

'I was literally away for –'

'Too long,' finished Soames. 'And now look at the state Saxton's in. He needs an ambulance. Go and ring for one.'

As Bundy stumbled out of the dormitory again, Soames pulled out his mobile and called Mason.

'You'd better come over to the school. Saxton's not going to talk. He's been badly beaten up and there's an ambulance on its way.'

'How the hell did that happen? I thought you were going to stay with him all the time? I'll come right over. I'll need to see Weinstock as well.'

'That sounds good to me,' said Soames. 'And I think you

should see Bundy. He left the kid on his own when I particularly told him to stay around. OK – I know it's my fault too.'

'Do you think Bundy's implicated?'

'I don't know.'

'Is this Saxton kid going to testify?'

'Not at the moment.'

'In the blinking of an eye . . .' said Mason sourly.

'Exactly,' replied Soames bitterly. 'And next you're going to say – so near and yet so far.'

Half an hour later, after Saxton's parents had been alerted and, accompanied by the distraught matron, the boy had been taken to hospital, Ted Mason, Alan Soames and Noel Bundy met in Kate Weinstock's office. No refreshments had been offered and the room was chilly. The downpour outside had stopped and there was a steady, doleful dripping sound from an overflowing gutter.

Weinstock had been calm and composed throughout the interview and Soames had the impression she was making her last stand. 'I've no doubt St Clouds will be able to see this through,' she said after Mason had related the new developments, carefully excluding the events at Bantry Bay.

'Not at the present rate,' said Mason. 'There's been a gross lack of responsibility at senior levels, Miss Weinstock, and I consider management very much at fault.'

'In the circumstances, we've tried to cope as best we could.' She was not in the least self-critical.

'The circumstances, as you put it,' continued Mason, 'have somewhat overtaken you. This boy Dan Saxton was savagely beaten up on school premises.'

'We're looking into that, aren't we, Mr Bundy?'

'I'm trying to, but the students aren't co-operating.'

'What else can I do?' Weinstock asked impatiently.

'If St Clouds *is* to survive, I think the parents will want your resignation.'

'They won't get that.' She looked away, not making eye contact with any of them, and Soames could feel her reeling inside, barely able to cope any longer, almost closing down.

'They might,' said Noel Bundy, looking at Kate Weinstock with an amused contempt that Soames despised. 'It's certainly something that I'd vote for.'

Kate Weinstock turned on him but her venom was weak and played out. 'All you've done, Noel, is to watch from the wings and make yourself coffee at the wrong moment.'

Mason came between them. 'We have a very serious situation and this is no time for mutual dirty linen. Pupils from this school have allegedly been sexually abused at Bantry Bay and that's why I've asked Colonel Darrington to join us. He should be here shortly. Meanwhile, I'd like to summarise what we already know.'

Soames glanced at Kate Weinstock and for the first time felt almost, but not quite, sorry for her. She was hunched up in her chair, gazing down at her coffee cup, beaten.

'Dr Griff must have discovered the identity of a member of the ring – or even members – and for that reason he was murdered. Douglas Cass's killing may have occurred for the same reason. The pupils have not only been intimidated from the outside, but I'm sure they've used peer pressure to silence each other on the inside. I can understand why. It's the natural feeling of anyone who's been raped. They feel guilty, unclean, however much they were compelled, and would go a long way to stop anyone who wants to testify against the ring. Hence the injuries Dan Saxton received. Am I making myself clear?'

'Yes,' said Kate Weinstock with a feeble vigour. 'Now I'd like to make *my* situation clear. I've done everything in my power to reassure these boys, to get them to understand –'

'Absolute crap!' interrupted Noel Bundy. 'You ignored the situation until it was too late.'

'How dare you speak to me like that?' yelled Weinstock, suddenly losing control herself. 'It would be just as easy to terminate *your* contract as Mr Soames's.'

'I don't think so,' said Bundy. 'And you should be thanking Alan. He's taken the most initiative – far more than anyone else in the school. Far more than you.'

'That's because I'm a police officer,' said Soames quietly. 'Working undercover.'

'Seconds out,' muttered Mason.

There was a long blanketing silence. Bundy seemed dazed, Weinstock thrown and Mason inscrutable. Soames knew he should have cleared this with him first, but every instinct told him he had taken the right opportunity. Again.

'There's never a good time –' he said.

'On the contrary,' said Mason, to his surprise. 'I'm sure you've chosen absolutely the right time.'

'What a fool I've been,' said Kate Weinstock. 'I'd been wondering if you were part of this ring.' She seemed relieved.

'I wondered about that. Is that why you set me up?'

'I don't understand –' she began, but Soames knew she did.

'I think you do,' Bundy began.

'Let me handle this,' said Soames. 'Is that why you let me interview Peter Dawson on my own?'

'It was a risk worth taking.'

'With a child?'

Kate Weinstock didn't break eye contact with him. 'I had to take a risk,' she said. 'For the sake of the others.'

'Rubbish!' said Bundy. 'You don't give a damn for the kids – or their welfare. All you care about is your own position.'

'Was it legal to enter my school under false pretences?' asked Kate Weinstock. 'Was it moral to take risks with my pupils?'

'Perfectly legal,' said Mason. 'As to the risks – I'm afraid they had to be taken. Alan Soames – and that's obviously not his real name – was placed here as an undercover officer, liaising with the local CID and reporting to me. There've been two brutal murders. What else do you suggest in terms of intervention, Miss Weinstock?'

'He didn't save Douglas, did he?' she spat out bitterly. 'And he left them alone and unprotected at Bantry Bay.'

There was a knock at the door and Greg Jones, one of the care staff, appeared. 'Colonel Darrington is here – shall I show him in?'

Darrington glanced around him curiously. He was in full uniform and sat down without being invited. His presence brought a new authority into the room as well as a sense of relief. A greater sanity had arrived at last.

191

Mason went over and shook hands with him, but no one else moved. 'Colonel – I believe you've met Alan Soames. But that's not his real name. He's an undercover officer who was placed in the school a few days ago. I'd appreciate total confidence on that.'

'Of course.' Darrington wasn't in the least put out. 'That was a good idea. I wish we'd had the notion ourselves.'

'We're having difficulty turning up any hard evidence,' said Soames. 'The boys are too afraid to testify.'

'I've heard what's been happening.' Darrington betrayed emotion for the first time. 'It's appalling. Do you have any names?'

'Billings and Repton.'

Colonel Darrington started. For a few moments he obviously had difficulty in absorbing the shock, but then he looked determined. 'Can you back that up?'

'It's not going to be easy – without statements from the boys concerned.'

'Our own investigations haven't thrown up anything. Everyone's file has been checked and double-checked.' But Darrington didn't sound defensive, only deeply mortified.

'I should tell you that I spoke to Billings myself this morning and I'm satisfied he's part of the ring.'

'How the hell do you know?' asked Colonel Darrington, momentarily thrown.

'By getting Billings to believe I was of the same persuasion,' said Soames, glancing at Kate Weinstock who hurriedly looked away.

'Undercover work clearly has its bad moments,' said Darrington.

'It certainly has,' agreed Soames.

'Billings's tacit admission won't stand up in court,' said Mason, 'but it's a start.'

'I appreciate that. Is it possible for our people to handle the interrogation?'

'Billings will simply deny that he said anything incriminating.'

'What *did* he say?' asked Darrington.

'He agreed that the ring had been burnt out in Swanage and

192

was interested in another opportunity I suggested. He later confirmed his interest in a telephone call to me.'

'Any tapes?' asked Darrington.

'I'm afraid not.'

'And the murders?'

'That's more difficult,' said Mason. 'We suspect there could be more members of this ring involved.'

'In the army?' Darrington's voice shook slightly.

'Not necessarily,' said Soames.

But Colonel Darrington didn't look relieved.

Kate Weinstock rose to her feet and left the room, reminding Soames of Shafiq. They shared a similar dignity. No one attempted to stop her.

Darrington turned to Noel Bundy. 'The only way forward for St Clouds is to get itself a new management team.' He paused. 'Maybe the same applies to the Royal Rangers. I'm considering resigning my own commission.'

No one knew what to reply.

'How are the boys in the town affected?' asked Soames.

'I don't know,' said Mason. 'I've got this gut feeling that it was the St Clouds pupils who were targeted. Living away from their families makes them much more vulnerable.'

'Can I ask you some questions, Colonel?' asked Soames.

'Go ahead.'

'Did you know your wife is considering adopting Bernie Lofts?'

Darrington hardly reacted. 'I wouldn't be surprised.'

'Why?'

The tension sharpened and Bundy looked increasingly uncomfortable, as if he wanted to leave the room like Kate Weinstock but hadn't got the guts.

'Gaby's a very lonely woman.' Darrington paused. 'Lofts was one of the reasons for the break-up of our marriage, but I must stress he wasn't the only reason. We'd been growing apart for a long time, and as my responsibilities at the base increased so the cracks became wider. She's always had her own – vulnerability, and, of course, we weren't able to have children. Here at St Clouds there are dozens of children from broken homes, all of them needing reassurance, comfort and love, and there was

193

Gaby, in much the same position. She has a great deal of love to give, and when I didn't reciprocate – or started *not* to reciprocate – Lofts was an obvious candidate.'

'Thank you for being so frank,' said Soames. He was impressed.

'This isn't the time for holding anything back,' said Darrington. He paused. 'I was passionate – am still passionate – about what we're trying to achieve at Bantry Bay, but this filthy business could have put paid to all that.'

'Do you *have* to resign?' asked Mason.

'I don't see any other choice. If you're right about Billings and Repton, I harboured them, and, as you say, there may well be others.'

'Just to return to Lofts for a minute,' said Soames. 'How well do you know him yourself?'

'When Gaby and I were together he was always round the house. Frankly I tried to avoid him.'

'Did he dislike you?'

'I would imagine so.'

'What was your own opinion of him?'

'There's something very manipulative about Lofts and a lot more besides. I felt he'd got his feet well under the table as far as Gaby was concerned.' Darrington spoke without expression, as if he was giving objective evidence to a tribunal.

'Were you worried about their relationship?'

'I was becoming concerned.'

'Do you think Lofts saw Mrs Darrington in a sexual light?'

'Possibly.'

'Did you warn her?'

'Countless times.'

'And?'

'She was very angry and resentful. In the end I gave up – and of course I'm under such pressure at Bantry Bay it doesn't leave much time for unresolved domestic problems, however volatile. But I was wrong.'

'Have you ever considered Lofts might have a link with the ring?'

Darrington looked startled. 'No. It never occurred to me. Has he?'

'We're not sure.'

'In what capacity?'

'He could have been involved in a selection process.'

'Christ! Who with?' Darrington was considerably alarmed.

'It would be easy to say Billings and Repton, but there's no evidence.'

Mason intervened. 'We've been wondering about Hinton.'

'The youth club chap? How far does this fucking ring stretch?' said Darrington angrily.

'A long way,' said Mason, glancing at Soames. 'Did you know your wife phoned the police and alleged that Lofts had been sexually assaulted at Bantry Bay?'

Darrington didn't answer immediately. When he did, he seemed to have lost confidence. 'No. I certainly didn't.'

'Lofts later denied everything and we reckon he was either being leant on, or was being manipulative.'

'It could have been either.'

'Exactly,' said Mason, and then continued. 'So we decided to put in an undercover officer.'

Darrington didn't reply.

'But we're still at an impasse,' said Soames. 'At first I couldn't get any of the boys to come forward, and then Saxton agreed. Now he's been silenced.'

'Could one of the *boys* have killed the Head?' asked Darrington quietly. 'Or Cass?'

'It's possible.'

The room seemed to have become smaller.

'What would the motive have been?'

'For what they knew,' said Soames.

'The ring could be run like a series of terrorist cells, deliberately limiting knowledge of identity. But what about this youth club chap?' asked Darrington.

'Have the MPs got to him?'

'Their powers don't stretch outside the base. But there should have been more liaison between the MPs and the police.' Darrington turned to Mason. 'I didn't enforce that enough and, for obvious reasons, I was wrong. The army is a sealed world of its own and doesn't always recognise the problem, so that's my

195

resignation issue. But I'm not going until we've nailed these shits. Is there anything else you want to ask me?'

'I'd like to ask some more questions about your wife,' said Soames.

'Fire away.'

'She's been liaising with me since I arrived, fully aware of my identity.'

Colonel Darrington gave a faint smile. 'The old girl *has* got herself into deep waters.'

'She's been helpful,' said Soames cautiously, 'but I'm sure her relationship with Lofts has clouded her judgement.'

'I'm not surprised.'

'To what extent do you think he manipulates her?'

'Even at her most vulnerable, Gaby's no fool. If she thought Lofts had a link to the ring I'm sure she would have come to you – just as she called the CID about his alleged assault.'

'Do you think they've had sex?'

Darrington looked more puzzled than shocked. 'That would put a very different complexion on things.'

'Do you think it's possible?' persisted Soames.

'Unless the wretched Lofts forced himself on her, it would have been quite *im*possible.'

Soames stared at him in amazement. 'What makes you think that?'

'I don't think. I know,' said Darrington drily. 'She didn't have any interest in the subject. That's a rather more basic reason why we drifted apart and I'd hoped not to have to mention it.'

Before anyone could speak, Noel Bundy asked, 'Am I needed any more?' He seemed deeply embarrassed and uneasy.

Mason glanced at Soames who said, 'Perhaps you should go and comfort Kate Weinstock. If you feel you can fulfil that role.'

'I'm not sure I can.'

'Do you want to take over the school, Mr Bundy?' asked Mason suddenly. 'If the governors appointed you?'

'I'd be very interested in doing that.'

'One last question, Mr Bundy,' said Mason. 'Why did you leave Saxton alone? When you were particularly asked not to do so?'

'If you're implying I was in collusion with the pupils – that I *wanted* Saxton to be attacked – the answer is no. But I wasn't swilling coffee for long.'

'So what were you doing?' asked Mason.

Bundy was silent.

Mason looked at him impatiently. 'What were you doing?' he repeated.

'I was waylaid by Lofts,' Bundy replied reluctantly.

'For God's sake, why didn't you tell us that before?'

'Because I'd hoped to avoid telling you,' Bundy muttered. 'It's very personal – like Colonel Darrington's admission about his wife. But since you press me I have to say he was threatening me.'

'In what way?' asked Soames. He hadn't anticipated any more revelations.

'He'd discovered I was sleeping with a female member of staff. One of the assistant matrons. Do I have to reveal her name?'

'Not at the moment, but you may have to later,' said Mason.

'I'd prefer to protect her if possible.'

'When you say threatening – what exactly do you mean by that?' asked Soames.

'Lofts has been trying to extort money from me.'

'Have you given him any?'

'Not so far.'

'Were you going to?'

'I don't know.' Bundy turned to Mason. 'OK, I've been a fool –'

'Like a lot of other people round here.'

When Bundy had gone, Edward Darrington glanced at Soames and Mason. 'That could be useful. Something to grind Lofts with. What a nasty piece of work he's turned out to be.' He paused. 'But I'd hate to say I told you so to Gaby. Is there any other way I can help you?'

'We've some way to go yet,' said Mason. 'We need witnesses – and until we can get those we're stymied.'

'So what's the next step?' asked Soames.

'I think you should speak to Lofts again and then Hinton.'

They all got up, an oddly assorted trio. Kate Weinstock's abrupt departure had left each one of them feeling as if the balance of power had been irrevocably disturbed.

'You've done a good job in a short space of time. I'm very grateful to you.' Darrington shook Soames's hand.

'We need to get a result.'

'We'll work together, and I'll keep you informed personally. I'm sorry that hasn't happened before.'

'I still don't see why you have to resign, sir,' Mason said hesitantly.

'The army will need a scapegoat.' Darrington walked to the door briskly. 'And besides, the responsibility is mine.' He paused and then looked back. 'I'd like to thank both of you for doing my job for me.' Colonel Darrington gave them both a faint smile.

'He's got a point,' said Mason.

'He's a brave man,' replied Soames.

Mason abruptly changed the subject. 'I'm going to put Gaby Darrington under surveillance. We need to try and find out what the hell's going on between her and Lofts. Any ideas about a vantage point?'

'There's a couple of classrooms above the cloisters that aren't in use,' replied Soames.

'Maybe the decorators need to move in,' suggested Mason.

'I'll make some arrangements with Bundy. I'm sure he can be counted on to be discreet, like the oily bastard he's turned out to be.'

'Now *you've* come out,' asked Mason, 'are you going to come clean with everyone?'

'I'm going to start with Lofts,' said Soames.

After liaising with the acquiescent Noel Bundy, Soames waited in the interview room for Bernie Lofts to arrive, remembering his interview with Peter Dawson earlier that morning – a disquieting event that now seemed light years away.

Soames's mood was one of intense anxiety and his shoulder

was aching badly. Despite the fact that he had suspects in his sights at last, they still seemed insubstantial. Closing his eyes for a moment, leaning back on the hard chair, trying to ease the pain, Soames waited.

'Excuse me, sir.'

'Eh?'

'Excuse me . . .'

Soames opened his eyes to see the pock-marked angel who hadn't bothered to knock.

'You in pain, sir? Was it the assault course, sir?' Again the mocking grin.

'Probably. I slipped while I was on the wall and dislocated my shoulder. Sergeant Billings had to snap it back into place.'

Lofts winced.

'Puts your teeth on edge, does it?'

'Something like that, sir.' Lofts was calm, laid back, but had lost his sanctimonious aura and his acne had erupted badly.

'I need you to be completely honest with me,' said Soames. 'If you're not, you could face charges.'

'What charges?' Lofts asked too casually.

'Obstructing the police in the course of an investigation.'

'Is that really a charge?' he sneered.

'You bet it is – and there could be more. For instance, how about threatening behaviour and attempted blackmail?' Lofts, for once, looked disconcerted and Soames felt a pleasurable rush of triumph. 'Noel Bundy?' he prompted.

'I don't understand.'

'I think you do. He's already spoken to me.'

'It was a wind-up.'

'Like the alleged assault at Bantry Bay?'

Lofts was silent.

'You can't go on like this, you know.'

'Go on like what?'

'Lying and manipulating.'

Again Lofts was silent, but there was a stubbornness to him that was childish.

'So how about coming clean?'

'About what?'

'Bantry Bay.'

'I told you – I was winding her up. Nothing happened.'

'Why *were* you winding her up?'

'She'd annoyed me.'

'How?'

'I told you – she said she was going to adopt me.'

'And?'

'She decided against the idea.'

'Why?' This was new.

'I suspect her husband put the boot in.'

'I thought they were separated?'

'He still tells her what to do.'

Although Lofts avoided eye contact, Soames was gradually becoming convinced that he might just be telling the truth.

'Are things bad at home? *Your* home?' he asked more sympathetically.

'Yes.'

'In what way?'

'I'm not wanted and never have been.' His tone was flat, cold, rigidly factual.

'Why aren't you wanted?'

'I'm not like my mother and she doesn't like me. She doesn't like what I am.'

'What are you?'

'My own person,' Lofts said quietly.

'You wanted the Darringtons to adopt you?' Soames asked, deliberately getting it wrong.

'I wanted Gaby to adopt me.'

'You don't think you're too old?'

'I'm not too old to want a real mother.'

'Is that how you see her?'

'She's been good to me.' Lofts's eyes suddenly filled with tears.

'But you felt she was rejecting you?'

'She's being forced to. Her husband's a bastard.' The statement was curiously matter-of-fact.

'Just because he doesn't agree to the adoption?'

'He left her high and dry.' The cliché made him sound less convincing.

'Do you know the reason for the break-up of their marriage?'

'He's only interested in his career.'

Soames tried another tack. 'We've got reason to believe –'

'Wait a minute.' Lofts looked as if he'd had some kind of revelation. 'You're not a teacher, are you?'

'No. I'm a police officer.'

Lofts stared at him blankly, the tears drying on his cheeks. He looked as if he was trying to focus on a new concept but failing to grasp the idea.

'I knew all the time,' he said at last.

'I don't think so.' Soames laughed at him and Lofts blushed.

'Why were you posing as a teacher?' Lofts sounded pompously disapproving. 'Are you going to admit that to the whole school?'

Soames smiled. 'I'm sure you'll do that for me. Anyway, as I was saying, we've reason to believe that a ring of pederasts is operating in the Swanage area and that the murders of Dr Griff and Douglas Cass have some connection with that operation.'

'What connection?'

'They probably knew the identities of key members of the ring. So did Dan Saxton, who was badly beaten tonight. He's in hospital.'

Lofts nodded.

'Do you know who beat him?'

'No.'

'Was it you?'

'Of course it wasn't.' He stared at Soames, but his eyes were blank, giving nothing away.

'Have you had any connection with this ring?'

'No.'

'Have you ever selected boys for them?'

'Don't talk shit!'

'Were you sexually assaulted at Bantry Bay?'

'How many times do I have to deny that?'

'Maybe many more times.'

'For Christ's sake –' But far from losing control, Lofts had grabbed it back.

Soames pushed harder. 'If you *are* withholding information – if you are later found to be involved – you do realise you'll face a long term of imprisonment?'

'I'm not a child.'

'Why don't you tell me the truth?'

'I have. I didn't touch Saxton or collude with him being beaten up. I didn't arrange it. I'm not a fixer for any ring. I wasn't assaulted.'

'And you sleep with Mrs Darrington?'

Lofts was obviously taken aback. 'We don't have that kind of relationship.'

'Do you know Billings and Repton?'

'They're the instructors on the adventure training course.'

'Did you know of the existence of the paedophile ring?'

'Not until you mentioned it.'

'What's your sexual choice?'

'I'm not gay.'

'You don't fancy little boys?'

'No way.'

'You don't fancy Mrs Darrington?'

'No.'

'How do you see her?'

'As a friend.' He paused. 'A motherly friend. Someone to see me through.'

'What would you do if you knew she was in trouble?'

'Try and help her.'

'How well do you know Ray Hinton?'

'I loathe the bastard.'

'Why?'

'Because he's a Holy Joe and a fucking hypocrite.'

'Why?'

'He tried to touch me up.'

Soames made no comment, and for a few moments he and Lofts held eye contact. Soames saw – or thought he saw – pain in the soft blue of the boy's eyes.

'When was this?' he asked eventually.

'At the club. I don't go there any more.'

'Where in the club?'

'There's a storeroom that leads out of his office.'

202

'You were alone?'

'Of course. What do you think? I was being watched by an audience of salivating fourth formers?'

'Why didn't you report the incident?'

'I was ashamed.'

'Because you liked being touched?' Soames risked trying to provoke him.

'Because I loathed being touched.' For the first time there was cold anger in Lofts's voice. 'Because I was ashamed of being touched. Isn't that enough? That's what all the other kids felt. That's why they kept quiet. Once you've been touched like that you feel invaded in the most filthy way.' As he spoke, Lofts became increasingly convincing. 'I remember when it happened the first time.'

'With Hinton?'

'No. When I was really young. Maybe about seven or eight. Do you want me to tell you?'

'Yes,' said Soames, sure that for a while at least the game was over and some kind of truce had been called.

'My dad had given me a model glider for Christmas and I couldn't wait to try it out. It was Boxing Day and there'd been this fine powdering of snow, but you could hardly call it a white Christmas. I wanted to be on my own with my glider. I didn't want to share it with anyone and I was afraid other kids I knew would be out on the rec. Luckily it was a really cold morning – bitter, with a knife-edge wind. I can still remember how the cobwebs in the bushes were like – sort of glazed with ice.'

Lofts spoke softly but clearly, and Soames could almost feel the bitter cold of that morning.

'We'd been to church on Christmas morning – just the three of us – and there was this church warden, Mr Dacre, who always made a fuss of my mother. She'd had a streaming cold and Dacre sat us all by the radiator.' He paused. They were no longer making eye contact and Lofts was staring at the darkened wall as if it was a window of memory. 'Anyway, I began to fly my glider, but that cold wind kept knocking it out of the sky and I was getting really fed up. Then I saw this man standing watching me, just in front of a line of silver birches. He was wearing a black coat and a balaclava. I could see his breath, little puffs of steam on the freezing air, and he had his hands in his pockets. He started slowly walking towards me, and at first I was really scared. Then I saw the man was Mr Dacre and I stopped being scared. He was an adult, wasn't he? Someone I knew. He could be trusted.' Lofts sounded deeply bitter. 'Maybe he could sort out the glider. Anyway, he came over and he had the knack and the glider flew well and after a while he asked if I was cold and I remember my teeth were really chattering. Mr Dacre said he had a flask of cocoa over by the bench and I looked in that direction and I saw a bench but no flask. There was no one around. Just us. So I went over to the bench with Mr Dacre and we both sat down and then he said what a silly old fool he'd become. He'd left the flask in the car, so rather than go back to the car-park now why didn't we just cuddle up a bit and he put his hand on my knee and the filthy thing travelled up my leg, right to my balls and he began stroking them and I felt as dirty as he was being, as if I'd asked him to touch me like that, as if it was my fault.' Lofts's words, which had been tumbling over each other, suddenly came to a gasping halt. 'He violated me. Do you see?'

'Yes,' said Soames. 'I do see.'

'He made me dirty.'

'Yes.'

'Then he went away, and when I saw him again at church the next Sunday he smiled at me. The smile was like – like he licked me. Can I go now?'

'For the moment.'

They both got up abruptly, as if there was nothing left to say.

'Did Dacre ever touch you again?'

'I took care he didn't.'

'By never being alone with him again?'

'Something like that.'

'Tell me what really happened. Not with Dacre, but up at Bantry Bay.'

'Nothing happened.'

They were back to the familiar impasse.

'Think about it.'

Lofts opened the door. 'I should have someone to protect me against people like you,' he said with considerable venom.

'You don't need protection from me,' said Soames quietly. 'Only other people – and maybe yourself.'

When Lofts had left him, Soames called Ballard Youth Club on his mobile and, to his surprise, found Hinton still there.

'You're working late.'

'I've been getting up to date with my paperwork.'

'I need to see you.'

'When?'

'Now?'

'It's very late.'

'I need to talk to you right away.'

'I'll be here,' Hinton sounded compliant. 'I'll be waiting for you.'

'I'm going down to see Hinton,' said Soames when he had run Mason to earth in the refectory, talking to Noel Bundy. 'He's still in his office. I'll take my car.'

'I'll come with you,' volunteered Mason.

'I'd rather you didn't,' said Soames. 'Do you mind waiting here? I may need to call you.'

Mason walked down to the front door with him. 'Anything on Lofts?'

'He told me how he was first abused. When he was talking he seemed to be a different person. His real person. But I got this feeling – this really bleak feeling – that he'd been infected and he was passing the infection on.'

'Deliberately?'

'No. He's just a carrier.'

'What about Bundy?'

'Lofts enjoys winding people up. It's a habit.'

'Even with Mrs Darrington?'

'He's genuine about her. That's one thing I can be sure about. They both need each other.'

'And sex doesn't rear its ugly head?'

'You know, Ted, I don't believe it does.'

'Why did he make all these admissions?'

'Lofts told me he'd been – abused by Hinton.'

'Everybody's doing it,' said Mason.

'Not quite,' replied Soames. 'But enough to be frightening. Forget I used the word infection. It's more like a virus.'

'Do you think he's beginning to crack?'

'I don't think so.'

'Just manipulating, as usual?'

'Not even that.'

'What then?'

'He was just telling me how it all started for him. Nothing directly to do with this ring.'

'Is there a controller?' asked Mason. '*That's* what we need to know. After all, Weinstock controlled St Clouds. Who controls the ring?' Soames didn't reply, and Mason continued, 'How are you going to handle Hinton? Come heavy?'

'I'll play him by ear.'

'We're getting there,' said Mason hopefully. 'Take comfort from that.'

'But we have to make things stick. What about Saxton?'

'The hospital say he's comfortable, and Weinstock has gone down to see him.'

'Is that advisable?'

'I couldn't think of a good reason to stop her.'

'What kind of shape is she in?'

'Distraught.'

'By the crisis – or the threat of losing that control?'

'For her the two are interlinked, aren't they? Anyway, while I'm waiting to hear from you I'll try and talk to some of the boys. Sitting around isn't in my scheme of things. And I'm going to leave a couple of officers on duty here tonight. Do you think we could have another strike?'

'Only a massacre would stop the rot now,' said Soames.

17

The night was still dripping with rain when Soames drove down to the youth club and parked his car in a side road. Walking across the wet streets, in his mind he heard Lofts talking about Mr Dacre again and again.

Soames knocked on the door, and finding it locked knocked again more loudly.

Hinton opened up at last and as Soames stepped inside he smelt the whisky on his breath.

'I'm sorry to barge in on you at this late hour.'

'I'm pleased to have the company.'

Hamlet's absence was immediately noticeable.

'Where's the parrot?'

Hinton laughed mirthlessly.

'Have you strangled him?'

'Hamlet's become a little hard to bear in the present circumstances. I put him in the meeting room. Can't you hear?'

Soames could. 'Who's a pretty boy then?' reached them only distantly, slightly muffled.

'Do you want a drink?' Hinton pulled out a bottle of whisky from the desk drawer. 'I know what you're thinking.'

'Do you?' asked Soames.

'Doesn't suit the image, does it?'

'Not really.'

'The Holy Joe image.'

'Was that assumed?' asked Soames.

'No, but it's hard to maintain.'

'Why?'

'So much has run out of control.'

Again that word control. But who was controlling who? And how many?

'I feel the same way. Weinstock's sacked me.'

'Why?' Hinton asked rather perfunctorily.

'Getting over-involved.'

'Is there a reason?'

'Isn't that one good enough?'

'No,' said Hinton patiently. 'I mean – why *did* you get so involved?'

'Because I'm an undercover police officer. It's my job.'

Hinton stared at him, clearly discomfited. But there was something else. Was it relief? 'Do you want that drink now?'

'No, thanks.'

'Mind if I do?'

'You've had a skinful already.'

'I need a skinful and I've told you why.' Hinton paused. 'So you're an undercover officer? Does Weinstock know?'

'I thought it was time to stand up and be counted and now I've got a question to ask you. Lofts claims you assaulted him.'

Hinton shrugged. 'He's making a habit of these accusations. Hasn't he accused you yet? If Lofts is to be believed, the world is entirely made up of predatory pederasts. His world, anyway. The guy's off his trolley and always has been.'

'You didn't touch him?'

'Not in a million years.'

'What is your sexual choice, Mr Hinton?'

He grinned at Soames. 'Since it's confession time, I'll have to say I'm gay. Surprise, surprise! Now all we need is Miss Weinstock to admit she's a dyke.'

'Do you have a sexual interest in young boys?' asked Soames, confused by Hinton's nonchalance.

'Isn't that typical? Step out of the closet and you're immediately a paedophile.'

'So why should Lofts make these accusations?'

'I told you. Because he's a sick fantasy merchant. He needs help.'

'That's not really a good enough answer, is it?'

'OK. I take your point. Now listen to mine. I should have gone to Weinstock before, but I wanted gainful employment with the youth wing.'

'What would you have said to her?'

'That Lofts was harassing me.'

'In what way?'

'He's been trying to blackmail me.'

Soames laughed uncertainly. The whole thing was circular. He was always back where he started. 'You too?'

'Who else is there?' Hinton seemed surprised.

'A member of staff at school.'

'Now can you see how sick this kid is?'

'What was he blackmailing you for?'

'He has a video.'

'What of?'

'A survival night at Bantry Bay.'

'What's on it?'

'Cass going into a hut with Billings. Very compromising.'

'The hut in the valley?'

'You've been there?'

'Of course.' Maybe the labyrinth wasn't impenetrable after all, thought Soames, suddenly more hopeful. But if this *was* confession time, was his confession to be trusted? 'So why is he trying to blackmail you?'

'Because I was standing outside the hut.'

'And then?'

'I went inside.'

'Why?'

'To check on the group who should have been in the hut already.'

'And were they?'

'No. Repton had kept them back.'

'Why?'

'He was told there was a change of plan and they were to build bivouacs in another part of the valley.'

'Why weren't you told?'

'At the time it was passed off as a communications failure.'

'So you were alone in the hut with Cass and Billings?'

'Momentarily.'

'Who videoed you going into this hut?'

'Lofts.'

'How long were you in there?'

'A couple of minutes. I realised there'd been a mistake and so I went back up the valley.'

'Did Billings explain why Cass was with him?'

209

'He said they were looking for some empty water bottles. He wanted Cass to help carry them back to the bivouacs.'

'Did *you* help with the bottles?'

'No. I couldn't see any.'

'And so you left the hut first?'

'Yes – I went back to the bivouac site.'

'So Lofts had taken an opportunity to stitch you up.'

'Why not? Surely he's the world's greatest opportunist?'

Soames looked at him curiously. 'How do you square your private life with your Christian commitment? I mean – you're an evangelist, aren't you?'

'For the last twelve years I've been a member of the Covenant Church – a born again Christian.'

'And before that?' asked Soames.

'I was a rent boy.'

Soames felt the shockwaves course through him. Why was Hinton telling him all this? Was he simply trying to provide a scenario? An 'honest-to-God I'll tell all and not be ashamed' defence?

'I was a teenage rent boy,' repeated Hinton. 'You're going to get my tabloid confessions, Mr Undercover Man.' He seemed very assured, almost amused.

'Are they so tabloid?' asked Soames.

'Beyond the *News of the World*, let me assure you of that. I was a foxy little bastard.'

'Why are you telling me all this?'

'Because of Lofts's blackmail. I realise what a dangerous situation I'm putting myself in. But then I'm in a dangerous situation already and always have been.'

'How did your religious conversion come about?' asked Soames, changing tack, wanting to see how consistent his story might be.

'In the end I got sick to death of the life and, of course, I was terrified of contracting AIDS. I had the classic rent boy upbringing of course – community home and then the streets – and then the storybook break. Quite a collection of clichés, isn't it? I met a minister – and not in the line of duty.' Hinton poured himself some more whisky.

'Who was he?'

'His name was Tim Drayton, a minister of the Covenant Church. I told him what I'd done and that I truly repented. It may seem over-simplistic but I did want to repent, and it really happened. I'm a born again Christian now, with a strong desire to put the world to rights.' He drank some of the whisky. 'Or do you still see me as an ex-rent boy, up to salacious sordid sodomy at the youth club?'

Dimly they heard Hamlet squawking. 'Who's a pretty boy then?'

'Hamlet's persistency is an ironic everyday touch, isn't it?' said Hinton.

'And the whisky?' asked Soames.

'I'm afraid.'

'Who of?'

'Lofts has really got it in for me. Like he's had it in for other people too.'

'What are you talking about?'

'I think he killed Griff – and maybe Cass as well.'

Soames despaired. The lies wrapped sinuously around the truth, as the ring wrapped itself around the boys. But the ring was dying and as a result there were accusations, counter-accusations and accusations again. The destructive game was bitterly fought, opaque and many-faceted. Predictably, it was defeating Soames yet again.

'You think or you know?' he asked carefully.

'I overheard Lofts talking to Cass. He was furious about a video having been "left around in a locker" for Griff to find. Cass was upset. Very upset.'

'When was this?'

'The night Griff was murdered.'

'When he said "left around in a locker", did he mean at the school?'

'There aren't any lockers down here.'

'And that video would have been incriminating for Lofts?'

'Incriminating for someone.'

'Why should *Cass* have this video?'

'I wish I knew.'

'I want you to co-operate with me.' Slowly an idea was begin-ning to form in Soames's mind – an idea that would rival even

Bernie Lofts's manipulative machinations. 'Are you afraid of Lofts coming here?'

'He's already on his way,' said Hinton.

'Why?' Once again Soames felt he was lagging behind.

'I want it over.'

'What were you going to do?'

'Get the truth out of him.'

'How?'

Hinton shrugged hopelessly. 'The whisky's dulled my genius,' he admitted wryly.

'Let's try mine,' said Soames. 'What time is he coming?'

'I said I'd see him here at ten.'

'I'll keep out of sight and you do your best to make him incriminate himself. If he thinks you're alone we're in with a chance. Do you think you can handle that?' Soames gazed at Hinton thoughtfully. He had a gut feeling there was something wrong with all this, but there was no time to find out.

'I'll try.' Hinton was very agitated now. 'Go into the meeting room and leave the door ajar. You should be able to hear every golden word. And switch off your mobile,' he added.

Soames laughed. 'That *would* be the classic clanger.'

As if on cue, his mobile began to ring.

'It's Lofts,' said Mason. 'He's just left the school on his bike.'

'I'm expecting him. You got your surveillance team together quickly, didn't you?'

'For the moment *I'm* the surveillance team, and I haven't been wasting my time either. From this classroom I've had a pretty good view of Mrs Darrington's house. No one has come and no one has gone. Still – it gives me something to do, doesn't it? Hinton come up with anything?'

'Quite a lot. But I can't tell you now. We're waiting for Lofts.'

'Do you want back-up?'

'Not at the moment, but you'd better stand by.'

'Are we about to get a result?'

'We might be. I'll call you back.' Soames put away his mobile and gazed at Hinton who had poured out more whisky. Then he

212

put the bottle back in the drawer. 'Lofts is on his way. Are you sure you can handle him?'

'Absolutely certain.'

'So why did you need the whisky?'

'Because I'm a coward.'

'Lofts is a schoolboy.'

'Lofts is a demon,' replied Hinton thoughtfully.

Soames stood in the darkened meeting room, which smelt of sweat and cleaning fluid, leaning against a filing cabinet just behind the office door that was open a fraction.

Hinton's revelations had made him disorientated, but Soames had the feeling that his exploited past was the strength that was driving him on, and not his squeaky clean religion. Maybe facing up to Lofts would be his final redemption.

Then Soames heard the familiar voice and his stomach tightened, a stab of pain searing his shoulder.

'What did you want at this time of night?' asked Lofts. 'I had the hell of a job getting out of school.'

'I wanted to warn you,' said Hinton. 'This can't go on, you know. You need help.'

'Why don't you sod off! Is that all you –'

'I think you've overreached yourself, Bernie. You can't blackmail Bundy *and* me. It's too much for one greedy little schoolboy, surely?' Hinton sounded more nervous than threatening.

'What are you on about?' For the first time Lofts seemed slightly uncertain.

'All you have is a video that's purely circumstantial evidence.'

'If it's so circumstantial, why didn't you want me to show it to Weinstock?'

'What about that much more salacious video – the one especially made for the perverted pleasures of the ring?' said Hinton. 'I'm sure it's chock-full of familiar faces.'

Soames strained to hear as the voices seemed to get softer.

'You should know,' Lofts sneered.

213

'That's why you need help,' Hinton persisted.

'We're both in the shit, Ray. You're going down. Just like the others.'

'You were very careless with the ring's video, weren't you, Bernie? You let Cass steal it from your room and that was so fundamentally stupid that you're lucky to be alive. So Cass took the video to Griff and when you found that out you went straight over to the house and killed him, didn't you? You even got his blood all over that fucking parrot.'

'What the hell are you on about?' Lofts was still scoffing.

'And then your second big mistake was to imagine you could keep Cass quiet. Was that because you fancied him so much?'

'It's your word against mine,' said Lofts confidently. 'I didn't kill Griff. I *had* to kill Cass –'

'Enter the fairy godmother,' said Hinton as Soames stepped back into the office, looking as uncertain as the others felt. It was a strange confrontation, with Lofts incredulous and Hinton apprehensive.

'I'm afraid I can't grant you three wishes,' said Soames. 'But I can see into your future.'

Lofts was standing by Hinton's desk. He suddenly looked like a frightened child, caught out in a game he shouldn't have been playing.

'I've listened to what you both said,' said Soames. 'But there's a discrepancy.'

'Discrepancy?' asked Hinton brightly.

'Let's be fair.' Lofts's voice was high and shrill. 'I killed Cass. But Hinton killed Griff.'

'Can you prove that?' asked Soames, almost affably.

'No.'

'I can. It's all to do with that discrepancy I mentioned.'

'Lofts is very disturbed.' Hinton spoke slowly, as if they had to understand every word. 'He killed Griff and Cass – and would have gone on killing if I hadn't taken the risk of us all meeting up like this.'

'Who's a pretty boy then?' squawked Hamlet from his banishment.

'Bernie Lofts is everyone's suspect, isn't he?' said Soames. 'What's that phrase – mad, bad and dangerous to know?'

214

'You've got it in one.'

'I'm not sure I have, Mr Hinton.'

'What is this so-called discrepancy then?'

'You said Hamlet was covered in Griff's blood.'

'I said – Lofts told me he'd –'

'You didn't say that,' Soames cut in. 'You said, "You even got his blood all over the parrot." But the problem is that gruesome tit-bit never reached the press. No one except Miss Weinstock and the police knew about Hamlet's indignity, and I'm sure Weinstock would never have mentioned anything so distasteful to anyone.'

Soames knew that the discrepancy was small, and that, as usual in this investigation, it wouldn't stand up in court.

'There's something else,' said Lofts with sudden, childish glee. 'Something you can check on if you like. Hinton hid the knife he killed Griff with.'

Soames was gazing at Hinton whose eyes had glazed, his lips working without making any sound at all. 'Where?'

'Here in the club.' Lofts was confident. 'There was no mention of the murder weapon being found, was there? So I broke into the club and checked it out very thoroughly one night. The search paid off. I had my insurance policy.'

'What is this nonsense?' asked Hinton.

'We'll just have to check the fingerprints, won't we?' crowed Lofts.

'Where is it?' demanded Soames.

Lofts walked out of the office and back into the club. Soames followed with Hinton behind him. He knew he had to be very careful for the slightest misjudgement now could be fatal.

Lofts opened the door of a small room at the end of the corridor that was piled with chairs. In a corner Hamlet watched them quizzically from his cage. He looked pleased to have company.

Then he began to flutter nervously as Lofts opened his cage and began to dislodge the seed-covered base.

In the cavity was a long-bladed knife, covered in dried blood.

'Don't touch it!' said Soames.

'I wouldn't be such a fool,' replied Lofts, wheeling round on

215

Hinton with his familiar sardonic grin. 'I want to tell the truth,' he added. 'That's all.'

'He doesn't know the meaning of the word,' said Hinton. 'You've heard what I had to say, Soames. I'm innocent of all this. All Lofts will tell you is a pack of lies.'

'All the same, I'd still like to hear them,' said Soames gently.

When they got back to the office, Hinton was silent behind his desk while Lofts and Soames sat on a couple of chairs facing each other. The rain began to lash down again outside.

'It's true I was sexually assaulted at Bantry Bay.' Lofts spoke in a small, clipped, neutral voice. 'So I wouldn't have any more to do with them.'

'Who?' asked Soames.

'The ring.'

'You *were* part of it?'

'So was Hinton,' said Lofts.

'You fucking liar! I want a lawyer.'

'I'll see you get one,' said Soames. 'But for the moment Lofts seems to have talked his way out of a trap.'

'Hinton and I set the kids up. Billings and Repton took them on from there,' continued Lofts.

'Were there any other army personnel involved?'

'Half a dozen.'

'Is that all?'

'How many more do you want?' asked Lofts with a hint of his old irony.

'You're prepared to name names?'

'I am now.'

'Why did you work for them?'

'I got paid. It was a job I'd learnt to do.' Lofts sounded almost matter-of-fact. 'I thought Gaby was going to adopt me and I could leave all that shit behind me.'

Soames was struck by the fact that Lofts was exactly echoing Hinton's scenario. The ritual passing on. Was there no end to it? For any of them?

'So what went wrong?'

216

'I got leant on, didn't I?' said Lofts.

'Who by?'

'Hinton and Billings. They said they'd kill me if anything got out.'

'So you kept quiet.'

'Wouldn't you?'

'Tell me what you know about Hinton.'

'He'd been in rings before.'

'He's lying,' said Hinton. 'He's a pathological liar.'

Lofts and Soames ignored him. He seemed suddenly redundant, just a faint echo on the air of all this retribution.

'You allege Hinton killed Dr Griff?'

'Yes. And I killed Cass. He was going to tell.' Lofts sounded younger, a boy dealing with a potential sneak. 'I couldn't keep him quiet any longer and I was afraid it would ruin everything. I just wanted Gaby to adopt me. It's the only thing I'll ever want.'

'Why did you blackmail Bundy?' asked Soames. 'Is he involved in all this?'

'No. He's just what I call little man syndrome. He's a petty tyrant, like Hinton. I regard them both as playthings.' Lofts giggled and Soames realised he'd never grown up, nor was he ever likely to. Somewhere Lofts's development had been arrested. Could that have happened on a recreation ground in Surrey?

'Now you can see he's sick,' said Hinton. 'He goes for the jugular – just for the fun of it. It's an instinct.'

He still sat behind his desk, staring at its scarred surface. The rain beat down outside and the uncurtained windows were misting up.

'There's something else,' said Soames.

'What?' asked Lofts sourly.

'Who's in charge?'

'Of the ring?' Lofts laughed. 'Is your maths as bad as your English? A ring can't have a top. Aren't you thinking of a triangle?'

'Haven't you ever heard of a ring master?' asked Soames. He picked up his mobile and called Mason.

*　　*　　*

217

An hour later, after Lofts and Hinton had been taken away and he had fully briefed Mason, Soames drove back through the rain-washed streets to St Clouds. The fresh downpour was long over but water still seemed to be running everywhere. He got out of the car and listened for a moment, finding the sound oddly comforting as he walked through the grounds towards the cloisters and his flat.

The black Daimler with the Royal Rangers pennant was parked outside Gaby's house and there was no sign of a chauffeur. A light shone in the bedroom upstairs.

Soames knocked, and after a while Gaby came down, the porch light making her face grey.

'Something's happened,' she said.

Colonel Darrington lay on the double bed, part of his head blown away. The service revolver was still in his hand. There was blood and other matter on the ceiling and all over the bedspread.

'Why did he do it?' asked Soames.

'We talked. He wrote it down for you.'

A white envelope was propped up on the dressing-table.

Apart from the carnage, the room was quiet and orderly with a vague hint of rosewater. Gaby was composed. In fact she was more than that, thought Soames. She seemed relieved.

'It's over now,' she said.

'Hinton and Lofts – in that order?' asked Soames.

She nodded. 'It was a weight off Edward's shoulders.' The trite remark seemed to have a special dignity of its own.

'Did he have to do it here . . .?' Soames's question trailed away inadequately.

'He needed me, for once. I'm glad he felt he could come home.'

'Did you know he was a pederast?'

'It's such an ugly word.'

'It's a very ugly business.'

'He never wanted sex – not in the right way. I've always known I repelled him. But there was much more to it than that.

218

There'd always been incidents, not in Swanage, but elsewhere. At first he wanted me to help him – just like he did tonight.'

'He told you?'

'I've known him for a long time.'

'Why didn't you tell someone?'

'I did.'

'You mean – you told Mason about Lofts's allegations – wasn't that rather indirect?'

'There seemed no other way.'

'You created another labyrinth.'

'I'm sorry.'

'There's one last piece not in place.'

'What's that? I'd like to help. So would Edward.' Gaby Darrington spoke simply, as if there could have been no other course of action.

'If Lofts was so involved, why did he make the allegation?'

'Because he wanted it to stop. Like I did.' She paused. 'I'm sorry I couldn't bring myself to give Edward away more directly, but I did what I could.'

Soames's anger seemed distanced, as if he had taken a drug that had isolated pain. 'You were as responsible as any member of the ring. You stood by and let Griff die – and then Cass. There could have been more.' Then Soames saw a glimmer of light. 'Wait a minute. Who *did* make that assault on Lofts?'

'That's why I didn't speak. Couldn't speak.'

'Christ!' Soames went over to the bed and looked down at what was left of Colonel Darrington's heroic features. *These pederasts are everywhere, and in the most unlikely places.* The phrase beat in his mind.

'At least I can help Bernie.'

'I'm afraid that's not true.' Soames wondered why she was so blinkered. Was it deliberate?

'OK, I know he'll be detained for a long time. But I can visit him – I can be here for him.' Soames was silent, and Gaby asked uncertainly, 'Do *you* think I can help him?'

Again Soames couldn't think of a reply. Then he said, 'It's hard for him not to pass it all on.'

She nodded. 'I'm going to try.'

'Do you really understand what he's done?'

'Don't be stupid. I'm not a fool. I know exactly what he's done.'

Soames remembered that he had once thought her glib. 'I'm very sorry,' he said, and went over to the dressing-table and picked up the envelope. 'I'll take this to Mason,' he said, and then hurried down the stairs, leaving Gaby Darrington alone with her husband.

Kate Weinstock knelt by Dr Griff's open coffin in the chapel of rest. The tape that played religious musak was slightly distorted and the sound was grating on her. She glanced round, wincing at the plastic flowers, the faded Pre-Raphaelite prints and a sign that said NO SMOKING. Worse still, the undertaker seemed to have rouged Rowley's waxen features so heavily that he looked like a whore.

Getting to her feet, Kate placed the spray of roses she had brought from a local florist on the shroud. Leaning over the coffin she kissed Rowley's cold cheek and whispered, 'I'm sorry I didn't say how much I loved you.'

Kate Weinstock walked slowly away, contemplating the imminent hell of the bungalow she was about to buy in Bournemouth. She supposed she would do good works. She supposed she would regain just a little control.

EPILOGUE

'Will you be glad to be going home?' asked Creighton at the final debriefing a fortnight later.

'Anything but that flat,' said Boyd. 'I'm not cut out for institutions. Maybe I'll get used to the peace and quiet.'

'Would you like a bit of company?' asked Creighton rather hesitantly.

'You'd like to go for a drink? I was thinking of –'

'A little bit more long-term than a drink, Danny. Just for a week or two while you take a rest.'

Creighton left the room and when he returned Boyd could hardly believe what he was seeing.

'How?' he asked, and then, 'Why?'

'No one wanted the thing and there was talk of putting him down. I knew you wouldn't want that.'

'No?'

'If you give him a temporary base – before the next job – I'm sure someone will give Hamlet a home.'

'You can guarantee that?'

'I'll try my aunt. She's away at the moment but I'll talk to her when she gets back. She's a very compassionate woman.'

'She'll have to be.'

Boyd gazed down at Hamlet who was still subdued and didn't speak.

'Maybe's he's gone silent.'

'I don't think so,' said Creighton.

As Boyd drove home, Hamlet was in his cage, wedged on the back seat. On the whole, he thought the parrot had had a comfortable journey and he'd tried to drive as smoothly as possible.

As Boyd pulled up outside his house, he turned round to see Hamlet watching him, beady-eyed and accusing.

'Who's a pretty boy then?' he squawked.